They were all out in front together on the charge up San Juan Hill, wondering how many of them would be alive when they got to the top...

FATE BAYLEN: A young Arizona cowboy from the Bell Rock Ranch in Oak Creek Canyon.

LIEUTENANT COLONEL THEODORE ROOSEVELT: A valiant soldier born of a rich, respected family.

THE NINTH CAVALRY: They came from all over the South and out of the slums and ghettos of the North. They were the Regular Army, professional soldiers led by Regular Army officers.

Henry Wilson Allen wrote under both the Clay Fisher and Will Henry bylines and was a five-time winner of the Golden Spur Award from the Western Writers of America. Under both bylines he is well known for the historical aspects of his Western fiction. He was born in Kansas City, Missouri. His early work was in short-subject departments with various Hollywood studios, and he was working at MGM when his first Western novel, *No Survivors* (1950), was published. While numerous Western authors before Allen provided sympathetic and intelligent portraits of Indian characters, Allen from the start set out to characterize Indians in such a way as to make their viewpoints an integral part of his stories. *Red Blizzard* (1951) was his first Western novel under the Clay Fisher byline and remains one of his best. Some of Allen's images of Indians are of the romantic variety, to be sure, but his theme often is the failure of the American frontier experience and the romance is used to treat his tragic themes with sympathy and humanity. On the whole, the Will Henry novels tend to be based more deeply on actual historical events, whereas in the Clay Fisher titles he was more intent on a story filled with action that moves rapidly. However, this dichotomy can be misleading, since *MacKenna's Gold* (1963), a Will Henry Western about gold seekers, reads much as one of the finest Clay Fisher titles, *The Tall Men* (1954). Both of these novels also served as the basis for memorable Western motion pictures. Allen was always experimental and *The Day Fort Larking Fell* (1968) is an excellent example of a comedic Western, a tradition as old as Mark Twain. His novels—*I, Tom Horn* (1975), *San Juan Hill, The Raiders,* and *From Where The Sun Now Stands* (1960) in particular, remain imperishable classics of Western fiction. Over a dozen films have been made based on his work and both *The Day Fort Larking Fell* and *The Bear Paw Horses* are currently in development. At his best, he was a gripping teller of stories peopled with interesting characters true to the time and to the land.

"I am but a solitary horseman of the plains, born a century too late and far away," Allen once wrote about himself. He felt out of joint with his time and what alone may ultimately unify his work is the vividness of his imagination, the tremendous emotion with which he invested his characters and fashioned his Western stories. At his best, he could weave an almost incomparable spell that can involve a reader deeply in his narratives, informed always by his profound empathy with so many of the casualties of the historical process.

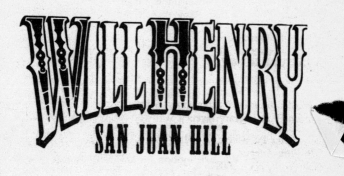

WILL HENRY
SAN JUAN HILL

LEISURE BOOKS **NEW YORK CITY**

For Richard E. Roberts

A LEISURE BOOK®

July 1996

Published by special arrangement with
Golden West Literary Agency.

Dorchester Publishing Co., Inc.
276 Fifth Avenue
New York, NY 10001

WILL HENRY
SAN JUAN HILL

Chapter One

On a warm sunny rock in the middle of Oak Creek just above Chavez Crossing, flat upon his back and free of care as the cactus wren which warbled in the sycamores above him, Fate Baylen waited for the Verde stage.

He was still undressed from his swim but there was no hurry about that; it would be noon and more before the ancient Concord, bearing his new Winchester carbine, would be getting down the canyon from Flagstaff. The lanky cowboy squinted upward beyond the red palisades of the rim, taking drowsy measure of the morning's beauty. Northward, a herding breeze nipped at a flock of sheepswool clouds, driving them to browse along the Little Colorado above Winslow. Southwesterly, there was no wind. The sky was a set piece of Pima turquoise. The high cumulus stood painted in place over Verde Valley and the Phoenix road. All about were the redolent aromas of the Arizona spring.

"April 25," murmured Fate, sleepily aloud, "1898. My, but she surely is one darb of a day."

Over on the south bank his buckskin gelding raised its head and snorted emphatically. Fate eyed the animal. "Was that a hostile sentiment," he inquired, "or did you get a nettle up your nose?" The buckskin stared at him, swung rump-to, resumed its feeding. Fate nodded thoughtfully. "You may be right, at that," he said. "There's two ends to everything. . . ."

The concession was not completely noble. Except for the horse, Seepwillow, there was not another useful conversationalist closer than Cottonwood, where Miss Mary McGarrity—sometimes—kept the Yavapai County School. However, since Miss Mary had a tongue alkaline enough to poison waterholes and had, in fact, never forgiven him for quitting her classes nine years before when he was fifteen and just learning to read well, Fate put up with his pony. But the effect at times, such as now, was somnolent. Presently the Verde cowboy was snoring, full-bore, oblivious alike to the beauties of the young spring and the boneheadedness of old horses. His next awareness was that of stage-coach wheels crunching in creek gravel. Bounding wildly to his feet, he dived into the foam-flecked eddy upstream of his sunning rock.

Knowing how long it took the stage to cross, he waited under water until he was certain it had reached the far side. When he stood up, however, it was not on the far side but parked squarely in the middle of the creek a rope's toss away. From his high seat, driver Gila Ehrenberg waved and said cheerfully, "Good morning, Fate. My, but you're white where your winter drawers was."

Fate went back under, wishing he might drown and be swept away and that they would not find his body until next spring. But the need to breathe overtook his natural modesty. This time, though, he raised only his head above the edge of the rock, cursing Gila in unrounded phrases which were as heartfeltly returned. An incensed ticket-holder, a dry-goods drummer from Denver, put his head out the coach window. "Confound it, driver," he complained, "I should think you would show more respect for the lady!" Atop the coach, Gila winced guiltily. "Ma'am," he called down, "I purely hope we ain't offended you. I wouldn't linger a minute if I thought you was apt to be overstrought by the scenery, nor the noise, neither one."

"That's a double negative, Gila! And there's no such word as 'overstrought.' " The response from below was immediate and stringent. It was followed by a lecturing finger wagged out the window at Fate. "You get out of that snow-melt water, you hear me, Fate Baylen? You'll catch your death!"

Fate grinned happily. "Miss Mary," he said, "I am surely delighted to hear you sounding so well. How's the new crop of kids at school? Dumb as ever?"

"Dumber!" chirruped the Cottonwood schoolmarm. "Arizona breeds them tough in mind as well as muscle. A good thing, too, what with the news in today's paper!"

"Blast it, driver," broke in the Denver drummer, "I got a wife and eight kids to feed! Let's get a move on!"

"Waal," said Gila admiringly, "you been busier at home than on the road. However, I got a schedule to keep, too. Hang on."

"Whoa up!" yelled Fate. "How about my new gun you was supposed to fetch down today?"

Gila checked his tensing teams. "Yeah, I brang it for you," he said. "I'll leave it ashore. Here's something else you can ponder, meanwhile." He tossed Fate a rolled copy

9

of the Flagstaff *Arizonan*. "Knowed your dad would want to read about it," he said. "He was in the last one." Kicking off the brake, he sang the poppers of his whip about the ears and haunches of his wiry horses. "Hee-yah! Gittt—!" he bellowed.

The little mustangs dug in. Gravel and green water showered back. Ashore, the stage halted long enough for Gila to deposit Fate's gun, then it was gone clattering and harness-jingling into the juniper. Still watching after it, Fate sat down on the rock and opened the Flagstaff paper. From the side, the uncoiled headlines struck at him like black rattlesnakes:

U.S. AT WAR WITH SPAIN!
McKINLEY IN CALL FOR 125,000
VOLUNTEERS!

Below the headlines, bracketed by crudely printed woodblock eagles and American flags, appeared the motto, "Remember the Maine, to hell with Spain!"

Fate was electrified. He did not read the fiery details contained in the clarion dispatches from Washington and around the world. He did not need to. At a time like this any man knew where his duty lay. Heart pounding with rightful pride and anger, he stumbled out of the water and dressed.

Chapter Two

The parting with his father was brief, as Fate had known it must be. Emmett Baylen was not a man given to talk. When Fate showed him the Flagstaff paper, he frowned laboriously through the headlines and some little of the following text, then looked up at Fate and said slowly, "Do you remember what Stephen Decatur said, boy?"

Fate prided himself on his American history but this stumped him, so he said politely, "No, sir, I've sure forgot. What did he say?"

When he replied thus to the question, he saw Emmett Baylen stand tall and saw a look come over his weathered face he had never seen there before. " 'Our country!' " repeated his father, quoting the words with the dead certainty of moral law. " 'In her intercourse with foreign nations may she always be in the right; but our country, right or wrong.' " Fate stood there feeling the chill run up his back. It spread to his neck and jaws, and ached so hard

11

behind his ears that it hurt. After a long moment he said, "I'll go and get my things." His father only nodded and Fate started past him to the kitchen door. When he reached it he stopped and looked back. "Dad," he said, "I never knew you was up on your U.S. history."

Emmett Baylen returned his look. Once more the craggy head moved, this time in a fleeting headshake of denial.

"I ain't," he answered softly. "I don't know another word of it, nor figure that I need to."

Fate never forgot the picture of him standing by the ranchhouse porch, still and proud and staring far away down the meadow beyond Bell Rock and Schnebley Hill to Morgan's Stronghold and the Mogollon Rim. He never forgot it because it was the first time in his twenty-four years that he had really seen his father. And he never forgot it because in that last quiet moment before he turned away to his room and the gathering of his things, he knew what it was that his gentle Eastern mother, now eleven years beneath the whispering loneliness of the buffalo grass, had seen in unlettered, taciturn Emmett Baylen: she had seen a man.

This was the memory with which the young cowboy rode away from Bell Rock Ranch and his boyhood. It was a poignant good-bye and it kept him quiet many a mile along the outbound trail. Past House Mountain, past Cathedral Mesa, past Courthouse Rock, past all the dusty haunted landmarks of his youth, it went with him. But ahead lay life and excitement and a look at the outside world which he had never expected. By the time he reached the river and saw the town beyond, Fate's normal euphoria was rising like a hungry trout to the fly of foreign adventure.

When he rode into Camp Verde with his toothbrush and two ten-dollar bills rolled up in a brown paper sack, the

Phoenix paper was just in on the afternoon stage. Its front-page splash gave Fate the answer to the question he had come to ask: Where did a man go to enlist so that he stood the best chance of being on the first boat for Cuba? And what a vastly thrilling reply it was!

Theodore Roosevelt was to be commissioned lieutenant colonel in charge of volunteer cavalry and had announced officially his reported plan to raise a regiment of "college men and cowboys" to be known as "Teddy's Terrors." His idea was to recruit most of his fighting horsemen from the Western plains where he had hunted and ranched with such wide experience and full publicity. Of course, he had not yet resigned as Assistant Secretary of the Navy but his program for creating a mounted rifle and revolver regiment was already well under way. As "Teddy" confidently stated: "The organization will be completed and in Cuba within three weeks, there to engage upon a 'roving' campaign against the Spaniard."

There followed a list of places for Western men to sign up, and Whipple Barracks at Prescott leaped from the page. At once Fate rushed to buy a stage ticket. But at the Camp Verde general store he found things humming.

The aging Concord that Gila had driven down from Flagstaff had chewed up an axle a mile out. The only other available coach was a Celerity model, which had just come up from Phoenix. The Celerity was a lightweight coach with a canvas roof and would not carry top riders. Inside, it took just eight passengers and since Fate's place at the ticket window was number twenty-seven he saw plainly that it would be Friday, four days away, before he might hope for a seat on the Prescott Special. But he was determined and a straight-line thinker. Stepping away from the window he addressed his more fortunate fellow ticket holders in his friendly, warm-hearted manner.

"Boys," he said, "Gila is just bringing his fresh teams around. The Whipple stage will be leaving in five minutes. Plenty time to sort out who's going to Prescott and who ain't going to Prescott."

The crowd grew quiet. It began to drift in on the speaker. "Hold it," ordered a voice low with authority. A fish-eyed man wearing a tied-down revolver and a tin star stalked over to join Fate. "Houck Oatman," he said. "Deputy Sheriff over to Payson. Sort me in."

"Just a minute, that ain't fair, damn it!" objected one of the hesitating low-number holders. "The law ain't no right taking sides!"

The cold-faced deputy thought it over. "That's so," he finally admitted soberly and unpinned the star. "Now, then, who else is going to Prescott with Private Oatman?"

"Me," announced a bearlike prospector, waddling over. He had one blue eye and one brown eye and a mesquite thicket of whiskers. He was sixty if he was a day but he was a pioneer legend in those parts and Fate made room for him with patent respect.

"Thank you, Mr. Shodzak," he said. "We're beholden."

One other, a limping, infirm-looking youth came forward. He wore Texas stovepipe boots with silver spurs which rang beautifully when he walked. "Name's Billy Hester," he said with a shy smile. "I aim to go."

Fate gave a start. "Billy Hester from Sonoita?"

"Why yes, sir," replied the boy, blushing.

Fate prided himself on being able to ride. He had taken second money at Prescott on the Fourth of July the past three years. But this pale kid, with the possible exception of Tom Darnell, of New Mexico, was the greatest saddle-bronc rider in the world. Fate put out his hand uncertainly. "Fate Baylen, Camp Verde," he said. "Maybe you've heard of me." The other youth's face lit up. "Why, sure!" he cried. "You're the one does so well up to Prescott!" Fate, at the summit of his fame, modestly confessed that he was, indeed, that very one. The two might subsequently have summered right there in the general store discussing the bronc-riding business had not some fool put his head in at the door just then to bawl, "Better get aboard, you Teddy's Terriers!" and started the stampede for the stage.

In the first rush Fate and his friends were beaten back, rudely repulsed with boot and fist and loud guffaw by the winning majority. But reinforcements were on the way. Emil Shodzak burst from the store, seized the onside rear wheel of the stage, gave a mighty upward heave and toppled it over. The shouts and curses of the defenders rang desperately. Those of them who could leaped to safety as the tilting vehicle heeled over and sank into the dust of Main Street. Before they could regroup, Fate had armed his small force with the last four pick handles from the sidewalk barrel in front of the store and taken possession of the field. The enemy rallied briefly. Some ripped boards from the walk. One broke off the handle of the horse-trough pump. Another unbuckled the wooden leg he had earned thirty-odd years earlier at Shiloh. All hands swung with a will and a wide variety of Rebel yells, but now it was Fate and his friends who had their backs to the fallen coach and shortly the recently militant majority had absorbed all the pick handles its members were in the mood for. Terms were proposed and accepted. The stage was righted, its teams hooked on, its remaining seat space filled by lot. The only casualty of any consequence was old man Shodzak, who had sprung his back overturning the Celerity and who would now have to wait for another ride and another war. With his rioting passengers sorted out and seated, Gila Ehrenberg came out of hiding, scrambled up to the box, yelled at his spooky teams, and got the Prescott Special rolling. It appeared for a moment as though it would be an angry, unhailed farewell, but just before the Celerity disappeared around the river bend the battered losers had a saving change of spirit. Coming together loyally in midstreet, they raised on high their arms and cheered in a forgiving shout of "Give 'em hell, you Teddy's Terriers—!" and so the start was made auspiciously, after all.

No further trouble was encountered. They made Cottonwood by sundown, had supper in Clarkdale, started up the Mingus Mountain switchbacks to Jerome under a jewel-bright moonrise. At the Summit Roadhouse Gila pulled his teams to one side, announcing a half-hour rest for the horses and advising the humans to get down and loosen up whatever needed loosening up. Fate's group went into the tavern where the friendly cowboy found himself lined up at the bar next to Houck Oatman. Naturally he made some opening sociable comment. The older man endured about thirty seconds of this, saying not a word himself. Then, when Fate paused to take a breath, he gave him a look as frosty as the winter wind and asked quietly, "This the first time you left home, kid?"

"Why, yes, I believe you might say it was," replied the latter. "Of course, I've been to Flag and Prescott but they ain't nothing. Why you ask?"

"You look a little old for first-traveling," said the deputy, "but maybe you'll learn."

"Oh, sure," said Fate, encouraged to think the thaw had set in, "I'm a first-rate learner, Mr. Oatman."

"Learn this then," said Houck Oatman. "Keep your damned mouth shut."

It was here that two of the Camp Verde ticket holders, who had taken on previous stimulant at Cottonwood and Clarkdale, got into a technical disagreement on who was the superior specimen. By the time Houck Oatman had separated them with the butt of his Colt, the stage for Prescott had two empty seats, and the eastbound stage, passing fortuitously, picked up two consignees for the mining company hospital in Jerome. The vacancies did not go unbidden for. Watching Houck order the victims carried outside, Fate felt a tug at his shirtsleeve. "Name's Ben Gant," said the shabby-looking mountain man. "Just come down out'n the timber wanting a lift to Prescott so's me and Florence can jine up with Teddy and the boys. It 'pears you got some extry space now. How abouten it?"

"You and *Florence?*" said Fate interestedly. "Where's Florence?"

"Yonder," answered the shabby one. "Under the table."

Fate squinted hard but saw no one. "Oh, sure," he said, grinning, as he realized the other had been struck by Taos Lightning and was shooting blind. "You go fetch her out and we'll look her over."

By this time Houck Oatman had drifted back in to collect Fate. "What's going on?" He scowled, watching Ben Gant drop to all fours and crawl under the darkened corner table. "You teaching him to retrieve, or something?"

"Oh no, sir," replied Fate. "He's got a lady friend named Florence sleeping it off under there and wants to bring her along with him to Prescott on our stage."

"We're not taking any women to Prescott, you idiot," said Houck. "Outside—!"

"Hold on!" yelled Ben Gant, poking his head from be-

17

neath the table. "You ain't seen Florence yet!"

Before anyone could argue it further, the mountain man emerged tugging on a six-foot trap chain, the opposite end of which held an unflustered mountain lioness cub. Strolling regally across the room this sleek brute stared indifferently at Fate before turning to examine his hard-eyed escort. It was love at first look. The big cat, six or seven months old and three-quarters grown, gave a rasping "*Meowrrr!*" reared up, full-length, on the startled deputy, laid her face to his horsehide vest and began purring like a steam winch. "Keep that damned feline off of me!" cursed Houck Oatman.

Ben Gant smirked craftily. "Well," he demanded, "does she go, or don't she? What do you fellers say?" He looked past the deputy to the knot of stage riders watching from the tavern door. None of them said anything but it was obvious where the company sentiment lay. Florence, clinching it, wound herself house-catwise against Oatman's braced leg, rubbed her whiskers on the handle of his holstered Colt, fixed him with her jade-green eyes and uttered another piercing "*Meowrrr!*"

The deputy wheeled about, headed for the door. "My God!" he said hopelessly to himself. "Mountain lions, too . . . ?"

Chapter Three

In Prescott the saloons began just beyond the stage office, at Gurley and Mount Vernon, and ran from there on. Fate, however, had never been one to drink in self-defense. Thus, when Houck Oatman and the others started for the bracelet of lights encircling the plaza, he said he wanted to scout around a little and would see them later. Billy Hester decided he was of a like mind and that if Fate had no objection he would undertake to scout with him. Fate was delighted and the two younger men set out to see what they could see.

It was 3:00 A.M. At the 5,600-foot altitude the air carried an edge. The wind began to rise, whip them about the ears and snap and rattle their cowhide vests like tissue paper. After a turn of the sights along Whiskey Row, with detours to see the old log Governor's Mansion and the new stone courthouse, Fate and Billy believed they had had enough fun for one night. Fate suggested they seek out a hotel and sleep in style. Billy demurred, proposing instead that they go down to the stage office and sleep. It seemed he had overheard the Prescott agent, Fred Heffernan, tell Gila Ehrenberg that he would drive him out to the barracks at the break of day, so that Gila might be the very first in line to lay down his life for his country. Heffernan had said they would use the repair wagon, which had a large oblong toolbox built on its bed, and Billy figured he and Fate could dump out the tools and bunk in the box. "What you say, Fate?" he concluded diffidently. "You think it might work? We can get a night's sleep and a ride out to Fort Whipple, both."

Fate banged him between the shoulder blades. "I say you're a forty-karat genius, by damn!" he vowed. "Of course it'll work. Come on—!"

At the stage depot they emptied the toolbox on the work-wagon and climbed into it. Snugging under some empty feedsacks, they got comfortable against the opposite ends and said good night. But weary as they were, they found they could not sleep and so spent the remaining brief time before daylight smoking and talking of the war in Cuba. They agreed they weren't precisely certain what was going on between their country and Spain which called for a fight, or why the Cubans had to be rescued, or from what. But they were solid in their anger over the U.S. Navy's court-of-inquiry findings that the blowing up of the battleship *Maine* had been enemy work, and they surely agreed with the big New York papers that it was high time the U.S.A. opened up and showed the rest of the world that she didn't stand second at the trough to any of the other hogs, for damned sure not to those mackerel-snapping Spanish devils!

In this spirit of growing martial ire, the two young men

from Verde Valley and the Sonoita Plateau talked the stars dim, smoked up both sacks of Fate's Bull Durham, and dropped off finally, just as the fighting chickens were beginning to crow down in Mexican town past the railroad yards. Fate awakened in bare time to seize Billy Hester, push him down into the toolbox and clamp the lid into place above them, as Gila and Fred Heffernan came out the rear door of the stage office picking their teeth and checking on the sky to see what the weather would be. Ten minutes later the team was hooked up and the repair wagon rattling out East Gurley toward Whipple Barracks.

Chapter Four

Fate and Billy were arrested and escorted off the post when they climbed out of the wagon box. Disconsolate, they wandered across the road to the creek and to the encampments of the waiting "Terrors" which lined its banks. There they were speedily informed of the sagging prospects for Teddy's cavalry.

The Colonel was having troubles back in Washington, D.C. A scurrilous story had been spread that the cowboy army was not his idea at all. Some Iowa Senator was supposed to have beat him to it and introduced a bill into Congress calling for "Three regiments to be made up of expert hunters, riflemen, cowmen and frontiersmen and such other hardy characters as might care to enlist from the Territories . . ."

However, Teddy had shown his enemies the stuff he was made of. When the President offered him command of one of the three frontier regiments, he had humbly refused, claiming his lack of military experience forbade his accepting such an honor. He would, though, be cheerfully willing to take second-in-command to some more seasoned officer; say, only for honest example, Captain Leonard Wood of the Medical Corps. Immediately, a second shameful lie had sprung up claiming that Teddy and Leonard Wood were thicker than Chihuahua cow thieves. It was said that Wood's being McKinley's personal physician gave him an influence in The White House which would never harm old Teddy, and that old Teddy had known all along and very damned well that it would not.

This was not all of the glum news. Word had just been sent over to the creek camps by Major Alex Brodie, in charge of raising the regiment, that the number of men to be chosen had been cut from 1,000 to 350. Enlistment of this small lot would begin with daybreak tomorrow. Meanwhile Major Brodie had posted "five commandments" for acceptance:

1. Each man must be a fine horseman.
2. He must be a superior marksman.
3. He must bear a reference in writing as to moral character.
4. He must pass the physical examination of the Regular Army.
5. He would not be considered if he had been indicted for a major crime or convicted of a minor one.

Fate and Billy, considering these stern conditions, went back upstream to establish a camp of their own and to wait out tomorrow's call. Disturbingly, the call did not come next day, nor next. It was nearly a week before the rumor again raced the creekside. This time it held the urgent pulse of finality. The entire encampment went mean and edgy.

The hours dragged, whiskey flowed, fights broke out. Yet at last the sun was gone, the wine-sharp darkness fallen. Fires bloomed where the lucky ones who had found or stolen kindling held forth. Fate and Billy, having neither wood nor blankets, sat shivering against a windbreak boulder. Forlornly they watched the lights of Fort Whipple and shivered even more. What chance had they to be among the ones who went? Presently, more to seek spiritual than physical warmth, they set off down the stream. At the fourth fire they found a friend.

"Why hello, boys!" Ben Gant greeted them. "Come in and set a spell. Coffee's boilt and going to waste."

"Thank you, Mr. Gant," said Fate, glancing around. "Where's Florence?"

Ben Gant scrubbed his beard and wiped away what may have been a tear with the back of his gnarled hand. "Boys," he confessed, "I have done the dirtiest thing of my life to her. Got inter a game on Whiskey Row. Next thing I knowed I was betting the cat agin this city feller's stack of blues. I then drawed two trays to his three ladies and brace of johns." He wiped the offending eye once more. "Young friends," he sobbed, "it was worser not selling a good sheepdog."

"Well, maybe," agreed Fate. "But, say, why couldn't me and Billy ante-up and buy her back again?"

"No, no, thank you, lads," said the other bravely. "It's my shame and I aint atelling who brang it on me."

At this point a chilling voice well remembered by them all cut into the fireside warmth. "Don't bet on it, Ben," it said, and they turned to see Houck Oatman standing there.

"Why, bless my soul, howdy thar, Mr. Oatman!" declared the mountain man. "Grab a cup, she's hot."

Houck stared at him. "Who did you say won the lion?" he asked.

"Feller named Bob Brow," Ben mumbled. "Thanks," said the Payson deputy, and started away. Over his shoulder, in passing them, he added to Fate and Billy, "You two meet me at Gurley and Mount Vernon in one hour. Be there."

The boys were there. Houck, arriving within seconds, pulled to the curb in a rented buggy and ordered them in. Shortly he halted in front of a neat frame cottage.

"Listen good," he said. "In yonder is a friend of mine who can get you into the troops going to the training camp at San Antonio, Texas. There's no other way in God's world you boys can make it after what happened today: Major Brodie got final orders from Washington;   there's   only two hundred men going from Arizona."

Stunned, Fate and Billy followed Houck to the cottage door. Inside, a tall, wide-chested man in city clothes received them. Houck saluted him informally and said, "Captain, these are the two men I told you of."

"*Two* men?" said the other, eyeing Billy. "I see only one-and-a-half. That one's runt of the litter."

Fate, seeing Billy cringe, stepped indignantly forward. "Sir," he said, "that there is Billy Hester of Sonoita!"

It was the big man's turn to recoil. "No!" he cried. "The bronco rider? I take it back," he said, turning to Houck, "you did bring me two men."

Wheeling again to Fate and Billy, he told them abruptly, "You boys will be in my own company. I don't mind saying you're plumb lucky. You got two of the last three vacancies there were. Good night and get out."

He and Houck shook hands at the door and Fate, hanging

25

back to eavesdrop, marked that the deputy didn't say "captain," but "Bucky," and so felt these two had ridden a trail together older than the streets of Prescott. Climbing into the buggy and setting off at a trot, he asked Houck about it. The deputy surprisingly admitted the past association, saying feelingly, "His kind never forgets a friend nor fires wide at an enemy; you boys will learn that serving with Bucky O'Neill."

Bucky O'Neill! Fate and Billy exchanged gasps. There was no more famous man in Arizona Territory. That they had been taken into his personal troop was more than either could believe. Fate, however, would have a try at taking it in stride. "I wonder," he said casually, "who will get that final vacancy in our company?"

Houck at once pulled up the horse, halting the buggy under the corner street lamp. "Come on," was all he said.

They got out, wonderingly, and followed him around to the rear. Here he raised the lid of the leather luggage compartment and said, "Lean in and have a look; yonder's your last recruit for Company A, Arizona Cavalry."

Puzzled, Fate leaned into the trunk. "Damnation!" he yelled, drawing back. "What the hell you got in there?" His answer was the rattle of a familiar rusty trap chain and a hoarse-throated "*Meowrrr!*" some four octaves lower than a housecat's. Blinking sociably, Florence protruded her sleek yellow head into the lamplight. "I got her back," Houck explained dourly, "on condition she be enlisted on the company rolls as Florence Elizabeth Brow.[1] Bucky said

---

[1] In his book *The Rough Riders* Colonel Roosevelt says this lion cub was named Josephine. Perhaps she was by the time the Colonel got around to his memoirs. At Prescott she was Florence. Authority for the distinction: Mr. Robert Brow of that city, who donated her to the regiment while at Whipple Barracks.

to go ahead and do it. He thought it would be funny.''

Fate frowned and shook his head. ''Gee, I dunno,'' he said. ''A woman on the company muster? Won't that look like hell in the history books?''

Houck Oatman did not reply. ''Get back in the buggy,'' he ordered. ''I got to get you signed up yet tonight.'' Fate and Billy obeyed and it was only after they had driven well out Gurley Street toward Whipple Barracks that the Payson deputy looked over at Fate and asked in his deadly quiet way, ''Who reads history books?''

It had all the sound and sense of a good question, yet Fate found he had no reply to it. If it had been ''who reads newspapers,'' or ''ladies' magazines,'' or ''livestock journals,'' or just plain ''books,'' it would have been easy. He could merely have said, ''Why everybody.'' But history books? Damn. Who *did* read history books?

At Whipple they went at once to the post hospital for their physical examinations. Fate passed his but Billy was found to have tuberculosis and discharged. Dressed again, the two youths went outside and tried to talk it over but could not. They ended with the tears streaming down Billy's thin face and Fate standing there trying not to see them.

Houck came up just then. ''Kid,'' he said to Billy, ''I came away from my job in Payson so fast I didn't have time to line up a man to take over for me as deputy for Sheriff Young. I think you can handle it. Now don't argue, sleep on it. We can bunk in A Barracks for the night, have breakfast on the army in the morning. It will work out.''

Billy nodded, but could say nothing, and they set off across the parade ground. At the barracks they found three cots together and lay down in strained silence. In the morning Billy was not in his cot nor in the barracks. ''The kid's gone,'' said Houck, seeing Fate's alarm. ''Snuck out at

three o'clock A.M. I let on like I didn't see him go."
"What?" demanded Fate angrily. "Why didn't you stop
him?" Houck fixed him with his pale eyes. "What for?"
he said.

Fate blinked and bobbed his head. There it was again,
another of those good questions having no apparent answer.
They dressed and went outside, starting for the mess hall.
Suddenly Fate pointed ahead. Even though the sun had not
yet cleared Mingus Mountain, a long line of men was funneling into the recruiting building. By a side door of that
same structure, other men were issuing in much less happy
mood. Unhappiest of these was a lank specimen of familiar
rough look and language.

"He could be sent to Yuma for talking like that," said
Houck, and Fate nodded. "Gila!" he called. "Wait up and
shut up! What's the matter?"

The accused spun around. "Matter?" he yelled. "Come
here and see for your ownselves!" He pointed to the re-
cruiting-hall window, and Fate and Houck, coming forward, peered within. The volunteers were filing in front of
a rocky-faced sergeant who, if he approved the looks of the
individual, would bark, "All right, move on!" If, however,
he took exception to some unfortunate, he would wheel to
the bulletin board behind him and scowl at the welter of
wanted flyers which plastered its surface two and three
deep. Not once did he miss his man. Each time he went to
the board he came back with a picture. This he would hand
to the poor miscreant who, seizing his official portrait,
would depart in grateful silence by the side exit—all, that
is, save Gila Ehrenberg. "How do you like that, for the
luvva Gawd?" the latter now protested. "Why, it ain't
American. It ain't even Arizonian. Sonofabitch! I will jine
up with Cubia!"

"If you're half bright," said Houck Oatman, "you will shut your mouth and start running. Let's see your picture." Before the other could move to stop him, he lifted the crumpled Pinal County sheriff's flyer from Gila's shirt pocket and spread it out. "Wanted . . ." he began relentlessly.

"It's a black lie!" raged Gila futilely.

"Save your wind," advised Houck. "You will need it for digging out under the back fence. I just saw Sheriff Frank Gillespie of Pinal going into the Provost Marshal's office."

Gila turned gray. "All right," he said. "Whichaway is the back fence?" Houck pointed, and the old stage driver managed to draw himself up. "Good-bye, boys," he said, and then added with considerable feeling, "Give 'em hell, you Teddy's Terriers!"

"It ain't Terriers," Fate called plaintively after him, "it's Terrors." But Gila did not hear him. He was already a quarter of the way across the parade ground, gaining speed with every stride. He didn't turn to wave even when he was safely outside the fence, and that was the last that Fate Baylen ever saw of him.

Chapter Five

The following day, May 3, did indeed prove the day.

Fate was touched by one part of the leave-taking. He thought the presentation of the regimental flag by the ladies of the Women's Relief Corps of Phoenix was beautiful. When the shapely leader of the Corps stepped forward and transferred the silken folds into the arms of dashing Captain McClintock, and the Ladies' Full Chorus of Female Voices from the Territorial Normal School stood at attention and sang "God Be With You Till We Meet Again," he and half the regiment wept like babes. After that, there were the usual interminable speeches of hail and farewell but at last the final oration was delivered and done. The temporary sergeants ran up and down the ragged lines pushing and herding the new troopers into some semblance of military order. The regimental band played "We Won't Be Home Until Morning" well enough so that anyone could recognize it, and all the ladies from Phoenix and Prescott, as well as all the other good folks from as far as Ashfork and Wickenburg and Skull Valley, joined in the singing and marched with Arizona's "Iron Two-hundred" down to the railroad siding.

A happy incident occurred when the company was held up by Florence, now promoted to regimental mascot, taking off when jumped by a pack of yappy curs going through Mexican Town. Fate was detailed to round her up and when he reappeared with the young lioness on a leash the Prescott citizens who had stopped to watch the chase broke into echoing cheers. One of the young ladies of the Normal School overcome by the din, rushed from the crowd, tackled Fate, planted a kiss on him and hung on. Fate kissed back and Sergeant Houck Oatman finally had to order the company to march over them to break up the embrace. Realistically Fate did not resent the command. He hated to leave the girl, who could express herself about as well as any he had encountered, but he knew there was a train to catch and a training camp to get to. So he went manfully with the others and an hour later was on the cars steaming toward San Antonio. His cup was full, he believed, until later that afternoon when Houck Oatman stepped into the car he was riding and called out, "All right, men, attention! I need somebody with not too much brains to be my acting corporal. Baylen, step forward."

Fate stood up feeling eight feet tall. He followed Houck down the aisle and out of the car, proud as though he had just been made brigadier general. The cheers and jeers of his fellow volunteers hooraying him on his way meant absolutely nothing. Let them laugh and cowboy him all they wanted. Many were called in this world, but precious few were chosen. He had not been in the army forty-eight hours and he was already a noncom. You couldn't rattle apples like those, no matter how hard you shook the tree.

Outside the car on the windy, rocking vestibule, Houck issued the instructions for handling the hardrock miners, horse thieves, desert rats, drifters and owlhoot riders who made up the Prescott troops. Fate nodded but scarcely heard him. He was looking back over the soft gray of the Arizona uplands, heart and mind reaching toward the Bell Rock and his father. Ah, if Emmett could only see him now: *Corporal Fate Baylen, Troop A, Arizona Regiment, First United States Volunteer Cavalry!* Why, there was no telling how high he might rise in the ranks before they left San Antonio, or got to Cuba. Corporal in forty-eight hours was a terrifying start; well, at least it was sobering.

Fate's duty was to keep order in one of the cars which carried Troop A. It was work demanding a nice balance of friendly charm and blunt force. Fortunately the acting corporal had the two-way gift. His main chore, once he had established physical supremacy, became the answering of his comrades' endless questions on the days ahead.

How long would it take the train to get to San Antonio? How far was it from there to Florida? How long would they mess around playing soldier before they climbed on the boat and took off for Cuba? What was keeping old Teddy in Washington? Why wasn't he in Texas and raring to go? The way he had talked in the papers, he ought to have been there first off. What sorts of uniforms and what kinds of weapons would they be issued? Were the Cubans thriftless and barefoot like the Mexicans? Was it true they had colored blood in them for the most part? Did they really wear those white diaper pants shown in the newspaper pictures? Would they understand Arizona Spanish? Were their girls lookers or dumpy and squat? Either way, were they inclined to be cozy, or hard to corner? Did they cotton to *americano* men? How much was the Army going to pay them per month for being heroes? What did the Pope of Rome look like, and was it true he was actually a woman? Was it true Teddy Roosevelt had once been head policeman of New York City? Would they get decent horses in Texas? What about whiskey, women, wild life in general?

Fate stood up to the torrent of inquiries the best way he could, but by sundown was defeated. "Boys," he pleaded, "I am not your mother. Back off and give me a breather."

By then the heat and odor in the car was stupefying. The men were beginning to slump in exhausted slumber or to sit and gaze out the dusty windows like hypnotized birds watching the mottled snake of the landscape loop past. Before long Fate and Houck Oatman were the only ones awake in Car Six of the San Antonio Super. Houck let the wheels click for another mile, studying the sweating sleepers and the welter of flies, greasy sandwich papers, discarded boots and stale cigar butts amid which they sprawled insensate. "They stink," he said finally.

"I been thinking the same thing," Fate said. "I been in cattle cars, horse cars, hog cars—Lord A'mighty, even sheep cars—and I ain't never smelt nothing like this."

Houck shrugged. "We'll get so we smell like the rest; all it takes is time."

Fate shook his head decisively. "My dad never let me run shabby," he said. "He wouldn't permit a hand to light on our place who didn't get in the horse trough every Saturday. He fired the best foreman we ever had because he once went two weeks between troughs, and that in February and colder than a heifer's belly in a snowbank."

"Your dad," said Houck, "sounds like he had some sense."

"He still has." Fate grinned. "He talked me into leaving home, didn't he?"

Houck glanced over at him. His hard face seemed to soften just a moment. "You might do some day," he told Fate. "Thank you, Mr. Oatman," replied the Bell Rock cowboy. "I mean to try." Again the Payson deputy sized him. Presently he nodded. "Make it Houck," he said, "and shut up." Fate colored deeply. "Yes, sir," he murmured, and turned to the car window.

Outside, the light was going swiftly. Already the chill darkness was creeping over the high country. Fate saw some cattle standing still and humpbacked to the wind. They were on a sweeping rise of sandstone, set against a red tabletop mesa. The gray-green waves of the grama grass lapped at their flanks. Off to their right a lone rider watched them. As Fate's gaze found the rider, the latter struck a match and cupped it to his cigarette. Fate could clearly see the brief golden glow of the match light on his face and hands. At the moment, the engineer pulled two wailing mournful blasts on the whistle. Over across the grasslands Fate saw the rider rise in his stirrups and wave to the train, exactly as he himself had done so many times when standing watch or riding slow lazy circles around the bedding herd at duskfall. The whistle cried once more, fadingly, into the night, then trailed off into the rush and buffet of the wind outside the coach's rattling panes. Suddenly Fate was the loneliest he had ever been, and the most afraid. He turned to Houck Oatman wanting friendship, talk, rebuke, any human notice at all in that moment of aching need. But Houck's hat was down over his face, his boots propped against the frame of the seat in front of him. Fate could not bring himself to disturb the deputy's rest, respecting the latter's right to it and to his own thoughts of home and loved ones and the life he was also leaving behind. He faced back to the window, throat tightened, lips compressed. Houck Oatman did not stir, but from beneath his lowered hat brim his quiet voice reached out to Fate.

"You feel it harder because you're older," he said. "A man will cry where a boy will laugh. Go to sleep."

Chapter Six

Life in Camp "San Antonia" was a miracle of revelations for Fate Baylen and his fellow frontiersmen.

By May 10 the last troop, K, had arrived—college boys from the East—and the regiment, save for Teddy Roosevelt, was complete.[1] The sturdy men of the West were struck dumb with wonder and dismay by the sons of Harvard, Yale, Columbia and Princeton. But cow-country hospitality was not to be denied. When one New York socialite-recruit, known to be en route in the private railroad car of his millionaire father, alighted amid the horse droppings of downtown San Antonio wearing a dove-gray morning coat, pinstripe trousers, spats and a silk topper, his company commander—an ex-New Mexico sheriff—had

---

[1]The troops were A, B and C from Arizona, D from Oklahoma Territory, E, F, G, H and I from New Mexico, K from the cities and universities of the East, L and M from the Indian Territory.

the regimental marching band waiting for him at the depot. He was escorted with cymbal and trumpet back to the Exposition Building where, for lack of proper tentage, the troops were in temporary bivouac. Not only was he brought thus afoot to the site, but conducted fourteen times around it to the resounding cheers of his simple subjects from the Far West. He stuck it out, however, and proved eventually as stout a soldier as any in the regiment.

On the opposite side of the coin were the celebrities from sand and sagebrush. Among these were Rattlesnake Pete, a squawman living with the Moqui Indians, who claimed he knew the secrets of the sacred snake dance until the night his comrades supplied him with a live, scaly partner for the "lights out" waltz in the barracks of C Troop; High Note, the slender Choctaw boy with the beautiful singing voice, who came with a letter of commendation from his white school teacher, a young lady said to have been a good friend to Theodore Roosevelt "out West"; Benjamin Franklin Daniels, one-time marshal of Dodge City, who had half an ear bitten off and went by the solicitous name of "Gotch Ear"; Little McGinty, the bowlegged dwarf bronco-buster from Oklahoma; Pollock, the full-blooded Pawnee from Indian Territory, a chief's son and a vicious fighter whose manners, mind and tongue were pure as a girl's; Smith, the giant bearhunter from Elk Basin, Wyoming, who, it was maintained, had enlisted with a 900-pound grizzly cub which had failed to pass the physical examination because of poor eyesight, but had scored thirty-five points higher than Smith on the written questions; and McCann, the shy bookkeeper from Cochise, Arizona, who had been a famous buffalo hunter in his youth.

There were some real heroes of the land, such as J. B.

Armstrong of the Texas Rangers who had tracked down John Wesley Hardin, but mostly they were the faceless ones of no name and no fame whatever, men known only by pseudonyms: such as "Dude," a particularly hard and hairy cattleman; "Sheeny Solomon," a redheaded fighting Irishman; "Metropolitan Bill," an unlettered cowpoke who had never left the home ranch; "Prayerful James," the most profane man in the regiment, and "Hell Roaring Jones," the meekest recruit in camp.

In Fate Baylen's case, however, these colorful banditti of the plains were old medicine. He had brushed elbows with the Gotch Ears and the Hell Roarers; they were a part of his cowboy past. It was the Easterners who excited him at Camp San Antonio. Such college heroes as Dudley Dean, captain of the 1891 Harvard football team; Bob Wrenn, America's champion tennis player; Waller, the great high jumper; Devereux and Channing, immortals of the Princeton eleven; and Hamilton Fish, ex-captain of the Columbia crew, completely fascinated him. The sheer idea of all the education—four years on top of high school!—brought Fate to a point of rank wonderment toward the so-called "Harvard Cavalry." One in particular of these lords of the sheepskin attracted him. This was P. W. B. Van Schuyler IV, the blond boy who had marched fourteen times around the Exposition Building. He had the way of a king about him and Fate wished mightily that he could meet and talk with him, but naturally this would be impossible; there was simply too much social distance between them.

Two of the Regular Army officers made themselves memorable to Fate. They were Captain Allyn Capron and Captain Micah Jenkins.

Capron, commander of Troop L, was fifth in line, father to son, to serve with the Army. Tall, graceful, immensely strong, he had the widest shoulders, yellowest hair and most piercing steel-blue eyes Fate had ever seen. He asked nothing of his men, either dirty, dangerous or disagreeable, which he himself was not ready to perform in example.

Jenkins was also Army-bred. Commander of Troop K, he was the son and namesake of the famed Confederate general. A South Carolinian of genteel manner, he was a deadly if modest soldier. Unlike Capron, he did not lead by example but by the conveyance to his men of the iron line between officer and trooper and of the absolute duty of the one to command and the other to obey. Of the "amateur" officers, two also stood out. First was Captain William O. "Bucky" O'Neill, leader of Troop A, Fate's own. Bucky was a roving soldier of fortune. Ex-sheriff, ex-mayor, ex-newspaper editor and publisher, he was an extremely bold and ambitious man whose father had fought with honor in Meagher's Brigade in the Civil War. Bucky had a bull terrier's heart in a professional boxer's body and was more of a disciplinary problem to the overworked regimental staff than any common trooper in camp. No one, Fate was certain, would fail to remember Bucky O'Neill. It would be like trying to forget being hit and rolled over by a runaway locomotive.

There was also Lieutenant Woodbury Kane, second-in-command of Troop K. A Harvard classmate of Roosevelt's eighteen years before, he was the oldest junior officer in the regiment. Kane had enlisted as a private and begun his service humbly washing dishes for the New Mexico troops. But all too soon he was given his commission. When he was thus elevated, it was over the heads of at least a dozen Western candidates of superior experience for the job and complaints of Eastern favoritism spread through the cowboy ranks. It was a rightful bone of contention, Fate believed. Moreover, he knew it was one which would be chewed upon with plenty of teeth by the passed-over frontiersmen.

Teddy Roosevelt had called together this grandly conceived if totally unrealistic conclave of Eastern boys and Western men, foreseeing a Biblical mingling of the hosts at his command. But he had failed to show up in person to issue the command. Now, a fair part of Hell was due to break loose. It was ominously apparent to the Arizona youth that despite the happy refutations printed in the popular press and regardless of his own warm interest in the Eastern contingent, the "college men and cowboys" had not, as euphorically reported in the New York papers, "homogenized with a glad shout at the ancient shrine of the Alamo." The differences in social, economic and racial backgrounds were patently too hard-drawn. No matter the quick friendships formed by some of the men on both sides, for the main part the sensitive Westerners could feel as well as see the vast gulf between themselves and the "dudes" of the Ivy League. Fate would have liked it to be otherwise but Emmett Baylen had taught him never to close his eyes to a trouble that was morally obvious, so the Bell Rock cowboy saw the situation for what it was.

Jammed within the barnlike mustiness of the Exposition Building like shipping steers in a loading corral, possessing no single officer strong enough to control the integration of highly scrubbed Eastern with unwashed Western recruits, Camp San Antonio was bidding to become the single greatest unfought defeat in American military history.

There was utterly no ray of hope which Fate Baylen could see in this growing darkness of confusion and jealousy.

Then, like the sunrise, Teddy came. . . .

The first day Fate did not see him, nor did the camp at large. But the electric impulses which "T.R." never failed to generate were sparking wildly. Theodore Roosevelt was there! Now, by the Lord, things would start to hum! The men forgot the heat and the dust. They swung into their drills shouting the regimental ditty in hoarse cadences:

"Rough, tough, we're the stuff,
We want to fight, and we can't
Get enough—YippppeeeEEEE!!!"

Fate marched and yelled with the rest, and Lady Luck attended his cause; Troop A was selected to form the honor guard for next morning's review. At 6:00 A.M. the regiment stood assembled before the headquarters tent. Off on the right flank the regimental band held its collective breath waiting to exhale into tuba and cornet the moment the famed dashing figure should appear. Front center, the company officers sat their nervous mustangs. Fifteen minutes passed. Lieutenant-Colonel Roosevelt was an early riser—they had heard his reedy voice piping inside Wood's tent since forming up—but he was proving not to be an immediate shiner. Six-thirty came and the tension mounted.

Fate, fidgeting beside Houck Oatman, drawled aloud, "Say, you suppose his laundry's late?"

Houck flicked a glance at him. "Shut your damned mouth and stand military!" he snapped. "This is a review!"

Fate flinched. He had worked hard for Houck and would have thought their relationship had warmed a little. Apparently he was mistaken. "You betcha," he answered, and stood rigidly as ordered.

41

Five more minutes inched by. One of the officers' horses started to pitch and bucked off its rider. Another not only tossed its rider but stomped him. A third turned and bit through boot and legging to draw blood from its supposed master. The first trumpet in the band, having taken and held one too many breaths, fainted dead away. While his comrades were fanning him the sentries at Wood's tent shouted, "*Ten-shun!*" and with such a flourish as only he could arrange, Lieutenant-Colonel Theodore Roosevelt strode forth.

There was vast and sudden stillness. During this pause one of the Texas ponies elected to whinny loudly. It was the clearest horselaugh Fate ever heard. And it was not without some inspiration.

Teddy's cordovan boots shone like wet varnish. His campaign hat was pinned up flaringly on the left side with a pancake-sized regimental insignia. The U.S.V. letters on his stand-up collar glittered in the sun with twenty-four-karat magnificence. His golden spurs and the chains of his sword belt, adorned with blue and scarlet saber loop, rang with a wondrous jingle as he stomped forward to face his awestricken troops. It was here that Houck Oatman's bony elbow punched into Fate's ribs and he muttered, "Quit grinning; this is about as funny as a wagonload of dead squaws!" But Fate could not help thinking, all the same, that the Texas pony had a point.

Teddy Roosevelt just did not come up to the picture of him offered by advance press notices. His uniform did not fit him and he looked as odd and unsoldierly as it was humanly possible to do. He was short. He was wide. He was bandy-legged. He had no waist and no neck, and his head was the shape of a pig-iron stewpot. He had a jaw as undershot as a pugdog's and the lower teeth to go with it.

His uppers were even more spectacular. Showing continually above the protruded lowers, they were of the seeming number and brilliance of new piano keys. He appeared to be eternally grinning. Actually, since the jutting ledge of his large blond mustache bristled feistily at all times, it was impossible to tell just what he *was* doing with all those teeth. There were, as well, the famous steel-rimmed spectacles without which it was rumored Teddy could not find his stirrup to mount up. Or, as some uncharitably claimed, the horse under the saddle which went with the stirrup. But the thing Fate would remember longest about him was the way in which he stood, strode about or struck his various poses of importance. He gave the peculiarly fascinating tri-impression of a bull-necked duck, a belligerent bantam rooster and a pouter pigeon with its chest permanently inflated. For a chancy moment Fate thought again of the bad-mannered pony and almost laughed himself. But a second jab from Houck's elbow sobered him. He was standing as stiffly as any trooper in the review when T.R. at last addressed his waiting army of college men and cowboys.

His words were disarmingly few. The men must realize, he said, what they faced. They must be prepared not merely to fight but to perform the weary, monotonous labor incident to the ordinary routines of a soldier's life. They must be ready to face fever exactly as they faced bullets. They were to obey unquestioningly and to do their duty as readily if called upon to garrison a fort as if sent to the front. Work that was merely irksome and disagreeable must be accomplished as cheerfully as work that was dangerous and exciting. No complaint of any kind must be made. Each man was free to leave the regiment as of today and no official dishonor would attach to him. But for all who stayed there would be no backing out. From this moment the First

United States Volunteer Cavalry was at war. God bless America and God bless the cause in Cuba.

When he had finished he waved and flashed his toothy grin and vanished into Wood's tent before a sound could be uttered. Then the men broke loose and cheered for ten unbroken minutes. Bucky O'Neill had to fire his revolver into the air finally to gain order. He then led Troop A off at a smart trot, and the other troops, still yelling for their colonel, followed in turn.

Fate was as sold as any man in camp. All his former doubts of the war with Spain were dissolved in the single moment of Teddy's talk. Gone, too, were any thoughts of how odd the famous man might look or act. When he stood up there and spoke, then a man listened and looked with his heart. Then he felt the thrill of the time and place. Then he shouted and cheered as crazily as the rest, nor was his faith misplaced.

Within actual hours Teddy's orders were flying from the headquarters tent in volleys of verbal grape and oral canister. The Western troops lay down their previous lament of Eastern unfairness and leaped to do the new leader's bidding. The true commander was here at last and he was every bit the he-coon and hell-raiser as advertised. He even brought the regiment a new name—the Rough Riders— which in itself seemed to change everything as though by a touch of magic.

From nowhere appeared the tents, uniforms, spurs, leg-wraps, saddles, blankets, haversacks, canteens and cartridge belts previously missing from Camp San Antonio. The railroad virtually poured the lacking matériel of war into Texas on the heels of T.R.'s arrival. The procurement of horses— and good horses—doubled and redoubled in three days. On the fourth day the first cases of the wonderful new 30–40

U.S. Krag carbines began piling up at the supply dumps. These beautiful weapons, issued to no other volunteer troops, raised regimental morale 100 percent by themselves. On the fifth day Teddy held the first mounted maneuvers of his cowboy cavalry. Although a disaster as a military exercise it was another triumph for the "little Colonel." The entire 400 head of horses involved in the drill broke away in a range mustang stampede at the first "Forward ho!" and were not untangled for a full two hours afterward. But Teddy endeared himself to the cursing, laughing, disgraced "riders of the plains" by ordering a mass rodeo held on the spot to show the wild horses who was boss. In the ensuing wholesale understanding between men and mounts, Fate was voted third money by company acclamation, placing behind only the celebrated Tom Darnell of New Mexico and the equally noted A. R. Perry of Arizona. Teddy Roosevelt personally pinned upon the Bell Rock cowboy one of the three "busted surcingle" citations awarded in the field for "conspicuous bravery above and beyond ordinary human ability to stick with a McClellan saddle."

From the memorable afternoon of the rodeo Teddy's reputation skyrocketed. The already furious pace of regimental training became fanatic. Men actually fought for work. The officers themselves vied for any lowly chore, or dangerous, which might speed the day of departure.

On May 22 the regiment, fully uniformed in brown duck trousers, gray flannel shirts, canvas leggings and felt campaign hats, heard the reading of the Articles of War. The senior captains repeated the solemn words to their individual commands. The mass intoning of the litany silenced the regiment so that each clink of cartridge belt, each shuffle of booted foot, each least rattle of spur chain could be heard distinctly. Being a Sunday, religious services followed. A

45

choir of twenty cowboy voices, led by the same A. R. Perry who was the second best bronco rider in the West, sang "How Firm a Foundation" and "Onward Christian Soldiers." The sole accompaniment was trooper Cassi blowing the silver regimental bugle. The hymning could be plainly heard in San Antonio, a mile distant. It was the most stirring and lovely thing the men had ever witnessed. When Perry sang the solo lead of "Christian Soldiers," Fate joined his rough comrades in open tears.

Monday it was back to work with a vengeance.

Roosevelt inaugurated officers and noncommissioned officers "study classes." Fate's workday was thus extended to sixteen hours but he did not complain. Teddy had ordered it.

On May 24 the second of the full regimental mounted drills was held. It proved a disaster nearly equal to the first, sending 600 squalling mustangs pitching over the prairie en masse. But this time no rodeo followed. Teddy only waded into the mess, untangling squadrons and companies, working them back into mounted line and rerunning the charge again and again. When he quit it was so dark Fate could scarcely see his horse's ears but the men, bone-weary and ready to drop, still cheered Teddy to the prairie echo when, at last, his high-pitched order to "Dismiss!" rang down the darkened lines.

Another three days and nights of struggle to whip the Rough Riders into a regiment of cavalry ensued. Then, on May 27, a Friday, general assembly was blown just after supper. By 7:00 P.M. the regiment was standing tensely before the command tent. Colonel Wood emerged with Lieutenant-Colonel Roosevelt, Major Brodie and the remainder of his staff. Wood announced in his quiet way that he had a message for the regiment, which Colonel Roosevelt would read.

When Teddy strode forward, the stillness struck like soundless lightning among the troops.

"Men," he cried, *"we have received our marching orders; we leave in twenty-four hours!"*

That was all, and it was enough. The men, wild with long-delayed excitement, would not quit hurrahing and demonstrating throughout the camp. Only the repeated calls of the buglers brought a gradual cessation of the uproar. Saturday, all day, they broke camp. With nightfall the work was unfinished. Lanterns bloomed by the hundreds in the windy darkness. Dust and debris whistled through the hot air like bullets. Lights were blown out and could not be relit. The men worked on, cursing, laughing, Rebel-yelling, drunk with relief and eagerness. At 3:00 A.M. taps blew. It was Sunday, May 29, 1898. Fate could scarcely believe it, yet it was true. Teddy Roosevelt had arrived in San Antonio on May 16. In exactly thirteen days he had done what the Regular Army could not have done in thirteen weeks; he had organized, equipped and field-trained a full regiment of cavalry and was ready to place it aboard the railroad cars for Tampa, Florida and the waiting military transports of the United States Navy.

Thanks to Teddy Roosevelt, Cuba and the war lay but a week away.

Chapter Seven

From first light to last on Sunday and until dawn next day the troops labored to get themselves and their 1100 horses and mules aboard the seven sections of the train which would bear them eastward. Colonel Wood went ahead with the first three sections on Sunday. Roosevelt was left in command of the trailing four sections. Section Seven, with him and some special service troops, including Fate and Houck Oatman, acting company police, was ready to leave the San Antonio depot shortly after sunup Monday. In this weary moment, with the windowpanes of the town still blinking to the sunrise behind them, Teddy did something which proved to Fate that he deserved all the confidence and affection his cowboy army lavished upon him.

Fate and Houck were swinging aboard the end coach of Section Seven. In their custody was a soldier of Troop C, a boy only, and dog-sick with measles. As they entered the car, a pullman reserved for officers, all the curtains were drawn. One berth was not occupied. Its owner was just then coming down the aisle from the washroom. Houck saw him, took a firm grip on the sick boy, and said, "We will try to cover for you in some way. Shut up and salute when we do." The youth nodded weakly but was given no chance to show his mettle. Roosevelt blocked the way, stubby legs widest. "What have you there?" he demanded.

Houck saluted. "A sick kid, Colonel; from Troop C."

"Troop C?" Roosevelt's teeth clicked audibly. "They left yesterday afternoon. Well, the devil with that. Here, let me feel your forehead, boy." He put his hand to the youth's brow, wheeled again on Houck. "Sergeant," he growled, "put this man in my berth. I'll send in Dr. Church to look after him. Let me know what he says." He was instantly back to Fate, clapping a fatherly hand to the latter's wide shoulder, and saying, "Come along, lad, let's see if two old soldiers can find a seat to share."

Hours later in the gusty shadows of a trackside watering tower, Houck and Fate, on guard to see that none of the men left the car during the stop, paused to take last drags on their cigarettes as the whistle shrilled warningly.

Fate shook his head. "I still can't get over it," he said. "Him setting down in that troop car and sleeping in the same square alongside me. It was amazing."

Houck moved his head in lean agreement. "It sure was," he said.

Fate glanced at him quickly. "What you mean?" he asked.

Houck shot his cigarette spinningly into the muddy puddle at the tower's base. "I'll tell you," he said. "If he had just had us to take the kid along to Doc Church, Church would have taken care of him because he's the regimental surgeon and it's his job to do so. That would have been that and no medals handed out to anybody. But now what have you got? You've got 'Teddy' doing a noble deed, that's what. By this time half the train knows how unselfish the Colonel is. Christ Jesus himself couldn't beat him in an election held tomorrow morning.''

Fate had not heard the Payson deputy speak as long and heatedly on any subject but his own sympathies were all opposed.

"God bless it, Houck,'' he stormed, ''I can't believe it! You standing there saying such things about Colonel Roosevelt. It's downright shameful. How can you do it?''

"Easy,'' said Houck. ''I've worked a few more roundups than you, kid. Also, I was born brighter. You got a simple mind. It may help you to stay happy but it isn't ever going to win you any promotions, not in the Army and not in life afterwards; now, you remember it.''

"Remember what?'' said Fate, bewildered. ''Cuss it, Houck, I can't keep abreast of you. What you trying to say?''

The older man kicked at the cinders of the road-bed, pale eyes narrowing. ''God damn him,'' he said softly, ''he's a fourflusher. There's nothing lower in my opinion and I can't stand the sight of him. Get back aboard.''

Subsequent to the clash Fate was kept too physically miserable to brood over Houck's outburst.

To begin with, their coaches were ancient wooden bench models. One newspaperman told Fate he had ridden from Camp Chickamauga to Tampa with the Ninth Regular (Negro) Cavalry and that the colored troops had been furnished upholstered chair and sleeping cars. Moreover, they had been fed three times a day with extra coffee and hot rolls at every stop. This made an instant hit with Fate and his fellows who had been issued no food except one banquet of two weevily hardtacks and a "fragrant" slab of tinned beef. Yet on Tuesday their pleasures truly commenced. They were ordered to water the horses for the first time. The work of unloading and reloading the wild Texas ponies in the 4:00 A.M. blackness was incredibly difficult. The cursing Westerners required six hours merely to get each mount up to the trough. It then required two additional hours to fight the mustangs, squealing and biting like cornered coyotes, back into the prewar, narrow-bed stock cars. The real joys were still ahead. It was after this Tuesday watering that the civilian crowds commenced to gather along the right-of-way clamoring to see "Teddy." From the moment this phenomenon presented itself the journey assumed the aspects of a theatrical tour.

The audiences were large and overwhelmingly enthusiastic. The press reviews were universal in damning the railroad officials, while praising shamelessly the amateur and unblushing star of the troupe, "our Teddy." Indeed, the late Assistant Secretary of the Navy was receiving standing ovations at every prairie freight siding on the line. Some of the smaller minds in the regiment felt it was his interminable taking of these unscheduled bows which resulted in the troop train's requiring an unprecedented four days between San Antonio and Tampa. It was circulated as a fact that the engineer of Section Seven wore out four pairs of gloves just reaching for the brake handle in order that T.R. might climb down and address the bucolic multitudes. Houck Oatman was forced to admit he had misjudged the Colonel in the beginning: at first he had believed that Roosevelt was after Wood's job but now he could see that this was all wrong; he wasn't after Wood's job, at all, he was after McKinley's.

Fate thought this bordered on the treasonable and said

so. Houck only moved his chewing tobacco from one cheek to the other. "You name me a quicker way to get into the White House," he said, "than to fight your way in. Start with George Washington and come right on up to U.S. Grant. You get the idea, kid?"

Fate scowled, turned stubborn. "You surely do dislike the Colonel," he grumbled. "What's he ever done to you? And how come you joined up if you thought he was such a lowdown fourflusher?"

"I gave him the benefit of the doubt, same as you and the rest did," Houck replied. "But he's a politician, kid, first, last, and forever. And they come in only one variety. Bad."

"Funny. That's what my dad always said."

"Sure, your dad was smart."

Fate would not see the validity of the snare he had set for himself. He shook his head. "Houck," he said, "let's us don't talk about the Colonel no more. All right?"

"Sure, kid, I know how you feel. I only ask one thing of you—watch him. Keep your eyes open and think. Not only about your friend Teddy but about this whole thing he's cooked up. It's queer as a twenty-four-cent quarter."

"Honest to God, Houck," said Fate, confused, "I can't get it straight why you joined up. You talk like a man that was drove into doing it. It don't make sense."

"For once you win," answered Houck Oatman. "It sure don't. Shut up."

They were riding the last bench near the vestibule on the troop car. Down the unlit aisle Fate could see the sprawled forms of the exhausted men. Beyond them the uncertain shadows of the night flicked and smeared past the coach windows. It was June 2, their third day on the train. They were somewhere in southern Mississippi nearing the Alabama line. During the night they would slip through the latter state, be in Florida by morning. They were running very late and there were to be no more stops for officer or man or thirsty livestock or any reason whatsoever. Fate shivered, looking about apprehensively. With the wind rushing by the greasy windows, the train whistle calling mournfully through the little hamlets and dimly lighted stations flashing past in the outer darkness, and with Tampa and the transports for Cuba lying only hours ahead, it was scary, and lonely. Lonely as hell. Many of the men down that aisle were not asleep but sitting with their eyes shut, thinking in the same way Fate was thinking. He wondered if their feelings were as uncertain as his own. He wanted to go down the car and talk with some of them but his temporary position with Houck's police squad fixed that. The Western troopers did not take to the idea of being "chaperoned" by any big lunk of a Verde Valley boy who had never in his ignorant life commanded anything more impressive than the sometime respect of his cowpony. Nobody, short of Teddy Roosevelt, was going to tell these strays from Bent Horn, Broken Bow, Big Piney, Bad Water, Bear River, Squaw Rock, Snakeroot, Steamboat Springs, Owlhoot, Wagontongue, Tensleep, Fort Pitchfork, or you name it, one damned solitary thing they did not want to be told. Not today, not tomorrow, not the middle of next month, not any time. Their hair was long and full of cockleburrs and they intended to keep it that way come Tampa, Havana, hell or high wind.

Fate grinned happily. It warmed him to think of the way the Rough Riders fought the bit. Turning from the window, still smiling privately, he caught Houck Oatman's frosty glance examining him. For no reason he blushed guiltily. "Howdy, Houck," he blurted. "Nice night out."

His companion continued to study him.

"I knew," he said at last, "that you had a simple mind. I just had no idea how simple. You're a real chucklehead, aren't you? What the devil you smirking out that window about?"

"Nothing much," admitted Fate. "Odds and ends."

"Odds mostly, I'd say," nodded the other. "You got a mother, Baylen? Alive, I mean."

"No, sir, I ain't. Why?"

"Good. I won't need to fret over bringing you safe home to her."

"No, that's so," said Fate, "I reckon you won't." He thought it over for a long time, then added soberly, "You know something, Houck? Speaking of folks, I mean? You would have made some lonesome boy a wonderful mother."

"I'm fond of you, too, kid," said Houck Oatman patiently. "You wake me up one more time shy of the Florida line, I'm going to belt you square in the mouth."

"Yes, sir," subsided Fate. "I didn't mean nothing."

"You couldn't," growled Houck. "Where there's no sense, there's no feeling. Give up and go back to your window."

Chapter Eight

In the swampy dawn the regiment reached Ybor City, outside Tampa. Here the railroad sided five sections of the Rough Riders' troop train, as well as the passenger special carrying Colonel Wood and his staff. The string of cars bearing the regimental mess kits and field kitchen supplies, however, was run off somewhere in the morning darkness and again the Westerners missed breakfast. Still, as the famished troopers began unloading and feeding their horses, they had to laugh. After all, it did make a strange picture seeing the ragged bales of hay and bulging oat sacks being brought out of their own coaches where the forage issue had traveled with them all the way from San Antonio stacked in aisle, vestibule and overhead baggage rack. Roosevelt, meanwhile, was raging. His high voice tearing at the railway officials riding in Wood's passenger section could be heard the full length of the sided troop sections. It was later said he made more enemies that day than in the entire

Cuban campaign, and Fate Baylen believed he had just cause. It was no great privilege to ride four days cooped in a wooden coach with forty men, sixty sacks of cracked oats and half a ton of prairie grass. According to Houck this sort of crazy planning was all Army fault, but Fate could not see it that way. With most of the regiment, he was greatly cheered by the sounds of Teddy "telling them off" back at the staff car. Yet the railroad had only begun to show its shoddy regard for the First Volunteer Cavalry.

It was now discovered that Tampa was not just beyond the bend but eight miles away, and had it wished, the management of the line could have disembarked them six miles nearer the city. There was nothing for it, though, except to saddle up and ride the remainder of the way.

The resulting march was without order or spirit. The bedraggled troopers straggled along the mucky wagon road cursing the falling mist. No troop guidons flew. No bugles rang. No Rebel yells echoed. Tampa proved a miserable huddle of Negro shacks and white-trash shanties: its sole verdure, sawgrass; its principal landscaping, sand dunes. The Rough Riders went through it at a growling trot. Eventually, they reached their destination, the abandoned drill area of the Sixth Cavalry (Reg) lying in a "dry swamp" behind the Tampa Bay Hotel. Here they got down to survey mournfully the campsite selected for them by their Army hosts. Only First Sergeant Houck Oatman seemed amused by the choice. Standing with Fate Baylen ankle-deep in the pungent mulch of Sixth Cavalry horse droppings, he drawled to his lanky companion, "Well, here we are, kid, up to our spur shanks in the Regular Army's opinion of Teddy Roosevelt and the Rough Riders. Any way you want to spell it, it still comes out—"

"Don't say it!" interrupted Fate, wincing at the thought.

"I don't rightly believe I could hear such a naughty word without weeping."

"You're faded," nodded Houck sympathetically. "We have crapped out for sure on this throw."

"Thank you for your understanding," muttered Fate. "A growing boy can bear only so much."

But once on the grounds, the natural sunshine of the Western disposition broke through, speeding the business of pitching the tents and setting up the picket lines.

The shelter-halves were erected, at will, in long wobbly lines, each line's mounts being picketed behind its tents. This arrangement put a picket line in *front* of, as well as *behind,* each shelter row. The proximity of the livestock struck some of the less eager warriors as "cozy," but no official complaint was lodged. Twenty-four hours passed. There was no news of the Navy and their troopships. First uneasinesses were aired. The Florida sun now came out of the arrival mists and began to bear down. The fly hatch left in the manure piles of the Sixth Cavalry came off magnificently. Swarms of southern greenbots assaulted the First United States Volunteer Cavalry with a viciousness not to be matched by the mere "buffalo gnats" of Arizona, New Mexico or the Indian Territory. Yet, once more, Teddy Roosevelt rose to the challenge. He reset the entire campsite so that each tent line's horses were picketed on its own side of the company street. In this stroke of clear-headed thinking, according to the New York newsmen resident in the swank Tampa Bay Hotel, "he brought unbelievable order out of incredible chaos." The same action led Houck Oatman to remark acridly to Fate, "You see now, kid, this way all you have to smell is the stuff from your own horse. If that isn't military genius, you will never see any. Like you always said, the Colonel surely is amazing."

There was also that summer a record hatch of tarantulas and centipedes in the Tampa sands. Added to the horseflies, heat, tropical humidity and further unexplained delay of the troopships, the poisonous "nightcrawlers" threatened to win the war for Spain before a solitary Rough Rider got aboardship for Cuba. The Western tempers were not improved by the next inspiration of tireless Teddy; the reestablishing of 4:30 A.M. reveille and 5:30 A.M. mounted drill. With all this the spoiling troopers had still to fight the third and greatest of the insect invasions of Camp Tampa Bay that summer—a groundfog cloud of vampire mosquitoes the size and fierceness of harpy eagles. One lean member of Fate's company declared that he had been "friendlier bit by hydrophoby bats," while another swore that he would "far ruther fight a pack of starved she-wolves inside a sewed-up gunnysack" than to face another sixty seconds under his shelter-half with the Tampa mosquitoes.

But it was not all "horse flies and spiders" at Camp Tampa. Recreation was an important part of the recruit's life, and in this area Fate left a name for himself.

Returning from Tampa and a minor courier mission for Captain O'Neill, he had halted his pony at the edge of the marshy field whereon a group of the Eastern college boys were battling with a skittery pigskin. The football uniforms were unpadded brown duck issue trousers, sockfeet and underwear tops. Bloody noses, skinned elbows and blued eyes were evident in healthy number. Yet the game had not even commenced to get genuinely rough, as the Eastern lads were immediately to discover.

Fascinated, the Bell Rock cowboy watched the fortunes of "his team," the Harvard eleven which was captained by young "Pete" Van Schuyler, the millionaire boy who had so interested Fate at Camp San Antonio. Yale's kicker—

the only player on either team permitted to wear footgear—
had just gone back to punt out of danger for Old Eli. Standing on his own goal line he got off a towering spiral
downfield toward Van Schuyler, playing safety for Harvard.
The latter moved out to field the ball, but the sun got in
his eyes and he missed the catch. At the same moment he
stepped into a gopher hole and sprawled headlong. Fate
could not bear it. A Rebel yell flew from his throat and he
vaulted off his startled pony. Dashing out upon the field he
scooped up the loose ball and called excitedly to Van
Schuyler, "Which way? Which way?"

The New York youth scrambled up and pointed toward
the advancing Yale monsters. "Follow me, cowboy!" he
ordered. Inspired by such fearlessness, Fate charged the on-
coming tacklers like a wild brahma bull. He shed the first
three by sheer power, shattered the next four by blazing
speed, and ran over the remaining enemy, as well as his
own teammates, by brute enthusiasm coupled with total
lack of talent for the game. The only player of either side
still standing between him and the Yale goal line was Van
Schuyler IV. With the latter leading the way he virtually
loped over for the game-winning points. He was still bow-
ing in acknowledgment of the spectator applause when a
grinning Van Schuyler tapped him on the shoulder and said,
"Better come along, cowboy. I doubt my pals will understand you didn't purposely leave on your boots and spurs
for that run."

Horrified, Fate recoiled. He had indeed made the touch-
down wearing his three-inch U.S. Cavalry "spikes" and he
knew, by instinct, that Van Schuyler was correct and that
in honorable retreat lay their only chance for survival.

"Mr. Van Schuyler, sir," he said, "I reckon you have
estimated them odds near perfect. You foller me this time."

He set off, reversing his field and charging the side-lines and up them to his standing pony. Leaping into the saddle, Bell Rock-style, he wheeled the wiry animal into a dead run back toward Van Schuyler. Scooping up his curly-haired hero, he spurred for the sawgrass swamp which bordered the field. Once safely lost in this cover, he and the New York boy were able to make it back to camp in good time for noon mess.

Captain O'Neill was well pleased with the promptness of Corporal Baylen's message-riding. He was a little puzzled, though, by a remark passed by a short blond soldier from Troop K who was with Baylen when he complimented the big Arizonan on the speed of his return from Tampa. "Yes, sir, Captain O'Neill!" said the Eastern lad, saluting and stepping briskly into the breach when Fate hung his head awkwardly and could not think of a proper response. "But then what would you expect, sir, from the greatest running halfback Harvard ever had?"

Chapter Nine

In the remaining time at Tampa, Fate acquired a disturbing assortment of "facts" concerning what lay ahead of, as well as immediately surrounding, the First U.S. Volunteer Cavalry.

For example, he heard there were no more than 20,000 regular troops in the country when McKinley declared war. Spain, on the other hand, was said to have 150,000 regulars in Cuba alone. Also, the Spanish soldiers were equipped with late model Mauser rifles firing the new smokeless high speed ammunition from fast repeating bolt magazines. Some of the U.S. regiments were still carrying single-shot trapdoor Springfields of Civil War vintage, and firing black powder. The First Missouri Volunteers had begun training in recruit camp with no shoes. The Thirty-second Michigan had not been issued any weapons. Many outfits had no uniforms, were still in the clothes they had worn to home-town armory or depot for the departure to Florida. Most of the commands had been given heavy regulation "dark blues," more suitable, as Roosevelt bitterly complained, "for service on the January plains of Montana than in the steaming jungles of Cuba." Even the dusty brown ducks of the Rough Riders were woven of the heaviest cotton manufacture, and their iron-gray campaign hats were of felt thick enough, according to the perspiring cowboys, "to turn anything short of a hand ax." And last, but a long ways from least, two of the Regular Cavalry detachments, the Ninth and Tenth Regiments, were colored men!

Most of the men, particularly the Southerners, believed that a darky simply would not fight. He would quit and run the minute he got the chance; he could not be depended upon for a single thing. Accepting this judgment, Fate was still personally curious about the "buffalo soldiers." He sneaked over and watched the Ninth, which was stationed next to the Rough Riders, drill several times. The truth was, although he did not dare say so, they were a crack outfit and made the Rough Riders look like nothing. The sight of the dusky troopers riding and obeying and behaving exactly the same, except a little better, than white soldiers, struck him as most intriguing.

On June 6 word came that, of Roosevelt's and Wood's regiment, Troops C, M, I and H would have to be left behind in Camp Tampa, along with most of the 1100 head of horses and mules brought from San Antonio. Not even Florence, the mountain lioness mascot of the regiment, was to be permitted to go. The Rough Riders were stunned. Fate could not believe it and felt sick for the poor devils who had come so far and worked so hard only to be told they would not be needed except to shovel manure and swat flies in Florida. Sitting glumly hunched before his shelter-half, he was subsequently cheered a little when Private P. W. B.

Van Schuyler IV happened by, undaunted, and called out happily, "Come on, cowboy, up and at them—I'm taking you to lunch at the Tampa Bay Hotel!"

The regiment had been given unlimited liberty to ease the pains of separation, so there was no reason for Fate to refuse this exciting invitation. He argued a little but the mere thought of such an adventure was heady stuff. He began to want very much to see what lay inside the towering façade of that famed seaside resort, and what there was about it which attracted all the high officers, newspapermen, foreign correspondents, army wives and handsome women of other callings who were in daily attendance at the Tampa Bay.

He was swept away in the end by Van Schuyler's enthusiasm. "Listen, Arizona, I saw a Georgia peach over there yesterday with her dress cut clear down to here, and let me tell you she was double whipping cream all the way! Come on, don't just stand there with your mouth open, Lofty. Girls may go out of style!"

The Bell Rock cowboy shook his head in despair. "Goddammit, I ain't even seen the eyelashes of a pretty woman since Prescott," he groaned. Then, a great and burning blush of resolve beginning to discolor his earlobes, "Sonofabitch! wait up; I'll go and slick some saddlesoap on my hair . . . !"

On the trip over to the hotel he thought nothing of the remarks his host made about "the girls," taking them to be general. It was only when they had walked up the broad veranda steps and entered the glittering dining salon itself that he discovered differently.

"There they are," said Van Schuyler. "Those two luscious ones at the table by the window. How do you like them?"

Fate did not hear him. He was staring at something else. At a table nearer them sat an enormously fat general dining with Colonel Wood. This had to be General William R. Shafter, commander of the camp and the man who would head the entire campaign in Cuba. At the adjacent table was Lieutenant-Colonel Theodore Roosevelt and two obviously embarrassed recruits. Teddy appeared either oblivious to the discomfort of the enlisted men or callous to it. For the first time Fate felt a doubt stir within him. "Say," he asked his companion uneasily, inclining his head toward Roosevelt's table, "how come you suppose the Colonel ain't eating with Wood and the General? How come he's with them soldiers? They somebody special or something?"

Van Schuyler glanced over at the table and laughed quickly. "Sure," he said. "They're something special all right; they're common soldiers. Think how it will look in the newspapers."

Fate looked at him. It was exactly the same thing Houck Oatman had said about the kindness to the young soldier who had been ill on the train out of San Antonio. But this was P. W. B. Van Schuyler IV, not some shark-jawed deputy from Yavapai County. He would have no rightful cause to low-rate the Colonel. He had a million dollars in the bank and four years of education past high school. He wouldn't be jealous of anybody on earth, not even Teddy Roosevelt.

"You actually think that of the Colonel?" he asked at last. Again his young guide laughed. "Willy Hearst will have it drawn from life by Frederic Remington and planted in the middle of the front page of tonight's *Journal*. Two hours later, and with a faked photograph made up from Remington's phony drawing, Pulitzer will have the *World* on the street in a five-star edition. Any wagers, Arizona?''

Fate set his teeth. "I ain't a betting man," he said. "Where we going to set?"

Van Schuyler scowled slightly. "Didn't you hear me just now?" he said. "Our girls are over there at that window table. The redhead's mine, the blonde's yours."

Fate's gray eyes widened. "Whoa up!" he cried. "You mean to tell me them gorgeous things setting there is waiting for me and you?"

"You know it, cowboy!" said the other. "Nothing but the very best for any friend of Pete Van Schuyler's. Let's close in!"

"You must be loco, Pete," said Fate, backing off. "I will see you in the sweet by-and-by. Good luck . . . !"

P. W. B. Van Schuyler made a belated college try at seizing him by the arm but the tall Arizonan was already plowing his way through the crowded foyer toward the freedom of the front doors. He hiked the eight miles back to camp and spent the remainder of the afternoon shoveling manure by choice. When he finally quit and went to the shelter-half he shared with First Sergeant Houck Oatman, he found his tent companion rolling his blankets.

"What's the matter?" he inquired dispiritedly. "You been transferred or throwed out?"

"Neither," answered Houck. "I merely got a friendly tip from Roosevelt's cook and am packing to avoid the rush."

"Oh," said Fate, "what rush is that?"

Houck regarded him acidly. "Well," he said, "it ain't to the Klondike."

"Cripes!" yelled Fate, beside himself. "You can't mean it! We're going to Cuba at last!"

Houck sighed heavily, depressed by his protégé's enthusiasm. "The cook says he overheard the order. Teddy's been given the inside track again. Our outfit's getting the jump on all the others. We will move out in the dark tomorrow morning. T.R. means to have us aboard our transport before the others hear the bugle blow."

Fate could scarcely contain his excitement. It was the grandest news ever. Then, numbingly, an associated thought cut across his stimulated intellect. "Good Lord," he said, "I got to warn Boone Gaskill!"

Houck shot him a hard look.

Boone Gaskill was the regimental moonshiner; a sly Georgia fox who owned and operated a whiskey still so ingeniously designed as to be transportable within the bedrolls of his six or eight best customers among the Rough Riders. He had been hotly pursued by Colonel Wood's entire intelligence section since the first green fumes of cooking sourmash had coiled through the camp at San Antonio, and to be presently seen in his company was tantamount to a charge of spying for the enemy.

"Baylen," said Houck, after the long, ice-cold stare, "for God's sake smarten up. Wood has enlisted a special U.S. revenue officer just to run down that crazy hillbilly whiskey maker. You get caught anywhere near that snake-oil distillery of his, you'll get twenty years. Now, you understand me, kid?"

Fate turned a fish-gut gray.

"Sure," he gasped, "I understand you fine. But it ain't goin' to do me no good. I'm the one in charge of the corkscrew copper pipe that draws off the final juice and drips it into the bottling crock . . . !"

Chapter Ten

By that evening word of the departure had been given official status by Wood, yet no orders to march had been issued. Roosevelt, nonetheless, went ahead with his preparations. At 11:00 P.M. the Rough Riders moved out. By 12:00 they were at trackside of the Port Tampa Railroad, leading to the bay and docks. Here they waited, laughing and talking in the darkness. Their train did not appear. It was now 2:00 A.M. Other troops began moving up and boarding the engineless troop cars on the nearby sidings. Still no train passed up or down the main line. Roosevelt sent out patrols to find general officers and inquire for clues. The patrols returned with the impression that the situation had degenerated into a first-served operation. Teddy's teeth gleamed in the light of the bull's-eye lanterns. He went at once to Shafter, returning with a signed order for another train on another spur of the line at 3:00 A.M. The Rough Riders started on the trot through the early morning blackness. The other troops aboard the stalled sided sections cheered them off with such encouragements as, "Good-bye, boys, too bad you couldn't make it," and "Keep the place cleaned up while we're away!" The Rough Riders did not return the sentiments. By then they were worried from Roosevelt down to the last private.

Arrived at the new rendezvous, they waited past three, then four, then five o'clock. No train appeared. Gray light was showing in the east. At a quarter after five Roosevelt gave the order to return to the main line below the point where the sided troop sections were loading. In position on either side of the track, he called up his company commanders. "Commandeer the first train moving up or down this line. I will not be left behind."

At these bold words the men cheered spiritedly. There simply was no one else like Teddy Roosevelt. If he had no orders he invented some. If he had orders and did not care for them, he made up his own. One thing; he did not stand still! "By damn," said Fate to Houck, "you got to admit it—he's a doer!" Houck made no reply.

At 6:00 A.M. a string of empty coal cars came chuffing up from the bay. The better part of a thousand Rough Riders jammed onto the track, halting the train. Its engineer shouted irately to clear the line. Teddy flashed his copyrighted grin and shouted in return, "Sir, your orders have just been changed. You are going to reverse this string of cars right back down to the docks."

The engineer threw up his hands. "But I'm empty!" he protested. "If I run back without a load the company will have my job!"

Again the famed teeth gleamed in the early light. "If a load is all you need, sir, you have it. . . . Men . . . !" Teddy wheeled. "Get on board. If we must start out to

Cuba backward, we shall do so. On the double now, into the cars!''

The Rough Riders swarmed into the dusty gondolas. Within five minutes the string of empties, now filled with bituminously black troopers from the West (happily calling themselves the Eleventh Cavalry—brothers to the Ninth and Tenth, Negro), was backing down the track toward Port Tampa.

But the Regular Army was not to be so simply denied. At the quay a three-star general pulled Teddy off his coal-car special and abruptly informed him that here was where the Rough Riders began to walk, and this despite the fact that the railroad continued along the quay to the transport berths. Roosevelt was irked but hardly defeated. He and Wood set off on the trot to find some other general officer who remembered the Assistant Secretary of the Navy. Instead, they found a Colonel Humphrey who, apparently on his own, was handing out transport allotments. He gave them their number—it was Number Eight, the *Yucatan.*

By this time, 7:00 A.M., the docks were choked with upward of 7,000 men. More were pouring down from Camp Tampa by the minute. Roosevelt, in his wildly improbable military manner, passed the order to his company commanders to lead a flying wedge charge of First U.S. Volunteer Cavalry, dismounted, straight out the main quay of Fort Tampa, to seize and occupy the 750-man transport *Yucatan.* The action, playfully written up by Roosevelt later as ''the first offensive of the War with Spain,'' was entirely successful. The Rough Riders not only boarded the *Yucatan* but held her against the determined assaults of two other outfits which also showed allocation papers to the Number Eight transport. Of these groups, the Seventy-first New York Volunteers alone contained more men than the *Yu-*

catan was designed to carry! The Second Infantry (Reg), the other "enemy force," abandoned the field when Roosevelt offered to allow four of its companies—because they included a regimental band—to come aboard and cruise to Cuba with the Rough Riders.

The rest of the day was devoted to loading the baggage of the regiment. With nightfall the *Yucatan* was ready to raise her hook and get out into the stream to await daybreak and sailing orders. It had required thirty-six of the most hectic, original quick-thinking hours ever put together by a resourceful commander for Roosevelt to get the Rough Riders aboard transport for Cuba that June 8, 1898. And when the *Yucatan* hooted hoarsely, cast off, reversed her screws and backed out into the summer darkness, the cheers for their bandy-legged little Colonel sent into the hot, humid air by the grateful cowboy soldiers thundered inland past the pine flats of Camp Tampa.

"My God," said Fate Baylen in awed tones to First Sergeant Houck Oatman, "listen to that. It would raise goose bumps up a salamander's spine. Ain't it grand, though?"

Houck continued to stare over the rail into the stifling gloom toward Indian Key, Cortez, and the mouth of Tampa Bay. Four hundred miles away, down across the westering route of Columbus, waited the isle of Cuba. He took time to gather his thoughts, to weigh his reply, and to phrase it in such a way that it would violate neither his own cynicism nor his promise to treat with due care his young comrade's opinion of Lieutenant-Colonel Teddy Roosevelt. At last he believed that he had achieved the solution. He nodded slowly and spat through his teeth into the night. "Yeah," he said.

Chapter Eleven

Dawn brought no orders to sail. The new sun came up pink and steaming. The mists cleared. The Bay of Tampa lay open and inviting. But "anchors aweigh!" did not resound among the black-painted transports and gray men-of-war guarding them. The entire flotilla sat in the stream bobbing and nodding like a stool of wooden decoys set out to mislead the passing migrant into believing that here waited an invasion armada, steam up and ready to sail.

The morning went with no information on the delay. Late that afternoon an announcement was made: R. A. Alger, Secretary of War, had telegraphed Shafter to wait further orders; on the previous Tuesday evening the converted yacht *Eagle,* cruising in the San Nicholas Channel, had sighted an armored Spanish ship-of-the-line accompanied by a torpedo-boat destroyer. The U.S. Cuban armada would need to swing at anchor while the Navy checked on the enemy craft.

Aboard the *Yucatan* the Rough Riders lifted their choicest prairie curses to match those of the 12,000 other American troops idled aboard the thirty-two transports. One day waned. Two. Three. Still the black troopships and their mouse-gray guardians drifted at anchor. On the *Yucatan* the Rough Rider spirit tumbled. The riders of rimrock, sage and lonely mountain meadow felt far more than their urbane Eastern brothers the confinement aboardship. To such men, born to the boundless land of "sky determines," the imprisonment was virtually intolerable. By 8:00 P.M. Sunday their morale had plummeted to its nadir. Fate, Houck and a group of their desperate fellows stood at the taffrail of their ship discussing the shrunken hand that fortune had dealt them.

The bunks of the *Yucatan* had been hastily roughed up of unplaned green lumber. They were full of resin, splinters, mill hair and hard knots. They were only seventy-two inches by twenty inches. Many of the long-coupled Westerners could not use them at all, and for those who could, the air below decks was poisonously foul. However, this was nothing. The Army had made, or had permitted the Navy to make, an arrangement whereby the civilian owners of the troopships, rather than the military, were to supply the food for the men aboard. As a result the Fifth Army Corps suffered privations from the inception of its loading. There was no edible ration. The shipowners supplied a repulsive canned "fresh beef" which Roosevelt later described: "There was no salt in it. At the best it was stringy and tasteless; at the worst it was nauseating. Not one-fourth of it was ever eaten at all, even when the men became very hungry." As well, there was no ice, no fresh meat, no vegetables. Daytime temperatures averaged above 100 degrees with relative humidity as high as a near-rain 98. The water in the ships' tanks was not fit for human consumption. Of it, the natty special correspondent for the New York *Journal,* Mr. Richard Harding Davis, wrote: "The water on board the ship was so bad that it could not be used for purposes of shaving. It smelled like a frog pond or a stable-yard, and it tasted as it smelt. Before we started from Tampa Bay the first time, it was examined by the doctors, who declared that in spite of the bad smell and taste it was not unhealthy, but Colonel John Jacob Astor offered to pay for fresh water for which Plant [owner of the Tampa Bay Hotel] charged 2¢ per gallon, if they would empty all the bad-smelling water overboard. General Shafter said it was good enough for him, and Colonel Astor's very considerate offer was not accepted. So we all drank Appolinaris water or tea. The soldiers, however, had to drink the water furnished them, except those who were able to pay 5¢ a glass to the ship's porter, who had a private supply of good water . . ."

Although Davis wrote from a safe distance—he had cannily arranged passage on another transport—he reported with accuracy and indeed, for him, admirable restraint.

It was the same situation of the porter selling "good" water which now engaged the profanities of the group gathered at the *Yucatan's* taffrail. Boone Gaskill had the deck. "If the little Yankee sonofabitch raises his price another two cents," complained the Georgia moonshiner, "he will be getting more for his goddam water than I am for my whiskey, and that's a purely sinful thing to contemplate." His comrades bobbed their heads vehemently. "I am thoroughly concurful," stated Little McGinty, the dwarf Oklahoma bronc rider. "But if you believe your situation to be desperate, consider mine: I can't stand to drink your whiskey without a chaser and the ship's water is deadlier than your rotgut. So a thoughtful man such as myself is enforced to buy both your painkiller and the porter's branchwater, or give up drinking entire. Maybe I'll take up tatting or smoking opium."

"I dunno about opium," said Bear River Smith, the hulking grizzly hunter, "but I know I can't stand these prices for drinking water. I got me a idear to go skin me a ship's porter."

"It's mean doings," nodded Fate, licking cottony lips. "I tried that buffalo waller extract in the ship's tanks and I will tell you, boys, I would not even dip a sheep in it, or offer it to a Indian. Phew! I will say that it is worser than Apache mescal or sweet milk!"

"I hear tell," put in Hell Roaring Jones, the diffident one from Meeker's Ford, Montana, "that some of the fellers are going to jump into the crick and swim for it. What you think of that?"

By "the crick" he meant the Bay, using a Westerner's limited definition for surface water, and replying now to his hesitant inquiry was First Sergeant Houck Oatman who, having served in his youth six years with General Crook and the Third Cavalry, was the solitary "old soldier" among them. "I will tell you what I think," he said, "and you can stuff it in your duffel sacks for the certain truth: there's none of us going to shear the porter, hooraw the shipowners, or jump overboard and skin for home. We will pay our nickel for a glass of good water, or our dollar for a decent piece of meat, or our dime for a shot of whiskey, or our six bits for a dry bed, or whatever else of graft and swindle can be dreamed up by the proprietors. Boys, you're in the Army now and you haven't begun to reap the benefits of your bravery. There's only one word to describe the joys of military service in time of war—horse manure."

"That's two words," objected Fate.

"Not the way I spell it," answered Houck.

"Oh," said Fate, and fell still with the others. As usual, Houck had boiled it down to the bone.

It was June 13, the day following, that the regiment drew its only issue smile of the Tampa Bay wait. On this date was released the text of a telegram sent Navy Secretary John D. Long by General of the Army Nelson A. Miles. Suggested the doughty old Indian fighter: IF IT WILL ASSIST YOUR DEPARTMENT IN THE SOLVING OF ITS EVIDENT INABILITY TO FERRY THE FIFTH ARMY CORPS TO CUBA, WE SHALL HAPPILY ORDER THE TROOPS DISEMBARKED, SUPPLY THE VACATED TRANSPORTS WITH GUNS, REVOLVING CANNON AND MORTARS, AND DISPATCH THEM AT ONCE TO THE AID OF THE NAVY.

Irreverent, irregular or apochryphal, this message evidently stung the admirals where they were tender. In thirty-six hours they had reassembled their scattered convoy of war vessels, provisioned and watered the transports and, at sweltering length, run up on their signal halyards the flags which conveyed to the various captains of the demoralized fleet the pulse-pounding instruction: "Now hear this, all ships, anchors aweigh!"

It was sundown, June 14, 1898, when the last of Shafter's transports swung into line down the channel from Port Tampa to the open sea, and the anti-Spanish armada disappeared into the Gulf of Mexico.

Fate alone found words for that supreme and fateful moment.

"God help them poor dumb Spanyerds," he breathed.

The five or six men standing nearest him, and hearing his fervent imprecation, nodded with clenched jaws of their own and thought, as Emmett Baylen's raw-boned son was thinking, that Spain was already as good as whipped, that she hadn't a Comanche's chance in Texas of standing up to the likes of Teddy Roosevelt and the Rough Riders.

Six days later, on the twentieth of June, having rounded the cold stone finger of Cape Maysí, run past Guantánamo Bay and swung to in the choppy waters off Santiago Harbor, the First Volunteer Cavalry was in position to make good the unspoken belief. That was Cuba lying there in the blue mists beyond the gaunt and lead-gray watchdogs of the U.S. fleet. This was it. The war. They had come as far as they were going. And in the strange hush which invaded the decks of the *Yucatan* with the sight of the island, the Rough Riders seemed to realize for the first time how very far they were from home. Suddenly the "poor" Spaniards did not appear nearly so poor, nor anything like so much in need of God's Christian assistance.

Chapter Twelve

Fate awoke wan and uneasy. The wind had come on during the night. The chop in the open seaway had increased to whitecap weather. The *Yucatan,* overloaded and poorly loaded, wallowed alarmingly. The men from the prairies believed she must go under and were scarcely quieted by the reassurances of the Eastern troopers. Fate sought out the quarters of Troop K and the counsel of his friend Pete Van Schuyler. The latter, as usual, had the latest, best information.

They were, he said, trying to decide where to go ashore. The Navy was supposed to have cleared the Spanish fleet out of Santiago Harbor but had not done so. In view of this plain dereliction of duty, General Shafter was forced to consider improvisations on the original plan. This, said the New York boy, might lead to all sorts of good fun; such as getting them all slaughtered in attempting to land.

When Fate, not caring for the sound of such talk, inquired as to the source of the news, he was told to remember that Lieutenant Woodbury Kane, Troop K's second-in-command, had been close to Teddy at Harvard College, and that he, Pete, had known Woodbury Kane for years. Thus, what Kane found out would be known to P. W. B. Van Schuyler IV and, if he kept his bloody mouth shut about it, also to Corporal Fate Baylen. Fate nodded soberly to this condition of secrecy and said guardedly, "Go ahead, Pete. I won't never say nothing to nobody."

"All right," agreed the other, "here's the situation: we either go back and put in at Guantánamo Bay or we steam along the coast looking for other spots. At Daiquiri, eighteen miles east, there's a good beach but not much protection. At Siboney, ten miles east, there's a better beach but no protection at all. Two miles west there's a place called Cabañas Bay. That's a beauty of a harbor, they say, but is under direct fire of Santiago's artillery. Now then, cowboy, were you admiral of this expedition, which of those daisies would you pluck?"

Fate shook his head in pure admiration.

"Damn, that's wonderful," he said, "to remember all that from only once hearing it. . . . Well, go ahead; what you think, Pete? I mean about a place for our boats to lay off and set us ashore?"

"I don't think anything," replied his companion, "except that we won't have long to wait. Look over there on the *Seguranca*."

Fate glanced at General Shafter's command ship. "By damn," he exclaimed, "them's the same string of saltwater signs they run up when we tooken off from Tampa Bay!"

"Sure enough they are," said Pete Van Schuyler. "Anchors aweigh, by God."

But he was wrong. It was only the *Seguranca* which

lifted its hook and steamed away. After a little while and as Fate and the New York boy were still watching the command ship dwindle hull-down to the west, Sergeant Tiffany of Troop K, a society playmate of Van Schuyler's, came by with the *real* news. Tiffany had, with Teddy Roosevelt, the same close relationship Van Schuyler enjoyed with Woodbury Kane. His press releases were therefore, if anything, better than those of Fate's blond hero. In this case, they were certainly so.

"That Navy brass which just boarded the *Seguranca*," said Tiffany, "was no less than Admiral Sampson himself. He and old Shafter really went around, the Colonel hears."

"Bully for them," sniffed Van Schuyler. "Go on; as long as you are giving us the latest war bulletin while it is still coming in, I would like to know how to arrange my affairs. If we are to engage the foe in anger and on dry land, I must wire Mother."

"It could be less funny than you think, Pete," warned the other. "Sampson wants the Army to storm El Morro."

"What?" Pete pointed toward Santiago Harbor and the forbidding cliff which housed the famed fortification. "My God, that's three hundred feet straight up!"

"Two hundred and thirty-three feet," corrected Tiffany. "But, as you say, straight up."

"Oh, that Navy!" groaned Van Schuyler. "What nerve!"

"Fortunately," said Tiffany, "our side has a bit of crust too. Shafter has told Sampson to go to Hell."

"Hooray for him. I didn't think Old Fatty had it in him. Ugh! What an animal."

"I dunno," Fate broke in. "It seems to me General Shafter is kind of a fooler. Fat, sure, but smart as a old, slowed-up coyote. I favor a man to be careful where being quick might come up fatal.''

"Shafter," countered young Van Schuyler, "is a complete boob. Ask anyone.''

"It's a fact," nodded Tiffany. "The Colonel was saying only last night that he has no more spine than a cup of hot custard.''

"Could be," conceded Fate. "Anyways, whereat has him and the admiral gone to now?''

"To talk to the Cubans, the insurgents, the ones we're down here to help. They're to meet General Calixto García and get his advice on where to land. The Colonel says if Shafter doesn't issue orders to go ashore by morning, he will take the Rough Riders over the side and swim for it.''

"He would do it, too," said Van Schuyler, "if he thought this collection of bowlegged Bayards could swim a lick.''

"What's a bowlegged bayerd?" asked Fate, eager to advance his education.

"Excuse the excess erudition," grinned Van Schuyler. "I meant cowboys.''

Fate regarded him cautiously. "You don't say it precisely like you was eating prime ribs," he said. "What you got again cowboys?''

"Not a thing, Arizona," said the Eastern boy, still smiling, "when I'm standing downwind of them. Present company always excepted, of course.''

"And what does that mean?" said Fate.

"It will come to you," his slight companion assured him. "Think of it the next time you get between your Prescott bunch and the nearest open porthole.''

"I already got it, Pete," said Fate. "Thanks very much. Good-bye.''

Neither of the Eastern troopers said anything. Both of them elevated their shoulders and rolled their eyes at one another to indicate that their untutored comrade was beyond help. Shortly, they had forgotten the incident. For Fate, however, it was the beginning of a long day. During it, he avoided everyone. He was not sulking over an imagined injury. The Rough Riders *were* a little gamey taken with the wind in the right direction. What bothered him was that Pete Van Schuyler, who had been such a good sport, would be so snooty about a matter nobody could help. Did these college kids think themselves above the other Rough Riders? Worse yet, was it possible they *were* better than the Western boys?

It was a tough question, one Fate would like to have put to Houck Oatman, but he could not find Houck and had to settle for Bear River Smith and Little McGinty, who got him into a penny-ante poker game with two halfbreed Choctaws from Troop L and Buck Dawson, the amiable chief packer for the regiment. So amiable, in fact, was the latter that he cleaned Fate of the sixteen dollars he had remaining of the original twenty with which he had left home, and then would not lend him five cents with which to buy a glass of good water from the ship's porter. Bear River saved the day by taking Fate with him to find Boone Gaskill. Boone owed Bear River two pints of whiskey and the giant grizzly hunter gave one of them to Fate. This was more than generous, since Fate, alone, could not have got near the source of supply. At Houck's insistence he had surrendered his custodianship of the copper coil pipe to Boone's portable still, and had ever since been suspect not only by the Georgia moonshiner but by all his faithful customers. As it was, Fate and Bear River retired to the aft cargo hold of the *Yucatan* and killed the two pints in about fifteen leisurely minutes.

It was perhaps 130 degrees in the hold, with no fresh air save for one six-inch porthole covered up by a pile of Alaskan-issue wool uniforms for the Regular Infantry aboard. Even Western woodsmen and cow-herders were not immune to such an environment. Fate didn't recall a thing until he awoke at sundown with his late drinking companion nowhere to be seen. It required all his native strength to haul himself up out of the hold and all his Baylen will power to keep from weeping real tears at the enormous pain hammering inside his head. He managed enough of both physical and mental control to stop a passing Troop L fellow and inquire after Bear River's fate. The man stared at him as though he were from another planet.

"Jesus," he said, "where you been? You didn't hear? The sonofabitch busted up out of the aft hold dressed in a Yankee colonel's uniform of the Second Regular Infantry and ordered both Wood and Roosevelt to surrender. Teddy took it good but Colonel Wood thought otherwise. Your acquaintance will spend the whole of the Spanish-American argument washing dishes for the sick mess, or swamping out latrines. He is out of action for the duration and you can collect bets on that all summer long." The soldier paused to peer at Fate. "You look a mite peaked yourself," he concluded. "Where was you when Bear River promoted hisself?"

Fate thought of the pile of dark blue infantry uniforms in the aft hold and groaned miserably. Damn it all, how was a man to know they were officers' uniforms? Or that Bear River would get into one of them and go look up Teddy Roosevelt and Colonel Wood?

"I dunno," he lied to the Troop L man, "but I think I

will go back there and burrow in until dark.''

''Not a bad idee,'' nodded the other. ''You smell like you tooken a bath in Boone Gaskill's still. Be sure you don't salute upwind of no officers. And don't try negotiating no terms with Wood or Roosevelt; it won't work.''

''Oh, my head!'' lamented Fate. ''I think I will go kill myself, or mebbe Boone Gaskill.''

''*Duck!*'' snapped his companion. ''Yonder comes Teddy . . . !''

Roosevelt was with Captains Allyn Capron and Bucky O'Neill, his constant shadows aboardship as in camp. Both were big men, the antithesis of their squat leader in romantic looks. Both were of his mercurial temperament, however, and no two lieutenants could have been chosen by the bantam-cock colonel who would serve as better examples of his own passion for the benefits of the strenuous life. The three now drew up and the Troop L soldier stepped aside, saluting awkwardly while Fate watched from behind a stack of pack-mule feedbags. ''At ease, lad,'' said Roosevelt in his high, quick way, proceeding to stand and chat with the restless trooper for five minutes, questioning him about home, family, future fears, hopes, wants and wishes. Fate had never heard such a heartwarming inquiry and wished that Houck Oatman might have listened to it with him. He would like to have asked the Payson deputy where all the newspaper reporters were who were going to write up this gentle and friendly deed of Teddy Roosevelt's there in the Cuban twilight? But when Roosevelt finally went on to join Capron and O'Neill, who had strolled ahead to wait for him, Fate set out to find Houck and discuss with him a more urgent matter; the prospect for tomorrow. He located the leathery sergeant just as full dusk was closing in over the anchored convoy, but before they could talk the *Segur-*

anca returned from her mission and once more the signal flags began to fly and the semaphores to flash and blink through the purple haze.

Presently the *Seguranca* moved out majestically to the east, and the troop carriers swung into obedient line behind her. The run was made at a fleet speed of four knots. All navigation lights were burning brightly. The cabin lamps and the light from the portholes below the deckline blazed bravely. No effort was made to disguise the direction of the invasion armada. The various regimental bands joined in the holiday spirit by blaring away at a gay variety of popular numbers, while the enlisted men sang lustily through the choruses. The freshly uniformed officers of the various commands exchanged courtesy dinner calls with one another and with the ranking naval officers of the accompanying warships. To Fate and Houck, resting and smoking at their favorite station near the taffrail of the *Yucatan,* it seemed a strange and disturbing way to run a war, and they were worrying about it out loud.

"I remember," said Houck, "a time when General Crook was away and this ambitious young jackass of a light colonel was left in command of the post. Crook himself was never anything but straight Army. This light colonel, though, he was one of those windmills who saluted with one hand and thumbed his nose with the other. Remind you of anybody we know?"

"Go on," said Fate, scowling. "I'm listening."

"Well," said Houck, "while Crook was back to Washington, this colonel decided to throw a Fourth of July party on the post. Crook, you know, was shy of people as a desert sheep. So this colonel figured the party would be good politicking. He sent out riders all over the area to tell the ranch families to come along in to the fort that Saturday night."

"What fort was that?" asked Fate, still frowning.

"Call it Cochise," said Houck.

Fate's frown darkened. "There wasn't no Fort Cochise that I remember," he challenged.

"Nor I," replied Houck. "I just said to call it that."

"All right," agreed Fate, "go on."

Houck watched him a moment as though weighing the invitation, then decided to accept it. "The colonel had his party," he said, "and it was a cinch buster. We had civilians to ride in from four counties. Some came a hundred miles and more. In July."

"That's somewhat," admitted Fate. "I guess they was powerful hungered for some fun."

"Yes," said Houck, "and they got it. It was never determined which Apache band it was, nor did it matter. But those red devils were definitely drawn in by the lights and the liquor and the sound of the colonel's band music. They caught those poor folks going back home that next Sunday morning. . . ." Houck jutted his jaw, spat again over the rail. "Goddammit, why can't men grow up? Why can't they get it through their thick heads that there's a time for singing and tootling horns and a time for shutting up and making sure their weapons are clean and they've got their orders all straight and understood?"

"I dunno," said Fate. "But what of it? You still ain't said what Colonel Roosevelt has got to do with that other colonel not knowing nothing about Apaches."

Houck looked at him, pale eyes burning. "He doesn't know one goddam thing about Spaniards, is what Colonel Roosevelt has got to do with that other colonel not knowing anything about Apaches!" he snapped, and got to his feet and moved angrily away down the deck.

When he had gone, Fate sat alone in the darkness, his

mind turning this way and that, trying to come up with a balance of reason which would explain why his trust of the Colonel was more logical than Houck's distrust of him. But he could not do it. The trouble was that he could see Houck's side as well as his own. It made the answer come tough. In the end, it did seem as though a man would just have to tackle it blind. He would have to follow his own faith and not listen to the facts. He would have to remember his father's farewell words about belief in country being above any persuasion. Doing that, he would know that Teddy Roosevelt was right and that right or wrong Fate Baylen was going to follow him wherever he led and that nothing else mattered except this loyalty to the U.S. and to the Cuban cause which he and Teddy were down here to serve.

Chapter Thirteen

The day came swiftly, flaming pink and gold out of the east and lighting the shores of the landing with glaring tropic brilliance. Inland, the nervous American soldiers could see only the high peaks of the Sierra Maestra and the nearer— much nearer—bunkers of steep hills which began behind the beach and seemed to thrust up everywhere from sea to mountains. The men, peering with shaded, keen Western eyes, could make out the spidery dock of the American Ironworks nosing out from shore where the invasion army would have to go in. It was a long way off and the Rough Riders knew they were going to have to get to it by small landing craft under heavy enemy fire from the hills backing the tiny thread of white sand, which their officers bravely assured them was "the beach at Daiquiri."

In Shafter's headquarters aboard the *Seguranca* the 300-pound Major-General, wearing his dark blue wool uniform and an immense white pith helmet, perspired over the terrors, real and imagined, of landing a green army upon an open, well-defended coast under circumstances wherein his transport ships could not, or would not, bring in their cargoes of men and equipment nearer than three and four miles.

On the *Yucatan* Roosevelt and Wood waited helplessly for word from the *Seguranca*. Both had been over to see Shafter earlier in the day and had come away when they realized that the mountainous general had no actual plan even at this last hour. Roosevelt, particularly, seemed certain that the landing would be conducted as had every phase of the raising and training of the invasion force, by the "go-as-you-please" method. Accordingly he went in that manner.

When the converted yacht *Vixen*, under command of Navy Lieutenant Sharp, a former aide in the office of the Assistant Secretary of Navy, steamed in under the bows of the *Yucatan* and hailed her cheerfully to know if there were anything the lieutenant might do for his old chief, Teddy was halfway over the side before the young officer's words got well clear of his megaphone.

A five-minute conference aboard the *Vixen* and Roosevelt was back on the *Yucatan* with the *Vixen's* black Cuban pilot. The Negro knew a way which would put the Rough Rider transport within a few hundred yards of the beach and much farther in than any other vessel in the convoy, including the *Seguranca* which was presently nearest shore at approximately a mile and a half off the dock. The *Vixen* would also, and meanwhile, go out to the warships of the Navy and let the right captains know that their former boss and great good friend, Teddy Roosevelt, was in pressing need of small-boat transportation to ferry his private army of college men and cowboys ashore ahead of the main rush, especially ahead of those crack units of Regular Infantry which Shafter was certain to send in first.

The colored pilot was as good as his word and got the big ship to within 200 yards of dock's end. And more. No sooner did the *Yucatan* swing to and drop her hook than Lieutenant Sharp and the *Vixen* reappeared shepherding a swarm of longboats for Roosevelt's pleasure in beaching his now cheering and exhilarated men.

Bold methods were still needed, however. Following the lead of the *Yucatan,* others of the fleet were now coming in to put ashore their own troops. The Rough Riders only cheered the louder and worked the harder. Expediency was the order of the day. The officer principally involved in this speeding up of an unfamiliar maneuver was short of stature, bull-necked, squeaky-voiced and squinting of eye. Coming on the trot to see why the few head of officers' horses and company pack mules were taking so long to be put over the side of the neighboring transport which carried them, the trademark teeth flashed and the bristled mustache stood forth like the hackle feathers of an aroused fighting rooster.

"You, there," he shouted at Fate Baylen, idly watching over the rail of the *Yucatan* the soldiers assigned to the livestock slings and steam winches of the faltering operation, "aren't you one of my San Antonio rodeo winners . . . ?"

Astonished to be remembered, Fate unblushingly admitted the charge. "By God, yes, sir, Colonel!" he shouted back. "And the proudest moment of my life, too, sir!"

"The devil with that!" snapped Roosevelt, daggering him in the chest with a stubby forefinger. "Do you have an idea of a better way to get those animals off that ship and onto the beach?" Fate, studying the hoist-and-sling procedure across the way, nodded laconically. "Hell, yes,

Colonel. Th'ow 'em overboard and let 'em swim.''

Roosevelt threw back his head and laughed. The sound, high-pitched, almost giggling, startled Fate. It was like a nervous girl. But Roosevelt struck him on the shoulder and cried, "Capital! Capital! Go to it!" and was off down the deck with his aides before there was time to worry about his high laugh or jumpy ways.

Catching a ride with a rowboat full of packsaddles, the young Arizonan set off across the water toward the stock ship. Midway, a Navy steam launch with a Cuban pilot came churning through the local traffic, almost running down Fate's small craft. Without thinking, Fate stood up in the rocking boat and complimented the Cuban in his native tongue. One hundred fifty feet away on the deck of the *Yucatan* Theodore Roosevelt stopped in his tracks, seized the megaphone borne by one of his aides, leaped to the rail. "Ahoy, there!" he shrilled. "Was that you cursing in Spanish, cowboy?"

"Yes, sir, I'm afraid it was," bellowed back Fate. "You want I should stick to American, Colonel?"

Once more the staccato laugh echoed. "No, no!" replied Roosevelt. "But we've been having the devil's own time finding noncommissioned men who can speak Spanish. You come see me when you're through over there, Corporal."

"Yes, sir," acknowledged Fate, "you bet. And I'll take special care of Little Texas, too, Colonel. You can dally and tie on that."

Little Texas was the favored one of Roosevelt's two permitted saddle mounts, the other being the rangy sorrel, Rain-in-the-Face. Little Texas was a bay pony no bigger than a forty-second minute, smart as a coondog, cute as a white-faced calf, meaner than a mother bear with triplet

cubs and caked breasts. But Roosevelt had not lingered to
hear Fate's glad promise to guard this treasure. He had
already disappeared in the press of his massing troops
amidship, before the lanky Westerner completed the vow.

Fate accepted the situation. He knew the abruptness was
not personal. The important thing was that Teddy had
picked him out to do a special job. Moreover, he had said
to come see him when the job was done. The prospect
stirred Fate's imagination. What did it mean? Did the Colonel actually intend taking Fate with him as an interpreter?
But that was nonsense. There must be plenty of men of
education and birth who could speak Spanish.

At the apogee of his bemusement, the escort gunboats of
lighter draft ran in and opened their covering fire for the
landing. At the same moment, decoy forces of naval de-
stroyers both up and down the coast from Daiquiri brought
their turrets to bear on the shore. The noise of the bom-
bardment set Fate's nerves ajangle. It seemed to him as
though the war would be finished before the clumsy oars-
men of his boat might bring him under the bows of the
stock ship. He urged them on with a mixture of salty talk
and abject pleading, and they managed, by some accident,
to scull the little craft up to the ship's ladder. By a second
accident Fate got onto the ladder without falling in, and
went up it with all the grace of a sailor boarding a bronco.
On deck, above, he bore down upon the laggard crew of
stock handlers in a bowlegged sprint which threatened to
pitch him back over the rail into the sea. Lurching up to
the surprised members of the New Mexico company doing
the work, he seized away from the sergeant in charge the
two range ponies which the latter was holding. Gripping
the two horses by their halters he hauled them to the chute
down which the troopers had been lowering them in the

web slings to the lighters below. Here he threw the animals by literal force into the bay. The little mustangs hit the water with a great splash and Fate yelled to the open-mouthed New Mexicans, "Come on, boys, grab a halter and start heaving! The Colonel wants to see nothing but bobbing horse behinds twixt here and the beach inside the next five minutes. He give me the job, so let's go . . . !"

The men seemed of a mind to obey but their deposed leader was not. He strode up to Fate and growled, "Oh, yeah? Says who?"

The Arizonan, having a closer look at the opposition, hesitated understandably. The New Mexico sergeant was as large, say, as Bear River Smith and as charming as Gotch Ear Daniels. Fate gulped and dug deep for inspiration. Survival seemed the natural selection of the moment. He swung from the deck and earnestly. His aim was flawless, its effect devastating. The huge Troop F noncom swayed and went down like a cut pine.

Fate picked up a fire bucket of sea water and sloshed it over the fallen one. The trooper sat up dazedly. Seeing Fate, he cocked his head to one side and put a cupped hand to his ear as though he were hard of hearing.

"Who did you say it was, pardner?" he asked. "I just caught the knuckles."

"Corporal Baylen, Troop A, Prescott," said Fate. "You all right, friend?"

"Why, certainly," replied the soldier, tottering to his feet. "How can you hurt a good man by fracturing his jawbones with a cement sack? Hand me them horses you want th'owed overboard. You have convinced me."

"Thank you very much," said Fate. "I appreciate your help a great deal. You see, I'm going to do some special confidential work for Colonel Roosevelt and am pushed for time. I'm to go consult him abouten it as soon as we are finished pitching this here stock over the side.''

The New Mexico sergeant stared at him. Then he looked beseechingly at his companions. They were of no help whatever, being as joggled as he. ''Jesus,'' he finally said, ''what an army!'' and fell to hauling horses up to the chute and kicking them over its edge into the churning green water below.

Chapter Fourteen

With evening of the first day, June 22, the landing was less than half completed. Many boats had been capsized and much valuable equipment, particularly rifles and revolvers, had been lost in the surf. Two colored troopers had been drowned. Bucky O'Neill had seen them go under and jumped in after them. He had dived for twenty minutes vainly seeking, at the risk of his own life in the pounding seas, to find and bring them up. Out along the dock where the main part of the lost guns lay on the cloudy bottom, other swimmers and divers were at work in equally dangerous undertakings. Trooper Knoblauch, an ex-New York stockbroker, led a handful of fearless comrades through six hours of deep swimming to recover nearly all the weapons. There were unnumbered similar acts of wellsung bravery. The landing operation was a nominating bonanza for Congressional Medals of Honor. That is, it was if one were to believe the voluminous words of the New York newsmen who covered it, or of the selfless Eastern officers—such as Lieutenant-Colonel Theodore Roosevelt—who directed it. If, on the disagreeing hand, one were to listen to an ordinary Arizona soldier—like Corporal Fate Baylen—then his report would indicate more unheroic hard work and overdoses of Cuban sun and salt water than acts of Spartan courage. But then, the Western and Eastern standards of values on such intangibles as risk and danger and unrefined guts were somewhat at variance.

Throughout the day Fate continued to hear these stories of American heroism, but for the life of him he could not join in the spirit of wonderment which pervaded the Easterners at their own and the Westerners' displays of dash and decision in face of extreme hazard. "Jesus Murphy!" he finally exploded, when interrupted at his assigned duties for the nth time, "don't nobody do no work around here saving for to be heroes? I wisht to hell you would send me three or four good cowards when you run acrost them. I would like some help in getting these goddam horses and mules put ashore."

Since he stood six feet four and, with his long black hair plastered wet and ragged to his head and his gray eyes striking sparks of flinty anger, looked convincing enough, he got away with his critical devaluation of the Rough Rider élan. Nor was he fooling about it.

It had all been fun thus far, there had been no enemy to face. Now they were in Cuba, and the Spaniards were only miles away. It was time to cut out the horseplay and get down to work, and these damned college kids did not seem to get the idea at all. Moreover, and worse, they had contaminated a lot of the Western troops with their football-game attitudes, and the landing had taken on the aspects of a contest to see who could get to the beach first, and to hell with how many head of stock or boatloads of guns were lost in the process. Fate wished he could find and talk to Houck Oatman about it, but the deputy had disappeared. Meanwhile the tall cowboy kept working and thinking and cursing to himself. It had all gone too easy, damn it.

The Spaniards, supposedly hidden in the hills immediately behind the beach, had not fired a shot. Neither had the blockhouse poised on the 1,000-foot peak which overlooked Daiquiri from the right. Most noted loss of the landing had been that of the rangy sorrel, Rain-in-the-Face. The animal had refused to follow Little Texas toward land and had swum out to sea and drowned. Others of the regimental stock had done likewise and a great number would have been lost in this fashion had not Fate put a cowboy stop to it by stringing several head together with a fifty-foot lariat through their halter rings and ordering them towed into the beach behind rowed small craft. Word of his quick thinking had got ashore and he had become a person of some reputation by nightfall. But for himself he was not taken in. He had failed his assignment by letting any of the stock drown and he had broken his personal pledge to Teddy by permitting one of his two mounts to be lost, even though saving the favored, better one of them. He regarded his own behavior as typical of that of the regiment. They had all acted like a pack of crazy Apaches and in his opinion deserved nothing of praise and one hell of a lot of honest criticism.

Other elements of the landing had been equally confused. Of the expected 1,000 Cuban insurgent soldiers promised by General Calixto García to aid the Fifth Corps in getting ashore at Daiquiri, not one had put in an appearance until day's end had safely established the absence of Spanish defenders in that area. Then, when the chattering insurgents had shown up, it was merely—so far as Fate and his Rough Rider comrades could see—to gain possession of the brand-new Lee-Enfield navy rifles which the U.S. had been forced to promise them as the price of their "loyal" cooperation in the common effort to save their own greedy necks from the supposed "vile" Spaniard. And it would seem that the Western suspicion of these particular local patriots was correct. Within thirty minutes of the free rifle issue, and that thirty minutes misspent by the shameless rascals in begging, borrowing or just plain thieving everything of *yanqui* manufacture to which they could lay their hands, the ragged native troops had faded back into the silent jungle hills from which they had emerged, leaving the American troops to ponder the amount of support, loyal or otherwise, they might expect from such baggy-panted allies. Fate was among the foremost of these pessimists.

The insurgent leader, an evil-looking Afro-Cuban named Benito Guadaña, had vowed to Wood and Roosevelt, who interviewed him, that he and his men would "be there when most needed." Understanding Spanish and having a regional distrust of dark skins, Fate was not altogether assured by this prediction. He was interested to overhear the insurgent chief's followers—while the latter was talking to Wood and T.R.—refer to the leader as El Guadañero. At the same time they laughed and pointed at the *yanqui* troops as though the U.S. soldiers and Benito's Spanish nickname had something quite humorous in common. However, since a good portion of this "jungle fun" was reserved for the Negro troops—the Cubans had never seen American colored soldiers and called them "smoked Yankees"—Fate was inclined to discount his suspicions of the native volunteers and to try to like them in spite of the prejudices of his birth and upbringing against anything which resembled

97

a Mexican and spoke Spanish.

He was not quite successful. He could not get out of his mind the nagging fact that there were two translations for El Guadañero. One meant *the mower,* and so went innocently enough with a man whose given Spanish name, *guadaña,* was literally *scythe.* But the other translation was *the reaper,* and that was an altogether different idea in English than in Spanish. It made Fate wonder, with considerable reservation, if this difference was not, after all, what the insurgents had been laughing about when they called Benito Guadaña "El Guadañero," and pointed to the American troops.

Yet, finally, he knew that he was very tired and could not make good judgments. He would ignore his fears and doubts of their Cuban allies, and particularly of their smiling, vacant-eyed *jefe.* He had an important appointment with Colonel Roosevelt as soon as supper was done and in the meantime he would just lie down and rest for a little while in the soft twilight. After he had seen Teddy and had a good talk with Houck Oatman, he would be better able to see the entire thing, including his foolish spookiness over Benito Guadaña.

The rationale was premature, indeed dead wrong: Benito Guadaña was precisely what his Spanish nickname implied in English, and the Rough Riders would very soon have cause to remember it, and him. But on that sunset of June 22, like the other 6,000 men who had come ashore before failing light and a rising wind had suspended the American landing, Fate was too worn out to take alarm over a barefooted regiment of small brown men in floppy straw hats and sagging white pantaloons. He would lie himself down and forget it. A good night's sleep here on the fragrant sands of this tropical island, lulled by the security of the campfires and the delightful odors of jungle trees and flowers wafted in on the breeze from the hills, would surely buck up a man. Tomorrow morning would show the insurgents and everything else in a clean, fresh light.

Again, his Arizona optimism was running ahead of the tide of history as stage managed by Lieutenant-Colonel Theodore Roosevelt.

It seemed to Fate barely ten minutes after he lay down in his shallow cot of beach sand that a friendly hand was on his shoulder and a low voice telling him to ''Roll out and look lively; Colonel's moving on. . . .''

Chapter Fifteen

But the soldier who awakened Fate in the lovely clear dawn of the twenty-third had been misled. Roosevelt was not moving "on." All of the cavalry, regular and volunteer, had been ordered to remain at Daiquiri. To General Lawton and the Regular Infantry had fallen the plum of taking the neighboring beach hamlet of Siboney, there to set up the base of operations for the push inland to Santiago.

The Rough Riders were shaken by this news. By noon mess a spirit of gloom had pervaded the entire regiment, and its effects were not lifted when the infantry outfits began forming up to march past their bivouac along the trail to Siboney. Roosevelt meanwhile had come to another of his "go-as-you-please" decisions. It was just after one o'clock when he strode out of the command hut and gave the unexpected order to break camp.

It was no mean feat of military inspiration to get up a regiment of 600 men and spirit it off in broad daylight, but

Wood and Roosevelt managed it, and in the moment of their success the fighting edge of the Rough Riders was rehoned ten-fold. Had they encountered the Spaniard anywhere within the first two miles of their march to Siboney they might have won the war alone and on straight euphoria. As it developed, they did not encounter the foe and the Cuban sun began to bear down. By 2:00 P.M. all shouting, singing and smart talk had been silenced. The day assumed the aspects of a Cuban inferno. No actual battle could have exceeded the stresses of the trail. The heat was the enemy and it could be endured in part only by the Negro troops and by the men of the Far West, to whom the furnace blasts of desert and short-grass prairie had given some immunity.

But both Wood and Roosevelt were agreed that, since theirs were volunteer troops and were being watched by the press corps and the general staff alike, the Rough Riders should not falter nor fall by the way, and should continue forward as long and valiantly as any regular outfit. This determination became contagious. Men of the iron stamp of Bucky O'Neill, Allyn Capron, Woodbury Kane and Micah Jenkins ranged the Rough Rider ranks with indomitable energy and constant cheerful encouragements. "Keep up, men, keep up and maintain company order, sirs!" became the rallying words of the afternoon. Hearing them, Fate and his dripping fellows panted like steers, grinned, growled, drank their sweat, ate its salt, sucked pebbles and stayed on their feet. Others did not. One-half the Regular Infantry on the trail ahead of them fell out from heat exhaustion. Going past the latter, the Rough Riders called to them, trying to lift their spirits with various well-meant jokes and crude talk of the kind intended by soldiers as friendly and reassuring. The sick and gasping regulars did not reply, or could not.

101

Fate remembered distinctly but two incidents of that trail. Both were tragic in their ways, though each was crudely humorous in that raw sense that anything may contain humor to men who are hot and thirsty and wickedly tired. The first concerned a regular of Tenth Infantry. This soldier, midway to Siboney, recalled that this was the exact day upon which his enlistment expired, and went forthwith to see his company commander to demand his release. He was given it and after relinquishing his government property set out to retrace his steps to Daiquiri. He began declaring as he went, and loudly, that he was leaving the United States Army "flat out and for damn well-rid final!" Unfortunately for him, Captain Allyn Capron and the head of the Rough Rider column was just then drawing up. Capron took the miscreant by the collar, lifted him bodily into the air and called out to his troops, "Boys, here is a yellow dog; show him the way to go home!"

With that, he shoved the fellow toward the hard-eyed men from the Territories. The poor devil cried out piteously but to no point. The Rough Riders bid him farewell all the way down the interior of their marching formation, each trooper who could contributing a personal blow to the leave-taking. When the man reached Troop A at the rear, he was stripped naked and bleeding from a hundred vicious welts. He did not look human and Captain Bucky O'Neill said quietly to his men, "Stand aside and let him pass; he has paid his way." Fate halted obediently with the others, waiting for the wretch to stagger on, but he wondered long after he and his comrades had marched on and left behind that spot of stillness, if many of them would soon, or ever, forget the moment of the yellow dog.

The second happening took place at the end of another hour of the hellish going. Colonel Wood, after sternly forbidding drinking from any of the streams forded during the march, now approached a lovely small river and was influenced by its clarity to consider both a halt and a watering of his dehydrated command. "Tell the men," he announced, "that they can fill their canteens here, providing they do not foul the water themselves."

At once the Rough Riders fell out and commenced to perform various wonderful feats of balance and restraint as they teetered from bank stone or brush hold in their efforts to dip full their canteens without contaminating the stream for those who would follow. As the last troopers were restoppering the carefully filled tins, a loud and happy splashing sounded around the bend from their position. Glancing at one another, the Rough Riders started upstream to investigate. Fate was among the first to break through the jungle growth and behold, not fifty paces above where they had filled their canteens, approximately half the Tenth Regular Cavalry, black and shining and birthday naked, bathing in the river. He and his companions stood and watched the Negroes silently and for a long minute. Then they opened and began to empty their canteens. The chugging of the water pouring out upon the ground seemed louder than all the carefree splashing of the colored troops. For some reason Fate remembered it a long time.

From that point the march was merely unmerciful. The molten sun set at last, bringing some relief, but Siboney lay still ahead. They ought to have reached it an hour before. Were they lost? Roosevelt and Wood could not tell them, for both leaders, together with the newspaper reporters headed by the natty Richard Harding Davis, "complete in a sack suit, a white puggaree, and cordovan tramping boots," were not with the column. They had gone on ahead of it to prepare a proper entrance into Siboney for the celebrated heroes of the Cuban campaign. That would be the Rough Riders, of course, and their impetuous lieutenant-colonel.

Meanwhile, Captain Capron was leading the regiment and no news came down the line from him.

That was the trouble with those infernal regular officers like Capron, growled Bear River Smith, who was stumbling along in the sudden tropic darkness with Fate Baylen and Little McGinty. They never opened their yaps and let a fellow know what the devil was going on. Now, Teddy, he was another side of steer beef. Him you could trust. He would tell you what he knew. He would do better than that, if need be; he would tell you what he didn't know but considered you ought to understand. A man appreciated that, he liked to be let in on things, to know how they were shaping up, what it was that was being attempted and how was the best way—according to Teddy—to go about it.

But this damned business of blundering along through the mother-loving jungle in the pitch of night in a foreign land, God knew how far from where they were going, and without food or even a drink of water since the last canteen, why, damn it to hell, it wasn't right. For the Regular Army, fine. They were paid to walk in the dark. But not the volunteers, the unselfish boys who had offered to shed their blood for nothing, and who weren't in it to make a career for themselves and retire rich on the government. God damn it, it was wrong. Something ought to be done about it. Where the hell was Teddy? He was the one. He would see that some sparks flew, and that they burned the proper ears and tail bones, by God!

But Teddy was gone and Colonel Wood was gone and Captain Capron would only say, "Keep up, boys, keep company order," and go right on leading the way confident as though they were still on parade at Camp San Antonio, Texas.

After what seemed like time enough to end the world, they came to the first sign of civilization—a string of friendly pickets put out along a railroad embankment to direct the incoming straggler traffic toward the encamped thousands already in place at Siboney. These lads, Regular Infantry with no great admiration for Teddy and his Terrors, would enliven their duty by sudden wild cries of warning as to Spaniards in ambush ahead, or cheerful screeches that Lawton had just been driven into the sea and the enemy was in possession of Siboney. No threats from the Rough Rider officers could subdue these ghouls and to ignore their yells was impossible. The empty stomach would clench and the weary nerves cry out at each new shout from the embankment. It was a dispiriting way to climax a march which had been such a hard fight all the way.

It was immediately after the men began to drop out that a courier arrived from Wood and Roosevelt. The message was brief but explicit: instead of camping near the ocean and General Lawton's infantry, as ordered by the latter, they were now to detour inland, circle Lawton, go into camp above and beyond his five regiments of Regular Army troops.

Capron's obedience to this unauthorized correction of the commanding general's instructions was instantly challenged by the young infantry lieutenant in command of the railroad pickets. This officer properly demanded to know by what authority Capron was altering his line of march. Capron countered by asking to know by what authority the junior officer questioned his movements. The youth answered that General Lawton had ordered all incoming cavalry routed beachward from this checkpoint, to which

Capron replied by giving as his authority General Joseph Wheeler of the cavalry, reminding the worried lieutenant that while Lawton might have the command Wheeler had the seniority and that "Fighting Joe" was hell to cross. Unhappily the lieutenant gave way. His conscience was hardly relieved nor his chances for promotion benefited when, half an hour later, a courier from Lawton panted up to his post with a special order stressing that absolutely no troops of Young's, Wheeler's, or particularly, "that fool Roosevelt's," were to be permitted inland of the pickets.

It helped not a great deal that the young lieutenant was subsequently able to intercept the remaining squadrons of regular cavalry. The main damage had been done. General Lawton's honest alarm at seeing Wood and "T.R." arrive ahead of their troops with their press corps in full dress, had not been implemented in time. The possibilities of military homicide latent in the combination of creaky Joe Wheeler, a volunteer ex-Confederate heirloom with a professional patina of thirty years disuse, and "go-as-you-please" Teddy Roosevelt with his enfants terribles from the halls of ivy and the haunts of the buffalo, came upon him too late. Fighting Joe had outflanked him. Shafter's explicit order to forbid any deployment inland, which might excite the enemy before the preparations for the general advance were complete, had been circumvented by deliberate insubordination.

For a general officer of the Regular United States Army it was nightmare food.

The Spaniards were reported entrenched and waiting a bare three miles inland of the beach at Siboney.

And Teddy Roosevelt stood half an hour's march closer to them than any commander in the Fifth Corps.

Chapter Sixteen

"It was one of the most weird and remarkable scenes of the war, probably of any war. An army was being landed on an enemy's coast at the dead of night, but with somewhat more of cheers and shrieks and laughter than rise from the bathers in the surf at Coney Island on a hot Sunday. It was a pandemonium of noises. The men still to be landed from the 'prison hulks,' as they called the transports, were singing in chorus, the men already on shore were dancing naked around the camp fires on the beach. . . . On either side rose black, overhanging ridges, in the lowland between were white tents and burning fires, and from the ocean came the blazing, dazzling eyes of the searchlights."

Such was the state of the beach at Siboney, according to R. H. Davis, when the Rough Riders arrived in their coconut grove camp long after dark on June 23. Indeed, it was ten o'clock before the pack burdens were put down and permission granted by the officers for the men to go down to the ocean and bathe. The officers were among the first to follow their own affirmation, the only injunction for all being Wood's stern order that no water was to be drunk until its source could be checked by the sanitation unit. Since the canteens of the regiment were still dry and there was no water at the Siboney camp—the Spaniards having cut the pipeline from the hills—this worked a great hardship on the men. But they obeyed the warning, respecting Wood's medical knowledge, and they were not sorry. The Rough Riders were the only organization which had no fever from the contaminated water being sold by the wretched Cuban people of Siboney to the thirsty soldiers of the Fifth Corps. Among Lawton's regulars the first cases developed within forty-eight hours and the spread of the disease continued for the duration of the campaign.

At surfside the weary marchers stripped naked and went into the curling white combers with a glad relief. For most of them—all of the Westerners—it was the first experience with salt water and the temptation to drink was a mighty one. A few tried it and got immediately sick, which discouraged the others.

Fate felt that the bath at Siboney saved his life. He had never had anything strike him as quite so wonderful. Within minutes the tingling bite of the sea water, coupled with the soft caresses of the tropic air ashore, had revitalized him. The result was much the same with the other men, the truly vicious effects of the daylight march from Daiquiri being for the moment rolled back by the combination of salt air, ocean foam, excitement, and the magnificent metabolism of youth.

After the first enjoyment, Fate looked about for Houck Oatman but did not see him anywhere among the hundreds of naked troopers upon the beach. Failing to find Houck, he extended his combing of the beach for anyone he might know—Pete Van Schuyler, Tiffany, Buck Dawson, Bear River Smith, Little McGinty, anyone at all who might tell him where Houck was. Luckily he found Tiffany, who was able to inform him that Houck had been selected among the scouts to go out with General Wheeler earlier that afternoon to probe the road toward Santiago. The troop captains had been asked to recommend their best men for such work, and Bucky O'Neill had put up Houck as "a manhunter by taste and trade, and a trailer by need and training." The Payson deputy had headed a scout detail made up of J. B. Merrick, one-time big game guide for Roosevelt in the Dakotas, "Post Oak" Prewitt, a West Texas mustang hunter, and "Blue" Calhoun, a small colored trooper of Tenth Cavalry, said by his commanding officer to be a superior tracker. Giving this information, Tiffany expressed some doubt of the inclusion of a Negro in such risky work. Fate nodded and said, "Yes, I don't reckon they'd ought to have left him go, but old Houck will handle it, never fear. What else you know, Tiffany?"

The Eastern trooper reached for his clothes. "I know I've got to get dressed and get back to the Colonel's tent," he said. "Your friend Oatman and his patrol are back. Seems they found a good way to go toward Santiago tomorrow. Why don't you come along and take potluck with us at supper? I'm sure the Colonel would be delighted to have you."

He meant it to be smart but if Fate understood him, he did not show it. "By golly," he answered earnestly, "I believe I may do just that, but not for dinner, thanks. Colonel asked me to come see him last night, but I was plum tuckered and fell off to sleep afore I knowed it."

Tiffany stiffened. He did not like being cowboyed by

cowboys. "All right," he said, "go ahead and be cute. See how much information you get next time, you damned farmer. I was only trying to be decent with you."

"Sure you was," said Fate, staring down at him with the calmest of looks. "You betcha."

"Go to hell!" huffed Tiffany and went off up the beach not at all certain who was ahead of whom.

Chapter Seventeen

Fate went up through the grove toward Roosevelt's fire. Well before he drew near, he could hear the sounds of social company. Halting among the palms, he studied the situation before intruding upon it. With T.R. were his particular cronies of the regiment. Fate recognized Captain Capron, Tiffany, Pete Van Schuyler, Sergeant Hamilton Fish, troopers Harry Thorpe and Munroe Ferguson. The latter three had all been members of Teddy's Oyster Bay Polo Team in prewar days, he knew, and he felt the strong urge to retreat from this personal gathering and come again another time. Yet what might he do? If Teddy had not forgotten inviting him to call, it would be a grievous mistake to ignore the ''order'' any longer. He was already a day late in obeying it. Did he dare risk further delay, or idle guessing at the quality of T.R.'s memory, or the meaning of his commands?

He squared his shoulders and started toward the campfire. He was still outside its light when Pete Van Schuyler saw him and moved to cut off his approach. "Hold it, cowboy," he said, putting his hand on his arm, "this is a regimental command post. Get scarce."

"But the Colonel asked me to come see him," protested Fate. "Hell, I ain't here collecting for charity, nor nothing. Come on, leggo my arm."

"Beat it," said Van Schuyler. "This is white tie and tails, Lofty. I'll tell the Colonel you called."

"I don't care," said Fate quietly, "if it's a camp meeting between U.S. Grant and Jesus Christ. I was told to come see the Colonel, and I'm here. Get out'n my way, Pete."

Van Schuyler did not yield. In fact, he reached for his Krag carbine, leaning against an adjacent coconut palm. Fate snared him by the back of the collar and dragged him, kicking and cursing, to the campfire. By this time the group there had noticed the scuffle, and Roosevelt himself had bulled briskly to the foreground to inquire into it.

"What is this?" he demanded of Fate. "Release that man this instant!"

"Yes, sir, Colonel," nodded Fate. "I ain't no real use for him, but he took a notion to lay holt of his gun and I felt morally obliged to persuade him toward more peaceful means." He let go of Van Schuyler and saluted. "Begging your pardon, Colonel," he added earnestly, "but I'm a practicing pacifist."

One or two of the men sniggered at the remark, but Roosevelt only scowled.

"What is it you want?" he asked brusquely. "Did you have a message?"

"He's got nothing but a colossal nerve!" broke in Van Schuyler. "I ordered him not to bother you, Colonel."

"You, sir," said Roosevelt, "be quiet. If you are going

to serve with me, you will speak when you are requested to do so. I don't give a fig if your father owns the Pennsylvania Railroad. Or is it the lease on all the land under Wall Street? No matter, sir, be still!"

Van Schuyler backed off into the darkness with no hint of a salute or an agreeing "yes, sir." Roosevelt, overlooking the breach of discipline, turned on Fate.

"Well, sir," he demanded, "what is it you want? Be quick, be quick."

"Yes, sir," said Fate, careful to salute. "It's me, Colonel. You told me to come see you. I'm a mite late."

The company at fireside tittered again but T.R. did not seem amused. "Who the devil are you?" he growled.

"Why," said Fate, "I'm the one you assigned to get the horses and mules over the side, back yonder to Daiquiri. Corporal Baylen, Colonel, Troop A, Bucky O'Neill's bunch."

"Ah, yes!" exclaimed Roosevelt, brightening briefly. "A damned fine job, too, Baylen. Damned fine."

"Thank you, sir," saluted Fate. "I am only sorry that I lost your sorrel, Colonel."

He saw the quick look of annoyance come to the other's square face, then the equally quick effort, and successful, to suppress it. "All right," answered Roosevelt evenly, "what else is it you wish to say to me?"

"Why, I don't wish to say nothing to you, sir; it was you wanted to say something to me. Don't you remember?"

"Frankly, no," replied Roosevelt shortly. "What was it about? Damn it, man, come out with it!"

"Yes, sir, it was about me speaking Spanish, Colonel. You said it was tough to find them as understood and could sling their language back and forth with them garlics."

113

" 'Garlics,' Corporal?''

"Yes, sir. That's what we call the Spanyerds, Colonel.''

"Oh, yes, of course. And I do recall the exchange now, Baylen. If it is all right with Captain O'Neill, you can start with me in the morning.'' Roosevelt's gray eyes grew bright behind the steel-rimmed glasses. "That is,'' he snapped, "if you have no objection to being where the bullets sing the loudest!''

Fate straightened, the thrill of the opportunity running through him. Before he could express his gratitude, however, Roosevelt had wheeled away and trotted back over to the fire. Fate, peering uncertainly in that direction, saw Colonel Wood and several officers hurrying up through the palms from the nearby brigade headquarters of General Young.[1]

Wood, ordinarily the least ruffled of professionals, was plainly wrought up. His sun-dark face glowed. His soft voice crackled. His swift words flew like sparks into the waiting tinder of his subordinates' rapt attention. Fate, drifting into the shadows of Roosevelt's tent to eavesdrop unobserved, felt his mind take fire with the rest.

Wood had just been over a secret battle plan with Young and all arrangements were understood. They would start with daybreak, Young leading off with four troops of First Cavalry (white) and four of the Tenth (Negro). Their course would follow the wagon road which led from Siboney to Santiago over the high ridge behind the beach. Wood, with

---

[1]S. B. M. Young, brigadier, commanded the Second Cavalry Brigade, consisting of the First and Tenth Regular Cavalry and the volunteer Rough Riders. The First Brigade was under Brigadier-General Sumner and contained the Third, Sixth and Ninth Regular Cavalry; both brigades under Major-General Joseph Wheeler.

the eight troops of Rough Riders, would follow the foot trail and mule path which paralleled the wagon road on the left and which rejoined it upon the far side of the high ridge about four miles distant.

The place of joining was noted upon the field maps as Las Guásimas, so called for the *guásima* trees which grew there in abundance. Directly beyond Guásimas was a miserable mudhut village called Sevilla. Beyond Sevilla the way to Santiago and to victory was all downhill.

The Spaniards were known to have their positions heavily fortified to cover the juncture of the trails at Guásimas, but waiting at the critical meeting place would be 800 Cuban insurgents of certain reliability under General Castillo. Their function would be to infiltrate the Spanish lines from both flanks, demoralizing them for the advancing Americans.

With any luck at all, the victory, and the place of the Rough Riders in their country's hearts and history books, would be secured within two hours.

But the time element was critical. Any delay or bogging of the attack could only bring up Lawton and the Regular Infantry. This, naturally, was to be circumvented at all cost. If Young and the cavalry were to be given credit for the grand smash, then they must win it alone, and early.

Fate was not so entirely lost in all this as to miss the implications and irregularities unstated. Even to a green soldier of Arizona volunteers it was evident that the plan of General Young was designed as much to gain opportunity for the first blow to be struck as it was to make certain the success of that first blow. When Wood said, "If we do not bring it off, the regulars will," he had said a very odd thing indeed. It made Fate uneasy and led him to wonder, at once, who was fighting whom and what for? Apparently he had

115

missed something along the line. The thought returned to his mind of Houck Oatman and the latter's dour warnings. Instinctively he glanced around, as though hoping to see his mentor from Yavapai County. It was only an action of nerves and thus he was doubly surprised to find it effective. Off to his right, having come up in Wood's wake, stood Houck and two or three of his scouts. Fate waved hesitantly. Houck's pale eyes stabbed in the direction of Roosevelt's shelter-half. Fate waved again, face alight. Houck nodded. A few moments later Fate heard a scrape of pebbles behind him and felt a quick touch on his tensed arm. "How you like it so far?" asked Houck Oatman, easing out of the crouch with which he had circled the tent. "You learning anything?"

Fate nodded smilingly. "Houck," he said, "I surely am pleased to see you. Where you been at?"

"Scouting the Spaniard," said the other.

"I know that. I mean since."

"Over with Colonel Wood."

"To General Young's tent?"

"Young, hell. You mean Joe Wheeler. He's the one that's running the show over there."

"Fighting Joe?"

"That's what they call him. The old man's a fanatic. He's in his dotage. He talks with fire in his eyes as though he was still waiting at Carrick's Ford for Phil Sheridan and the Union Cavalry. He's crazy. Thirty years crazy."

"I thought he was a hero. Everybody says he's a heller in a fight. The boys seem to love him, Houck."

"The boys are crazy too. But they aren't in command. It's Joe Wheeler we've got to worry about, and General Young is only his errand boy. The old man is calling this shot we're about to take, and he's doing it to grab all the glory he can, while he can. Wood and Young and the others are not likely to argue about a chance to be heroes, you can bet. They're all for the old fool. The sons of bitches!''

He wound up bitterly with the curse, and Fate shook his head solemnly and said, ''Houck, I don't see how you can call General Wheeler an old fool. I've read American history and he was a great general in the Civil War. He was one of the most fearedest cavalry leaders of them all, not even excepting Jeb Stuart. Why for you think he's so doddery and no-account now? Being a little agey ain't no guarantee. Some of them old devils is smarter than sin and tougher than shoe leather.''

Houck gave him his rim-ice stare and said, ''I'll tell you how come I think he's doddery; all the time up at Young's camp just now he kept calling the Spaniards 'the damn Yankees.' He wasn't funning either. It kept slipping out on him, and the others kept looking at one another whenever it did, and nobody laughed.''

''It's hard to believe,'' grudged Fate, ''him being Regular Army, and all.''

''Regular Army, hell!'' snorted Houck. ''He volunteered, and some idiot in the War Department took him up on it.''

''Well, General Young's regular.''

''Sure, and with guts enough to gamble getting cashiered against being promoted.''

''You appear to be set against the whole thing, Houck.''

''Kid, I was up there this afternoon. Those sons of bitching garlics are ready for us.''

''Well, hell, ain't we ready for them?''

''Some of us maybe.''

''What you mean?''

''Oh, Micah Jenkins, Captain Capron, Major Brodie.''

''That all?''

117

"Wood is all right. But he's a doctor. He's no more a combat officer than I am. Neither is Brodie, really. In our outfit you've got two regulars you can count on—Capron and Jenkins—and of the two only Jenkins is what I would call combat-ready."

"How about Captain O'Neill? He looks like a heller to me. I wouldn't be afeared to foller him no place."

"Bucky's brave as a bull. And about as bright."

They were down to it now, and Fate set his jaw and demanded, "Well, then, make it the colonel. Don't tell me he don't know what he's doing. He's been right every time so far. Why, goddammit, Houck, the Rough Riders wouldn't even be here if it wasn't for him!"

"Truer words," said Houck grimly, "were never spoke."

Fate looked at him. He knew he meant something more than the mere words, but could not figure out what it was. He was still scowling in the attempt, still doggedly shaking his head and biting his lower lip, when the older man nudged him and said quietly, "Meeting's breaking up yonder. Let's get out of here before we're spotted and put to work. I'm weary enough to sleep standing up."

Fate nodded, feeling the same need to break away from the situation. "All right," he said. "Let's bunk together somewheres. I want to talk a bit, Houck. I been missing our talks. There's things happened that needs clearing for me. Like tonight, say."

"Tonight," replied Houck, starting off, "is easy as apple pie. We're going to buck Shafter's orders and hit the enemy before Lawton can get his infantry up. If we win, we're heroes; if we lose, we're heroes. How in hell can you beat a parlay like that?"

Fate fell over a palm root and scrambled to catch up.

"I dunno," he said, "but I got a quaky notion watching Wood and the colonel just now, that something wasn't right. It don't hardly seem correct to me, for us to be taking on the whole damn Spanish army all by ourselves."

Houck Oatman answered him softly.

"Kid," he said, "it's not the whole Spanish army you've got to worry about. It's that one rifle bullet with your name written on it. Mauser, caliber-thirty, smokeless. You won't see her but she'll sing to you. Whisper is more like it. We drew a few up there today. They sound wicked. Like an old crone crouched in a corner and beckoning to you. 'Come here, come here,' they say. Singsonglike. Slithering. Like snakes in dry grass."

"Houck," said Fate, "cut it out. You sound spooked. I ain't never heard you talk like that. Leave off it."

"Sure," said the other, and then stopped and did a very strange thing. He put out his hand in the darkness and said, "Kid, give me your hand." Fate felt for and found his grasp, and they shook quickly. *"Remember that,"* said Houck, and turned and hurried on, not waiting for Fate nor looking back again.

Chapter Eighteen

Fate sat up, pulling the sodden blanket closer about him. Everything was wet and clammy. It was the first rain they had hit in Cuba and it had come on just as the hardtack and fat pork were being fried in the mess kits of the tired and hungry men. For two hours it had come down, then quit so suddenly that the dripping of the jungle growth which followed sounded eerily loud. Not so loud, however, as to drown out the curses of the Rough Riders at this untimely blow of fate which deprived them of their first bite in thirteen hours.

The fires refused to burn again after that. The fatback and wet biscuit were eaten cold or not at all. Fate would not touch his and had lain down with Houck to sleep in the spongy muck of the tall grass and roots. Now he was awake and staring through the intense black of the night wondering what it was that had brought him to the alert.

Then he heard it. An obscene scuttling and rustling, not

human, and seeming to come from all about him. He felt his flesh crawl.

He did not want to awaken Houck, yet could scarcely restrain the urge to do so. He could only guess at the time—two or three o'clock in the morning—yet he knew it was too early to get up. There was no sign of movement in the grove, save for the loathsome noise which had awakened him. Up toward Roosevelt's tent he could see a faint glow of banked firelight, and that was all. Around him in the gloom he could see no farther than the length of his own body, though he knew that within a hundred paces in all directions the complete regiment slept. The crawling noise began again.

He took a match and struck it against the inner surface of his webbing cartridge belt, the only dry spot upon him. As it flared, he cupped it before his eyes, toward the direction of the nearest scuttlings. He drew in his breath and held it until the match burned his fingers and he dropped it.

The creatures were foul and evil-looking. A light orchid color, they were the size of a small dog, naked, many-legged, staring-eyed and pincer-clawed. He knew at once they were the giant Cuban land crabs, and harmless. He had not seen any of them at Daiquiri but had been told by the boys who had, that harmless or not, they were enough to abort a sow-bear. This he could now agree to. He shuddered and cursed and felt in the dark for a rock or root. Finding a hard knot, he drew it back and hurled it at the cluster of creatures which had stared back at the burst of match flame.

A roaring voice, almost surely not that of the Cuban land crab, announced a solid hit.

"God damn it," shouted the victim, "who th'owed that

shoe? Jesus H. Christ, what has a man to do around here to earn a little rest? Come on, you sonofabitch, th'ow the other one, so's I kin locate you!''

Fate sank lower in his blankets, not admitting authorship. He didn't blame the poor devil, but he was in no mood for explaining to him his aversion to purple crabs in wet palm groves at 3:00 A.M. in the morning.

The uproar brought awake several other soldiers in the vicinity with the result that their movements and growls of complaint routed the invaders. After things got quiet again, Fate listened and could hear nothing but restless, heavy breathing from his comrades. He sat back up, found a palm trunk to brace his shoulders against, and resumed his worrying where he had left off when he and Houck came away from Roosevelt's fire. In his mind he marched over every mile of the way he had come: from the Camp Verde post office and general store, to Prescott, San Antonio, Tampa, Daiquiri and the beach at Siboney. It had all seemed so simple then. Each stop had made sense. Each journey between points had been but another measure of the whole adventure. Everything had added up to a clear total: *service to country in a just and noble cause.*

Now, though, something was missing. The answer did not go with the component parts which led up to it. The highlights of the long trek from Bell Rock Ranch to Siboney were all still sharp and black against his memory. But the sum total of the thing escaped him. It was, finally, one of those obvious questions for which no one had better or plainer answers than Houck Oatman. If any man in that dank coconut grove knew what they were doing there, it would be the pale-eyed deputy sheriff from Payson, Arizona.

Fate tried fighting it off but could not. He reached

through the darkness and found his friend's shoulder.

"Houck," he whispered, "you awake?"

There was a long moment's silence, then the cynical, acrid drawl answered thoughtfully.

"No, I'm sound asleep."

Fate nodded, as though the other could see him. "My dad always said that if you ask a idiot question, you ain't apt to get stuck with no genius answers," he muttered. "I reckon he was right. Excuse it."

Houck grunted his acceptance. "What's bothering you, Baylen?"

"You don't mind talking?" asked Fate hesitantly. "It's kind of a nowhere question. Likely you'll think I'm plain shook with the buck ague if I ask it."

"No," said Houck, "I don't think you're down in your boots, kid. It's brains you lack, not gizzard. What's your trouble?"

"I've been pondering it for most the night," said Fate. "It's a question that sounds silly but has me winging. To be honest, I been ducking it ever since we got to San Antonio and seen Teddy make his talk. Now it looks like we're square up agin it, and I still don't know the answer."

"Name it," said Houck. "Maybe I can identify it for you."

Fate complied slowly, frowning hard in the darkness.

"Houck," he said, *"what are we doing here?"*

He waited a long quiet time in the darkness of the coco-palm grove above Siboney Beach for the answer of the hard-eyed sergeant, but it did not come. Neither did he ask the question again. He did not have to.

Houck Oatman didn't *know* what they were doing there.

Chapter Nineteen

It was five o'clock in the morning.

No fires were lit. No breakfasts cooked. A few of the men had cold, congealed fat pork from the night before. They ate it and were glad. The others went out onto the ruts of the wagon road to Santiago with no more food in their bellies than they had lain down with the night before. For many of them, such as Fate Baylen, this meant nothing to eat since breakfast at Daiquiri thirty-six hours gone.

No man complained.

General Young had with him the Rough Riders and one squadron each of First (white) and Tenth (colored) Regular Cavalry—a thousand men, of whom six hundred had never fired a gun at uniformed enemy. Young seemed to think it was enough, or had been told by Fighting Joe Wheeler that it was. At the head of the Rough Riders, Colonel Leonard Wood appeared not to doubt the wisdom of the higher confidence. If he had reservations about the sneak advance, he left no document to record them. With Lieutenant-Colonel Roosevelt, it was the same. Fate, marching with Bucky O'Neill at the head of Troop A, watched the Colonel and was impressed once more with that strange sense of destiny which the latter inspired among those near enough to see him. Fate knew what it was he felt but he could not put a name to it. Had Houck been at his side, he would have asked him if he did not feel the spell, and, if he did, what he would call it. But Houck was far away, gone at 3:00 A.M., before first light, to scout the way for the secret advance of the cavalry.

It did not matter. Fate was strong again. Who would not be, seeing Teddy and hearing his high, cheery voice bantering with his fellow officers and with such enlisted men as marched close to him—men who needed the right word of encouragement from their commander? It was purely wonderful what being with Teddy Roosevelt did for a man.

The Santiago road led northward up a narrowing valley, becoming more obscured by brush and trees as it approached the ridge over which it must pass to Las Guásimas, Sevilla and the Spaniard. Following the road itself were Young and the two squadrons of regulars. By the hill trail to the left went Wood and Roosevelt with their regiment of volunteers. It was already hot at six o'clock. On the hill above the wagon road the climbing sun winked and glittered off the rifles of the Rough Riders toiling along the narrow mule track. The men at first laughed and joked about the difficult going and the fact the weather was promising to "turn off warmish." A little later they grew quiet; it was 6:30 and no sign of the enemy yet. On the wagon road below, Young's cavalry had pushed ahead and were lost to view.

At seven Wood and Roosevelt consulted their maps. A

first uneasiness spread among the troops. Fate, who had come up with Captain O'Neill—he was acting sergeant with Houck detached on scout—thought the contrast between Wood and his lieutenant-colonel, as they talked with the other officers of the staff, was notable. Wood, like Teddy, had been up all night. He still wore the yellow slicker he had donned to shed last night's heavy rain. His face was gray with fatigue, his voice croaked and broke repeatedly. He appeared to Fate as though he were ill. Roosevelt was chipper as a ground squirrel. He stomped and gestured briskly and positively. He showed no hint of strain, certainly none of hesitation. As against his superior's halting, weary attitude, his fresh vigor was magnetic. The troop commanders were patently drawn more to him than to Wood, and listened attentively to all he said.

The moment's uncertainty began to dissipate. It could not withstand Teddy Roosevelt. Presently the signal to go forward was given. The trail went sharply upward toward the high ridge and passage over it to Guásimas Junction. The climb was a hard one in the morning heat. Lungs were bursting and hearts pounding by the time of the topping-out. But the view from above was glorious.

Fate and his panting fellows examined it while they rested. The bay at Siboney seemed to lie at the very foot of the height they had just ascended. It gleamed like a blue jewel in the clear sunlight. Upon its glistening surface the transports and gray men-of-war stood stiff and brittle-looking as toys. The tiny village with its palm-thatched huts and whitewashed stores was as pretty as a painted picture. Fate thought the tiled red roofs and corrugated iron flanks of the two warehouses near the beach made a nice contrast with the houses. He liked, also, the way the graceful tall palms moved their fronds in the morning breeze.

"Damnation!" exclaimed Little McGinty. "It is purtier than the tits on a pink sow!" And Fate was forced to agree. Indeed, he was compelled to add a line of his own poetry to the occasion. "By Cripes," he said, "you're right, McGinty. From up here you would never guess how them huts stank at close range with that cow-manure adobe they got 'em smeared with. It's remarkable."

Boone Gaskill, the Georgia sourmash merchant, shifted his quid of longleaf Burley and spat a thin stream of amber over the mountainside. "Maybe now that we have rose above that hog-wallow rum and rotgut grape juice them little devils peddle," he said, "I may be able to get back some of my legitimate business. That sweet wine like to killed off some of my best customers, and that sugar-cane rum was scandalous. I seen one jug of it ate square through the bottom of a tin cup in fifteen seconds. Little brown monkey was selling it at a nickel a shot and you got your money back if the damn bottom fell out of the cup afore you could get it hoisted. That ain't free American competition and I am going to write my congressman, soon as we get down the hill."

Buck Dawson, the chief mule packer, nodded and sent a shower of his own plug juice after Gaskill's.

"I'm going to write your Congressman, too," he promised. "I'm going to have you hauled up for issuing poison drugs without a prescription, and for general assault and battery on my insides with a bottle. I would have you hung for selling whiskey to the Injuns also, save that you cain't call that stuff you sell whiskey."

"For mine," said Prayerful James, "I would rather gargle with panther sign and goat gland oil than to take another swaller of that swill you cook up. That is the goddamnedest throat reamer I've ever come acrost in my sonofabitching life. Jesus Gawd A'mighty!''

Hell Roaring Jones, who, to Fate's knowledge, hadn't spoken an audible word since the taffrail conference about killing and skinning out the ship's porter of the *Yucatan* for selling five-cent water, now nodded meekly and said, ''Yes, it is rather stout,'' and for some reason the men all thought that was very funny and everybody had a laugh and felt better.

Starting down the far side of the ridge toward the rendezvous with the regulars at Las Guásimas Junction, they were joking and cowboying with all the old spirit of San Antonio and Tampa. Twenty minutes later, having reached and been engulfed by the nearly impenetrable bottom growth, they heard the firing on their right and knew that Wheeler and Young had found the enemy.

They knew something else; and the laughing and the cowboying fell away. There really were Spaniards in Cuba. And they shot back.

Chapter Twenty

The Rough Riders hesitated. Where they were they could see nothing. The fire on the right was heavy, most of it the high whine of the Spanish Mausers. The heavier barking of the U.S. Krags was sporadic, then silent altogether. Had Young and the Regular Cavalry walked into a trap? Why the sudden cessation of American fire?

Wood and Roosevelt, Brodie, Capron, Jenkins and the other troop commanders talked tensely at columnhead. Without orders Troop A had been taken from the rear to midcolumn. Bucky O'Neill was following Roosevelt, when the latter, on the outbreak of the firing, had said to him, "Let's be going, Bucky, we won't see any fun back here!" T.R. was now coming back from the command meeting and Fate saw that he was greatly excited. "All right, men," he heard him call, "move up, follow me!" Then he saw him swing about, motioning to O'Neill and McClintock, who was commanding B Troop, to be quick. He had secured permission from Wood to take his two favored Arizona companies to the front. Upon returning now to columnhead, he was given the left of the advance, Wood himself taking the right. Ahead of the joint line, down each side of the path they were following, went a scout patrol.

Progress was slow and without evidence of resistance. The land about them had once been intensely cultivated by the rich Spanish and American sugar interests but had been laid waste by the Cuban revolutionists—the insurgents the Rough Riders had come to liberate—and it now lay still and ominous beneath the scars of liberty and equality.

Fate shivered despite the great heat. No land in primitive state is one-half so desolate as a land which has been tamed, then abandoned by man and reclaimed by the original jungle. Through the twenty- and thirty-foot regrowth of the bush, Fate could see the empty-eyed houses of the plantation owners standing in what had shortly before been beautiful clearings filled with the hum and bustle of happy, productive life. Now they stood eerily quiet, no life save that of the scuttling lizards and palm rats within their sun-speared darknesses.

Another sound, however, was heard increasingly before long—the mournful cry of the Cuban wood cuckoo. The bird's peculiar song put the nerves of the Rough Riders on sharpest edge. Benito Guadaña had warned the Americans to beware of it, since it was the alerting signal of the Spanish pickets. The U.S. troopers had grown used to the doleful notes of the bird en route from Daiquiri to Siboney, but now they looked at one another and peered hard into the blank wall of the jungle which enclosed them like a living shroud.

Were those cuckoos calling out there, or something else? Were they the Spanish Infantry, trained regulars acting

as snipers and waiting with their new Mauser rifles cocked
and aimed, to ambush the *yanqui* invaders?

Were they Loyalist local guerrillas, Cuban irregulars in
the employ of the Spaniards fighting to keep Cuba en-
slaved?

Were they perhaps their own friendly insurgent allies using the Spanish signal to confuse the government troops
defending the approaches to Santiago?

Why the devil didn't their scouts come in and tell them
something? Where were Houck Oatman and J. B. Merrick
and their picked patrol? They had left Siboney four hours
ago. They had only as many miles to travel to find the
enemy. They ought to have been back by six. It was now
a quarter of eight. Damn.

Off to the right, Fate saw the shell of a mansion. A thirty-
five-foot second-growth palm tree had thrust up in the middle of it, protruding like a fronded hand through the
ruptured tumble of the tiled roof. The trail narrowed suddenly here. Barbed wire began on both sides of the way,
channeling their path into the ever denser jungle ahead like
the funneling wings of a western brush corral for trapping
wild horses. The college men could not see it, but the cowboys looked at it, at one another, and cursed. They did not
like it the least bit.

Up front, Wood shared their distrust of the wire, and of
the continued stillness. He ordered the advance halted and
thrown off the trail. Fate's company was moved to the left,
under Roosevelt; Troops A, B and L being put into a gla-
delike clearing, entrance to which was given by a gate in
the roadway wire.

The men lay or sat down in what shade they could find.
The firing from the Regular Cavalry over on their right had
begun briefly again, then once more fallen still. The resur-

gence of the Krag's familiar deep-barking reports, even if short-lived, had a salutary effect on the American morale. The presence of the Negro troops with his and General Young's white regulars was given quick and easy blame for any show of nerves or uncertainty the U.S. forces may have evidenced. Further relaxing of anxieties among the halted Rough Riders led to the cheerful prediction that after a bit more blind marching through the *brasada,* they would all "right-about-face" and go back to the beach. Bets were shortly being offered, with no takers, that they would eat noon mess in Siboney. Tobacco pouches began to come out, loud talk and laughter to return.

Fate, letting down with his comrades, small-talked and ruminated about how hot it was and whether or not the clouds drifting in meant rain and what on earth was keeping Houck Oatman and the scout party. He joined in the guffaw which followed Little McGinty's guess that the boys had found themselves a hut full of female insurgents and had set about improving Cuban-American relationships at the mattress level. The sound of the laugh was still going around the circle of immediate listeners, when Colonel Wood's sharp order for "silence in the ranks" came down the line.

The men of A Troop fell still. Fate felt his belly pull in. He got up and moved forward, crouching and quiet, so as not to draw attention to himself. Halting near the group of officers about Wood and Roosevelt, he was able to get a close look at the body of the slight youth which two of the L Troop pickets had just brought in and deposited upon the ground. It was that of "Soldado," a loyal and cheerful young Cuban who had guided Colonel Wood and the Rough Rider column on the grueling march from Daiquiri to Siboney, and who had gone out in the blackness earlier that morning to "speak the Spanish" for Houck's scout patrol. Soldado was not a pleasant nor a reassuring sight. He had been knifed between the shoulder blades and was still warm and limp. Fate, listening as intently as he was watching, heard the one and sinister word *guerrillas* from the frightened Cuban interpreters with Wood.

Fate hesitated, trying to think—or not to think—about Houck Oatman and his scout patrol. Of course, Soldado's death did not necessarily mean trouble for Houck's detail. The little Cuban patriot might have lost some of his fervor for the cause. He might have deserted the patrol and been caught alone by the guerrillas. But he also may have stayed bravely with the patrol, then staggered a long way back with that knife stuck in him. Somewhere up ahead in the silent bush, Houck and the others might wait as dead and done as the valiant youth from Siboney. One thing was soberingly clear. The Spanish guerrillas, about whom the Rough Riders had been warned by Benito Guadaña, did exist. Perhaps this very moment they were watching Fate and the officers of the First Volunteer Cavalry; watching them and waiting for them to move on into the bush where they might arrange for them the same end they had provided for Soldado. Fate set his jaw and looked back at Wood and the other officers. As he did, the staff discussion became noticeably strident: a difference of professional opinion had obviously developed. Fate, staring hard, was distinctly surprised to observe that the primary trio engaged by Wood in this moment of doubt and danger was not composed, as one might expect, of Capron, Jenkins and Brodie, the regulars, but of Roosevelt and the two New York correspondents, Edward Marshall of Mr. Hearst's *Journal,* and Richard Harding Davis of the New York *Herald.*

Fate, of course, had heard about the incident on *Segur-*

anca when General Shafter, beside himself with staff work, had requested the reporters of the various papers to leave him alone, that he might get on with the business of the landing. It was at this point that an indignant, and gorgeously attired, R. H. Davis had informed the commander of the Fifth Corps that he, Davis, was no ordinary reporter but a "descriptive writer" of note and high distinction. The mountainous officer's reply had been unprintable for the first ten words and had concluded with the broad sentiment that he, Shafter, did not give a tinker's damn who or what R. H. Davis was; when he was told to get the hell out of the way, he was to get the hell out of the way. The action had resulted in Davis' attaching himself to Teddy Roosevelt and had formed the beginnings of his private war in print on General William Shafter. But all Fate knew was that here was a pesky newspaper reporter, or descriptive writer, who was now evidently handing Colonel Wood and Teddy Roosevelt the benefit of the same splendid military counsel which had got him thrown off the *Seguranca.* It struck the Arizona cowboy as mighty odd. More, it reminded him of what Houck had repeatedly said about T.R. and the press. As for the two newsmen: Marshall was polite, dignified and friendly, as Fate knew from having talked with him on the hard march from Daiquiri; Davis was Davis. He did not talk with enlisted men and seldom with officers below the rank of captain. Airing his concern to the two soldiers nearest him, Fate said to the first, "This here could be serious, don't you reckon?"

"Jesus," said the soldier, wiping his flushed and steaming face, "I ain't never seen heat to touch this. Ain't it fierce, though?"

The second trooper, taking off and throwing down his blanket roll—absolutely against orders—nodded and blew a spume of perspiration from the end of his nose. "Goddam if it ain't," he agreed. "It's pure hell. How would you like a gallon of ice-cold beer right now?"

"Oh, God!" groaned his companion. "You sonofabitch."

Fate looked at the two of them, feeling very uneasy. They weren't thinking about the war, or the Spaniards, or the dead boy in the grass, or the missing Rough Rider scout patrol, or a damned thing of real importance. They were thinking about cold beer.

He wanted to say something mean and small to them but did not. They weren't really to blame. After all, they were doing just what the officers, at least Wood and Roosevelt, were doing. He looked back at the latter. And his disturbance was not lessened notably. The "staff" meeting had deteriorated into a rest halt on the apparent and rather dubious theory of "when in doubt do nothing."

Wood and Roosevelt were standing together near the barbed-wire fence. Their companion officers were mostly seated or lying down in the grass around them. Wood was telling a dirty joke which had just drawn a good laugh, as commanding officers' jokes always do, and Roosevelt was talking with Edward Marshall, the *Journal* man. Fate, having stationed himself as near as he might to T.R., now drifted a step closer, hoping he might hear something of the strategy being offered Marshall by the second-in-command.

What he actually heard was a resumé of a "most delightful" luncheon in the Astor House with Mr. Hearst, the well-known owner of the *Journal,* in which Mr. Roosevelt had taken occasion to remark to the great man what a splendid young reporter was Edward Marshall. The latter was then responding with appropriate gratitude and, in his turn, reminding Roosevelt of the kindness with which he, Marshall, had treated the Rough Riders in his various reports. To this T.R. answered with a laugh and said, "Yes, and I could wish some of your colleagues might be as accurate—"

He had raised his voice deliberately to include Davis, who was talking with Wood, and the famed reporter blushed and set his jaw but did not look over at T.R., or in any other way acknowledge he had heard him. Fate guessed this barb had been earned by Davis through his critical writings of the mismanagement and blundering which had so far characterized the slapdash advance of the Rough Riders from San Antonio to Siboney. Marshall, being younger and far less known, had dared no such familiarities with Teddy's pets. In accordance, Fate supposed, he was now privileged to share T.R.'s confidences to a degree not given Davis. He also decided, and speedily, that if those confidences had to do with luncheons at the Astor House, Davis would do much better listening to Wood's officially funny stories than to Teddy's adventures in the cultivation of Mr. Hearst.

Neither activity, clearly, had the right association with the present position of a spread-out careless halt in a blind savanna of Cuban jungle grass. Not with the Las Guásimas Junction less than 300 yards beyond Captain Capron and his pickets, and the Spaniards reportedly dug in 600 yards beyond and *above* that junction.

Fate Baylen's uneasiness increased fourfold. Suddenly he saw Roosevelt look closely at the barbed wire near which he and Marshall stood. He heard his startled remark very clearly in the little stillness which ensued. "See here," he said, picking up a parted strand and showing it to his companion, "this is not broken, as I had supposed. It has been cut. And within the past hour.''

"What?'' exclaimed Marshall, leaning in to look. "How do you know that, Colonel?''

Roosevelt's blunt jaw protruded belligerently. "There was a heavy dew last night,'' he said. "A freshly cut end, one which was cut last night, or even in the early hours of this morning, would bear a light rust. This cut is absolutely clean and bright. The Spaniard has gone through here within the hour—or not later than sunrise. Colonel Wood—''

He turned to the commander, voice high and sharp. Wood, catching the note of urgency, moved over at once. Roosevelt showed him the cut wire and said, "What do you think?'' Wood looked up at him, and Fate could see his tired face tighten. "I think we had better get under cover,'' he replied, and turned to give the order.

But he was too late. The crash of the hidden Spanish rifle fire drowned out his warning even as its words left his mouth.

In afterthought Roosevelt was to write of the deliberation and coolness of his command at this moment. He was to tell in great detail how he led his gallant men: "I accordingly got all of my men up in line and began quick firing. In a very few minutes . . . the Spaniards retreated to the left into the jungle, and we lost sight of them.'' But he was seen by eyewitnesses other than Fate Baylen to behave in quite another manner than his own report would indicate. Wrote Edward Marshall, the most collected of the professional correspondents present: "Colonel Wood was as cool a man as I ever saw. He gave his orders with the utmost calmness and showed not one sign of undue excitement. Colonel Roosevelt, on the contrary, jumped up and down, literally, I mean, with emotions evidently divided between joy and a tendency to run."

The later memories of R. H. Davis and other melodramatists who were there were replete with praise of the manner in which the Rough Riders went forward, "fearless to the man, and not one straggler in the regiment." Each man, when hit, "fell without a cry, glad to find death in such a glorious cause." There were "no cowards and no malcontents on that field that day. No man who wore the brown or blue upon that hour of trail and under that murderous hail of Spanish Mauser bullets, faltered or fell back. All went forward uncomplainingly and acts of heroism were so numbered that to count them became, shortly, to count the number of men within one's view."

Fate Baylen saw a different regiment in a different jungle clearing, and with eyes trained from birth to see what they saw and to see it clearly and quickly for what it was, and not what he might have wished it was.

To be truthful, Colonel Leonard Wood did stand fast. His order, when it could be heard, was a simple directive for the troops to "chamber and magazine." He then sent Roosevelt and three troops into the thick bush to the right, himself taking the remaining troops into the open ground to the left, and leaving one troop in support of the center on the trail. Capron and L Troop were already engaged on the front and Wood went instantly with his troops to their support. Left alone, Teddy did nothing at first. He stood and watched his sappers cut the barbed wire which would let his command into the jungle on the right. He still stood, picking up and staring at the cut wires as though in a daze, while the first of his men—a dozen or more—followed Lieutenant Woodbury Kane of K Troop through the gap. It was Bucky O'Neill of A Troop who saved a possibly bad moment. The raw-boned Arizona adventurer knew well the signs of battle shock and was at his Colonel's side in three long strides. He put his hand on his shoulder and actually took from Roosevelt's hand the strands of wire at which he was staring. Holding back the wire as though he had replaced their commander in an onerous job, he waved his own men forward and at the same time said quickly to Roosevelt, "Let's go, Colonel, we're getting behind."

Fate, coming up rapidly at the head of A Troop, saw Roosevelt give a start and could tell that Captain O'Neill had said something to him, but did not hear what it was. The effect on Roosevelt, however, was electric.

He at once leaped the downed wire and cried out, "Come along, men! We're getting behind!" and dashed forward into the bush at a stumbling run. The men of Troops A and G raised a yell and went after him on the double. Within five minutes they were lost to sight of the rest-halt clearing and within another five minutes could not see one another. As for the enemy the only sign of him was the irritating, deadly slither of the Mauser bullets through the overhead tangle of vine and aerial root. But they did not mind that, now that Teddy had gone forward and the battle was on.

Fate went with the others, whooping and Rebel-yelling on the run. The crash of the Spanish fire increased. Here and there a man was hit and despite the later writings of the advance, did indeed cry out when the lead went into him. The Rough Riders only yelled the louder, ran the faster, fought the harder to get through the damnable growth which screened the enemy from the sights of their own Krag Carbines. Fate Baylen remembered the yelling because it was the most natural thing in the world for frightened men to do when charging, absolutely blind, into an enemy who outnumbered his side and had the advantages of elevation, fire power and familiarity with home grounds. But, again, Eastern and Western eyes saw a different fight.

Wrote the professionally intrepid Richard Harding Davis: "It was an exceedingly hot corner. The whole troop was gathered in the little open place blocked by the network of grapevine [*sic*] and tangled bushes before it. They could not see twenty feet on three sides of them, but on the right hand lay the valley, and across it came the sound of Young's brigade, who were apparently heavily engaged. The enemy's fire was so close that the men could not hear the word of command and Captain Llewellen and Lieutenant Greenway ran among them, batting them with their sombreros to make them cease firing. Lieutenant-Colonel Roosevelt ran up just then, bringing with him Lieutenant Woodbury Kane and ten troopers from K Troop. Roosevelt lay down in the grass beside Llewellen and consulted with him eagerly. Kane was smiling with the charming content of a perfectly happy man, exactly as though it were a polo match and his side had scored. . . . The same spirit that once sent these men . . . against their opponents' rush line was the spirit that sent Church, Channing, Devereux, Ronalds, Wrenn, Cash, Dudley, Dean and a dozen others through the high, hot grass at Guásimas, not shouting, as their friends the cowboys did, but each with his mouth tightly shut, with his eyes on the ball, and moving in obedience to the captain's signals."

Not having been bred to keep his mouth shut, Fate kept right on running and yelling with his bowlegged companions. He did not notice that an Eastern boy from K Troop took his bullets any more quietly than a Western lad from Troops A or G. Or that, when they had to, the college men dived any the less earnestly for cover than did the realistic sons of the sagebrush.

It was in truth a "hot corner" there in the tangle on the right where Teddy and his three troops were trying to find the Spaniard.

But it was not so lethal a heat as that on the left. Over there, in the van of L Troop, the stillness had already struck. Sergeant Hamilton Fish was dead and gallant Captain Allyn Capron, a Mauser bullet buried in his heart, was dying. Now they knew that the Spaniard not only was in Cuba and would shoot back, but that he would shoot to kill.

Chapter Twenty-one

Fate saw no more of Teddy Roosevelt on the right. Excited by the storm of firing on the left, the Lieutenant-Colonel abandoned his orders to push on the right and ran across the trail to find Wood and the harder fighting. A part of G Troop, with Captain Llewellen, followed him, as did Woodbury Kane with a part of K Troop. Bucky O'Neill, with A Troop, and Micah Jenkins with most of K, stood fast, both holding the "thicket," as well as feeling yet farther to the right in a cool-headed attempt to find and join the left flank of the regulars under Young. Individual soldiers from all three troops broke and ran after Roosevelt and his band but Fate had heard Wood give the order to bear to the right, and he did not chase off with the glory hunters. Had he been a private, he might have done so. But wearing Houck Oatman's stripes and serving as Bucky O'Neill's first sergeant on the line, he had no choice but to do as his captain was doing, obeying the unit orders of the regimental commander rather than the impulse to go where the big noise was being made and where the headlines undoubtedly were being written.

It was only minutes after the defection of Roosevelt that the K Troop guidon bearer, dispatched by Micah Jenkins to mount a nearby knoll, was able to catch the eye of Cavalry General Young's signal officer. The latter immediately acknowledged the presence of the Rough Riders by wigwag and then by hoarsely shouting voice, instructing Jenkins that General Young said to press forward with all energy; that he, Young, would secure the newly joined flanks in the center and attempt also to turn the Spanish line and drive it in across the advancing line of the volunteer cavalry. Cheered by such confidence from the regular command, the Rough Riders again tried moving ahead and up the grade of the ridge beyond the Las Guásimas road junction.

The effort cost them nine killed and wounded in ten minutes, and Micah Jenkins brought the assault to a halt while there was yet some cover remaining to his men. At the time that he did so, the men of the First and Tenth Cavalry, true to Young's promise, turned the Spanish flank and drove it in. Jenkins let the regulars cross in front of the Rough Riders to pursue the Spaniards, who were now in full retreat on the right of the American line. The regulars asked Jenkins and O'Neill to hold where they were, in support, and to this the Rough Rider officers agreed. Again, the brief action came out at odds with itself in the written records.

Of his practical ignoring of the order from Wood to explore and carry the right, not to mention the resulting actual abandonment of two-thirds of his command while he "explored" his personal whim to go see what Wood was doing on the left, T.R. was to say airily, "At one time . . . I was out of touch with that part of my wing commanded by Jenkins and O'Neill."

Adding his own special salt to the wounds of the aggrieved historians, who never have accepted his wondrous ability to appear in several places at the same time, he appended this modest appropriation to himself of battle credits belonging largely to Micah Jenkins and Bucky O'Neill.

"Soon we saw troops appearing across the ravine . . . we dared not fire, and carefully studied the newcomers with our glasses . . . we recognized our own cavalrymen. We were by no means sure that they recognized us, however, and were anxious that they should . . . so Sergeant Lee of Troop K climbed a tree and from its summit waved the troop guidon. They waved their guidon back, and as our right wing was now in touch with the regulars, I left Jenkins and O'Neill to keep the connection, and led Llewellen's troop back to the path to join the rest of the regiment, which was evidently still in the thick of the fight."

It would have historical significance, perhaps soul-shattering for the Roosevelt dynasty, to be able to read the reports of one or two of the Arizona volunteers present during these particular twenty minutes of what T.R. was later to call his "trying fight" at Las Guásimas.

It would be equally interesting to have, for comparison, the report of the professional soldier most directly involved. But Teddy rode, as always, with Dame Fortune smiling on him. Captain Micah Jenkins never corrected the record as to his part in effecting the critical juncture with the regulars on the right, or as to the precise whereabouts of Lieutenant-Colonel Theodore Roosevelt when the success or failure of that juncture meant the holding or breaking of the American line. Fate Baylen and the other common cowboys firing their Krags at grapevines and mango-tree limbs and dropping into the Cuban wiregrass to crawl on their bellies with their faces in the jungle rot praying for a chance to see just one Spaniard or to find a hole big enough to hide in for the rest of the fight, had no real idea of what was going on. They knew only that Teddy had disappeared and that things were in a hell of a shape until the regulars showed up on the right. As for Bucky O'Neill, a man who feared neither God nor Devil nor Teddy Roosevelt, his opinion would have been the most revealing of all. But Bucky was not to write it down. Over behind the high ridge frowning above Las Guásimas, a week later a bullet waited for Bucky O'Neill.

Chapter Twenty-two

In the lull following the crossing over of the regulars in front of Troops A and K, Mr. Richard Harding Davis discovered that his prize copy had disappeared. Inquiring after the whereabouts of Colonel Roosevelt, he was told by a not entirely delighted Bucky O'Neill that T.R. had last been seen "loping off to the left." He added that in case he, Davis, should locate the squadron commander would he please ask him "what the hell A and K Troops were supposed to do for the rest of the day?" To this Davis replied he would be glad to cooperate, if only a guide could be furnished him who might have some familiarity with the terrain on the left. O'Neill glanced around impatiently and caught Fate Baylen trying to ease behind a clump of dagger palm. "All right, Sergeant," he said, "you're nominated. Take Mr. Davis over to the Colonel."

Fate was tempted to plead ignorance of the left side of the battlefield. He would have done so, since he had a strong natural aversion to Mr. R. H. Davis, as well as to any unnecessary exposing of Fate Baylen's bulk to the sharp-eyed Spanish snipers, but a last-second thought of Houck Oatman's continuing absence changed his mind. He saluted and said, "Yes, sir, Captain. Will I stay with him or come back?"

"Stay over there," said O'Neill. "Stick with the Colonel. We'll catch up to you directly. *Cuidado, hombre.*"

"Yes, sir," said Fate. "The same with you, Captain."

He and Davis set out through the bush, going a way which Fate had located during the advance. The route swung back from the front in a looping arc, and came out in the same jungle glade where they had been resting when L Troop's pickets had drawn the Spanish fire.

Fate deliberately set a fast pace, because he did not care to talk with his companion and wanted, as well, to wear him out all he could. Davis had taken to issuing orders and conducting himself precisely like a commissioned officer of the regiment, even to the absurd extremity of directing fire at the front. He had somewhere appropriated a beautiful little Winchester carbine and had already been blasting away with it to the annoyance and, indeed, danger of his enlisted comrades of the First Volunteer Cavalry. This great bravery would humbly appear in his next report of the fighting in Cuba, Fate was certain, but the only thing the Bell Rock cowboy had personally observed of the noted descriptive writer's behavior which he would like to have seen printed in the New York papers was an act of considered valor which he was equally positive would not be included in the Las Guásimas dispatches: this was the promptitude with which Davis had found "his own hole" behind a downed palm log where he was quite protected between unaimed firings of his little carbine and loud shouts of encouragement to his more exposed fellows of the Rough Rider right.

By the time the Regulars had driven the Spaniards off and the reporter had crawled out of his retreat, he appeared personally to have led the right flank and miraculously suffered no visible damage in the doing.

Actually, Fate did not condemn this accomplishment. The only thing about it which he resented was the alert newspaperman's having found a better hole than his own. So, mulling it over, the cowboy soldier concluded that he simply did not appreciate New York reporters and that it was nothing he could particularly blame on Mr. Davis alone.

Nearing the rest clearing, his thoughts on the subject were interrupted by renewed bursts of very heavy firing on the left. His mind leaped at once to T.R. and to concern for the Colonel's safety and the welfare of the entire regiment. Coming out in the clearing, he had cause to redouble the sudden sense of misgiving which had swept over him.

The clearing was no longer a place of rest. Casualties had mounted within the brief minutes of the clash, and a field hospital and dressing station were being set up at the old ruins of the ranchhouse. At one glance, Fate saw that the Rough Riders were in more trouble than he had dreamed. A dozen troopers lay silent and bloody upon the ground about the building. Another two dozen leaned or sat or staggered about, still able to move but with their wounds soaking their brown ducks or streaming blood from the uncovered skin of face, hands or arms. There were only three medical corpsmen in attendance, no doctor in sight. One small Cuban mule, packed with slim panniers of medical supplies, drooped in the shade of the roofless wall. Some of these men on the ground were dead, Fate knew.

Others, he knew as surely, were dying. He stopped in his tracks, bewildered.

"What's the matter?" said Davis, unable to see past Fate's wide shoulders. He pushed forward, giving himself a view of the clearing and the field hospital. His eyes widened. "Great!" he cried. "My God, this is great! Let me through there. I must get to those men. Do you see Doctor Church any place? Hurry up, man! Get out of my way."

Fate moved aside, saying nothing. Davis sprinted past him, and across to the dressing station. Fate started after him. He caught up to him just as Davis was buttonholing one of the panting corpsmen, taking him from his work over a groaning Rough Rider. Before the corpsman could object to the interruption, Fate had firmly taken hold of the reporter's stylish uniform collar and quietly requested him to "leave off and come along."

"Get your hands off me!" commanded Davis indignantly. "I'm here to do a job!"

"Me too, Mr. Davis," nodded the Arizonan. "I hired on to get you to Colonel Roosevelt, and you're going."

He gave the descriptive writer a nudge to start him off in the right direction. Davis whirled angrily. Fate blocked him across the chest with a barred forearm, which had all the yield of a gun barrel. The impact seemed to sober the newsman, for he recovered himself and apologized for the "misunderstanding." He was a persuasive and a charming fellow and Fate was unable to hold any grudge longer than five minutes. "All right, sir, Mr. Davis," he said, "it ain't easy to be cool in a hot fight like this one: let's get on along and find the Colonel."

But he had gone as far as he was going with Mr Richard Harding Davis. Around the next bend in the trail, they bumped into a bent, powerful figure of a man staggering toward the clearing with a Rough Rider carried unconscious over his shoulder. The rescuer peered up at them from beneath his burden, and Davis burst out, "Church, old fellow! What the devil are you doing here?"

Evidently Dr. Bob Church was not in his "old fellow" mood. He completely ignored Davis, saying plaintively to Fate, "Here, soldier, will you please take this one on into the hospital for me? I've got to go back out for two others that were with him. Tell the corpsmen not to give any water to the ones with stomach and bowel wounds like this one. I'll be along directly." He gave Fate a second gasping look, and added, "Soldier, when you've got this man taken care of, will you come back and help me with the others? I'm about done in. Don't be too careful with that one you've got there; I think he's past help."

Fate, who had not looked at the wounded man, now adjusted the body over his shoulder, the arms and head hanging down his back.

"Yes, sir," he replied, "I will surely do it. You will be straight on along this trail, is that right, sir?"

Church nodded. "A little to the right, beyond the dry creek bed," he said. "Please hurry." He turned to go back to the front, but Davis suggested eagerly, "Wait old chap, I'll go with you; I'm looking for Roosevelt." The regimental surgeon shot him a mean look. "You won't find him where I'm going," he barked. "He's off to the left there somewhere. Brodie's been hit and Wood has given Roosevelt the command over there." This time when he turned to go, he did not stop when Davis called again for him to wait. The latter then came about, looking for Fate. The tall cowboy was already moving toward the dressing station with his blood-soaked burden. He did not reply to the newsman's belated shout, nor did he wait for him to catch up.

Five minutes after that he reached the shade of the standing wall and laid his burden in its stifling shelter. It was another two or three minutes before he could find a corpsman and give him Church's message, then persuade him to come over and attend to the wounded man he had just brought in. Wordless seconds later the corpsman had washed off the crusted blood and filth which hid the trooper's features and Fate was able to recognize him.

He felt the cold spread through him. He was sick and wanted to throw up. The corpsman looked quickly at him and said, "What's the matter? Ain't you ever seen one of them go out before?"

Fate did not answer him. He got up stiffly and walked away. It was a question which had no answer. Not for Fate Baylen. Not then, not ever. How could it have?

That was Houck Oatman dying on the ground over there.

Chapter Twenty-three

Church worked with Houck laid on an improvised table, a door held up by an ammunition box at one end and a pile of adobe bricks at the other. Fate watched him, hardly breathing. Since there were no corpsmen to spare from the remaining wounded, Fate held the granite basin of bloody rags and water, which was all the operative assistance Dr. Bob Church was given at Guásimas. Perforce, Church talked to the white-faced cowboy, the scalpel never ceasing to move as he did.

"These stomach wounds are the worst," he said. "I don't think I will operate them after this one. Poor devil. He's been knifed in the kidneys and shot from in front. The knife alone would have been enough, God knows, but these damned abdominal gunshot situations . . ."

Fate swallowed hard. "You doubt he'll make it?" he asked. "He's powerful tough, sir."

"You know him?" said Church.

"Yes, sir. He's First Sergeant Houck Oatman, of Captain O'Neill's troop. We come in together at Prescott."

"O'Neill's bunch, eh? Yes, now I remember. Isn't he one of the scouts who went out from Siboney this morning?"

"Yes, sir. Him and J. B. Merrick and four, five others."

"Merrick is back," said Church, wiping his face on his forearm. "Rag, Sergeant . . ." Fate wrung and handed him a piece of the bloody cloth, and the surgeon went on. "I saw him up the lane just now. With Roosevelt. Rag . . ."

A silence fell. Church worked more slowly now, and with a look of restraint. He kept glancing at his patient's face, watching it more than the movements of the knife. "Got one of them," he said tersely, and handed the slim bullet to Fate. "You recognize it?"

Fate took the bullet, peering at it closely. "Damn!" he said, low-voiced. "The sons of bitches."

"What is it, Sergeant?" said Church. "It's not a Krag and not a Mauser. Am I right?"

"Yes, sir," said Fate, lean jaw tightening, "you're right. This here is a smaller caliber than them."

"Here are two more," said Church. "Both the same. You know the gun they're from, Sergeant? Another rag, please."

Fate gave him the wrung cloth, put the long, slim bullets in his shirt pocket. "Yes, sir," he answered, "I know the gun. It's a Lee navy rifle, sir. The exact same kind we give them murdering Cubans with Benito Guadaña back to the beach at Daiquiri."

Church looked up quickly. "The devil you say! Do you suppose Guadaña's men are working with the Spanish guerrillas?"

"Yes, sir," said Fate, "I think they are."

Church did not reply, being busy again. Shortly he straightened and stepped back. "Rag, sir?" inquired Fate anxiously. Church shook his head. "Put him with the others over by the wall," he said. "Sorry, Sergeant."

Fate ducked his head, had to wait before speaking.

"Yes, sir, thank you," he finally said, and picked up Houck and carried him away from the table. At the wall he put him down carefully, making certain he would be comfortable. Then he looked at him a long moment.

"Houck," he said, "I dunno if you can hear me but I will say it anyhow. You remember we was talking last night back to Siboney about me and you and this here war? And you wasn't able to answer me when I asked you what we was doing here in Cuba? Leastways, you didn't say nothing. Remember?" He looked down as though he expected the stilled lips to move, the closed, pale eyes to open, the dry, caustic voice to speak again. "Well," he said, "you don't need to fret no more abouten it, Houck. I got the answer just now. You give it to me, Houck, and I reckon you knowed all the time what it was."

He paused, patting the deputy's cold hand.

"A man's got to be ready to lay down and die for his country no matter what. He can argue and bellyache all he's a mind to, right up to the time it counts. Then he has got to go the same as you went, not saying nothing, nor crying about it, nor resenting it in no way whatever. Just going ahead and laying it on the line straight out and for final. That's it, ain't it, Houck? It's why you didn't give me no answer back there in the dark at Siboney. You couldn't. There wasn't no answer back there. It was up here waiting with them sneaking Cuban guerrillas and them Lee navy bullets, or with the regular Spaniards and them Mausers, and you knowed it all the time. Ain't that so, Houck? Houck..."

"*Soldier...*" Fate felt the light touch on his shoulder and looked up. It was Dr. Bob Church. "He's dead, Sergeant," Church said softly. "Come on away from him."

Fate nodded and got up. "I knowed he was gone, sir," he said. "But we was talking the other night, him and me, about what we was doing here in Cuba. I asked him what it was and he didn't say nothing. I thought it was on account he didn't know. Now I reckon I was wrong."

"And you wanted him to know it, eh?"

"Yes, sir, I admit I did."

"Well, maybe they hear us," said Church. "A doctor would be the last to argue that. Let's go, Sergeant, I need your help and your friend doesn't."

"Yes, sir," said Fate, and followed him back to the door-slab table in the shade of the mulberry tree by the old standing wall of the ruined mansion at Las Guásimas.

He didn't remember how long he labored in the merciless sun. Nor could he recall the number of dead, the dying, nor the grievously wounded who were brought to the dressing station in the hours which followed. At sunset Dr. Church told him to clean up and go back to his outfit, and promised to speak to Bucky O'Neill about his service at the station that day. At the wash-up basin he talked with one of the corpsmen and learned a few other things.

The firing had stopped at 9:30 that morning. The enemy had retreated over the second ridge and the Battle of Las Guásimas had gone down in history at just over one and one-half hours in length. Casualties for such a skirmish had been heavy. Some of the newspapermen were calling it an "ambush," and blaming Wood and Roosevelt for blundering into the Spanish troops. The Rough Rider command was blaming the regulars and Young and Wheeler for jumping the gun and going against the enemy on the right before the volunteers could contact him on the left. There was some talk, spread by the infantry which had come up with the irate General Lawton late in the day, that both Wood and Roosevelt would be court-martialed; or, rather, would have been court-martialed, had the Spanish attack broken through between Micah Jenkins and Bucky O'Neill and the First and Tenth Cavalry.

There was more.

The mules carrying the regiment's brand-new Colt's automatic guns had been allowed to run off at the earliest Spanish firing, and had it not been for the great skill of Fred Herrig, another of Roosevelt's Far West hunting guides, in picking up their tracks and following them, the Rough Riders would have lost two-thirds of their artillery the first day. Still a problem, too, were their supposed Cuban Insurgent allies. Stories continued to come in from the battlefield as to the enthusiasm with which these local patriots appropriated American materiel in the heat of the fighting—some of it, the rumors claimed, from yet-living owners too weak from their wounds to defend government property. The entire picture was such as to hint that the aims of the insurgents were at least confused. It was not plain from their conduct in the first scrape just which side they were fighting on, the U.S. troops maintained. Indeed, it seemed they had not made up their minds one way or the other. A great crowd of them under General Castillo had failed their promise to support the advance of Young and Wheeler. They were known to be in the immediate vicinity but apparently had their "confusion" flags flying, for they simply "stood by," making no evident motion to come to the aid of their American benefactors. But there remained some honest doubt as to their guilt. Or so it seemed. Castillo had hotly declared that he had been convinced the retreating Spaniards were the Regular Cavalry of Young and Joe Wheeler and had not dared fire for this reason. By the time it had become clear that it was actually the enemy escaping up the ridge, he insisted that the Rough Riders had come into his line of fire and that he could not possibly volley at the Spaniards without hitting the Americans. It had required, far from cowardliness, a high order of bravery and discipline for the insurgents to withhold their urge to help. To this claim Wood had conceded generously. Roosevelt, Fate was more pleased to hear, had growled right out what he thought of the Cubans. It was like Teddy, Fate decided, to speak up and let the chips scatter where they would. And in this case it surely seemed there was every chance he was correct. At least in regard to one element of the so-called Cuban Insurgent force, there was extreme doubt of loyalty. Fate believed he had the proof of that particular force's treachery lying, with those bullets from Houck's poor body, in his shirt pocket.

Telling the little medical corpsman to be careful, and thanking him for his information on the fight, the lanky Arizona cowboy determined to go at once to Roosevelt. He would place before him the three Lee-Enfield bullets Dr. Bob Church had given him, together with the story of where they had come from, plus his own suspicions of Benito Guadaña dating from the beach at Daiquiri. Clearly he recalled Benito's Spanish nickname of "the Reaper." Also he recalled the throat-cutting gesture with which the Insurgent lieutenants had accompanied the use of the nickname, while laughing and pointing at the American troops.

The corpsman, a wiry Jewish youth from the East Side of New York City, raised his shoulders in a gesture of uselessness when Fate said good-bye to him and held out his hand to wish him good luck.

"*Ihh,*" he said, "so who needs good luck? What I would like is a transfer to the Navy. Or at least back to the base hospital at the beach. I'm no hero. To look at these men today . . ." He trailed off, but took Fate's hand nonetheless, and wrung it earnestly. "Good luck to you, too, cowboy," he said. "I hope we don't meet again."

"What's your name?" asked Fate. "I'd sort of like to remember it."

The Jewish boy laughed. "What's to a name?" he said. "I forgot mine already. But if you want me, ask for O'Toole. It ain't my name but I answer to it. Just like 'Sheeny Solomon,' over there." He pointed to one of his two fellow corpsmen, a giant redheaded Irishman with china-blue eyes, freckled fists and the pure look of Killarney to him. Fate laughed too and said, "All right, thanks. O'Toole. I'm Fate Baylen, of A Troop. Maybe we'll meet up again. Anyways, take care."

"Sure," said O'Toole. "What else is there to take? Poison, maybe?"

When he found Roosevelt's tent, Fate had to wait for half an hour. There was a great fuss of officers about the place, including Colonel Wood. It struck Fate as odd that the commotion should be at Roosevelt's tent, rather than Wood's. Then, having time to think about it, he knew it wasn't odd at all. Roosevelt, no matter that he was second-in-command to Wood, was far more famous. Everyone knew Teddy. But as for Leonard Wood, Fate had never heard of him until the Rough Riders were formed up and he had read in the newspapers of Teddy's unselfish act in refusing the command of the regiment. So it wasn't so strange now that most of the troop commanders and all of the reporters were at Teddy's tent. Besides, Roosevelt's cook was the best in the regiment. Right now, Fate guessed, at least if the officers felt as he did, a good meal would be worth two regimental commands.

The chances were that the Arizona cowboy never would have got near Roosevelt had not Dr. Bob Church happened along just then and seen him standing by. "Hello," said Church. "They got you blocked off from the front? Come along with me." He took hold of Fate's arm and next thing he knew he was standing in front of Teddy Roosevelt and his officers. It was very quiet and Dr. Church was saying to Roosevelt, "Colonel, here's a man wants to see you, and a man I want you to see."

He quickly told them of Fate's hard work at the station and, spying O'Neill in the audience, added, "As for you, Captain, you had better promote this fellow to lieutenant and fire the rest of your staff. He works like a mine mule and fears nothing. Not even newspaper correspondents." He gave R. H. Davis a brief nod, as the officers laughed without knowing why they did so. Davis colored deeply, and did know why. "Sergeant," Dr. Church concluded, "am I right in guessing you and I came up here for the same reason—to talk about Lee Navy bullets?"

"Yes, sir," said Fate, surprised that the surgeon should be so keen and have had the time and strength to worry about those few bullets from Houck's body after all the terrible work he had done with the other suffering men that day. "I thought the Colonel ought to know about them particular bullets and where we got them."

Church nodded and dug in his uniform pocket and dumped seven of the small-caliber Lees on the camp table before Roosevelt. He looked up at Fate when he had done so, and the latter moved in and added his three bullets to the pile. Church then told the story. When he had finished, Bucky O'Neill came forward and put his hand on Fate's arm. "I'm plumb sorry, Baylen," he said in his low drawl. "I know what you and Houck thought of one another. We'll both miss him."

"Yes, sir," said Fate, "we surely will, Captain. Houck, he thought the world and all of you, and I allow it wasn't one-sided, sir. He was a grand man."

Roosevelt, who had been standing by the table staring down at the bullets, chin in one palm, the other hand braced on the table, now swung around.

"Bucky," he said, "what the devil do you think?"

O'Neill moved his broad shoulders, his face hard as rim-rock. "I think Baylen's right," he said. "That goddam Benito Guadaña never did strike me good. I mean he looked wrong. I don't doubt he's robbing our dead and shooting our scouts either for what they have on them, for pay from the Spanish, for the pure hell of it, or for all three. One thing for damned certain; I would sure as hell find out, if it were me."

Colonel Wood nodded and spoke thoughtfully.

"There are always guerrillas in any war," he suggested. "I don't suppose these are any different from the whiskey sellers and gun runners we had to contend with on the plains. Neither do I imagine that to pursue them, as you would seem to wish to do, Captain, would do the least good. These fellows, if they are in truth operating in the pay of the Spaniard and against us with our own weapons, will never be caught. They are in their own land, even in their own home neighborhoods more than likely, and I see no prospect for success in detailing any pursuit at this time. What do the rest of you think?"

He turned to his listening staff. Most of its members

merely moved their heads in assent to his position. One or two frowned but said no more than the nodders. Micah Jenkins spoke, and so did Bucky O'Neill, the former doubting that it was altogether wise to ignore the activities of a well-organized guerrilla force which could quite easily be in their rear as well as their advance. O'Neill vehemently followed his original thought that guerrilla hunting ought to be made the first order of the next day.

Wood still demurred and Roosevelt kept his counsel to himself. It was later to be claimed by his detractors that his silence that evening was due to the fact that he had been instrumental in getting his good friend and former Navy superior, Secretary Long, to furnish the Lee rifles to the insurgents, and that the treachery with which the latter had apparently betrayed this personal charity had so shaken him that he was literally unable to comment upon it. Fate Baylen knew better. Whether or not Teddy had any part in giving the guns to Benito Guadaña's Cubans, he had repeatedly expressed his doubts of the local allies from first landing at Daiquiri. If this expression made his original evaluation of the Cubans invalid, then Fate never heard him try to weasel out of the responsibility, and he did not believe any of the rumors against him, then or later.

In the present case, Micah Jenkins accepted Wood's views with the unflavored obedience of the trained regular officer. But Bucky O'Neill was made of undisciplined stuff and did not always keep his voice down nor his emotions at right-dress. *"Oh, hell!"* he was heard to comment very audibly, before striding to Fate's side and dropping his tones to point-blank range. His outbreak drew a relieved laugh from the somewhat tense staff, and served to cover up his ensuing conversation with Fate at the table. For this, the latter was glad, since the ex-sheriff of Yavapai County did not choose his words with marked elegance.

"Pick up your bullets, Baylen," he growled through clenched teeth, "and let's get out of here! We can't argue with these dudes."

They went swiftly off through the darkness. After a ways, O'Neill stopped and rolled a cigarette. He was an endless smoker but now Fate could tell from his aggravated motions that he wanted to talk. He offered the sack of Bull Durham and the rice papers to Fate. Both men squatted down in the tall grass and smoked in silence, the understanding and acceptance of the moment typical of Westerners resting by the trail and thinking where its next loop might lead them.

It was Bucky O'Neill who spoke first.

"Baylen," he said, "did Houck ever talk about me? I mean about himself and me?"

"Yes, sir. He said him and you was in some tolerable tights a long while back. He said you owed him one."

"Yes, more than one. Several I'd say. Baylen . . ." He hesitated, and sat a moment puffing on his cigarette. "I want you to do something for me. I'm not ordering you to do it, I'm asking you. It's strictly between us. Nothing to do with the regiment. It's for you and me and Houck Oatman, you understand?"

"No, sir. But I'm willing to listen."

"Good."

There was another wait, while O'Neill licked and lit another cigarette. Fate wondered during the pause what it could be that his troop commander had in mind for him. It went without saying that it would be something where a man could get shot if he didn't keep his nose to the wind. With Bucky O'Neill's kind, they didn't play it any other way. Finally, the other man spun the second cigarette away and began making the third.

"I was born in St. Louis," he said suddenly. "The year was 1860, and I guess it must have been a poor one. I am a graduate of the National Law School of Washington, D.C., where I worked like a mongrel dog for my education. Yet when I tried for a commission in the Army, I was turned down. I went out to Arizona then, with no better luck. I ran a few newspapers. The *Miner,* the Phoenix *Herald, Hoof and Horn.* Couldn't settle for that and did three terms as sheriff of Yavapai County. That wasn't it either. I ran three times for Congress from the Territory, and got smashed each time. Wound up Mayor of Prescott, the only office I was never beaten for. In between lickings, I tried a few other things. That's when I crossed trails with Houck . . ."

He fell still, shaking his head, thinking back.

"I've always felt I would make it big one day, Baylen. Houck and I used to talk of it. He always insisted I would wind up in a box for my troubles. I never could believe it. Had a charmed life, I felt, and still feel." He shook his head again. "Yet here I am in the damned volunteer cavalry with no more chance of making it than I had in Arizona or Washington, D.C., or the Army. I wonder what Houck would say to that. I have meant to ask him a hundred times since Whipple Barracks, but somehow . . ."

He quit again, sucking deeply on his smoke and blowing out with a great sigh. Fate felt sorry for him but kept quiet, having no reason to say anything and wondering, still, why O'Neill—*the* Bucky O'Neill—would talk to him on such a night, in such a way, and in such a far-off foreign place as Cuba.

"You know what I saw over there on the left today,

Baylen? After Jenkins and I took our boys over there, when Roosevelt found out Capron was gone and sent out the word for Troops K and A to come up and side him in a hurry? It was pretty poor doings. I saw stragglers by the score, men just lying down and doing nothing. I saw Lieutenant Greenway running up and down a line of our men—*ours,* Baylen, not the regulars—hitting them with his hat to get them to stop firing. They were shooting crazy, at nothing, and would not heed spoken orders. Roosevelt was there, and kept jumping up and down and yelling like he had a bee in the gee-string. But it was young Greenway who went in and shut off those panicky men. It wasn't Roosevelt.

"Wood was blown, too. I saw and heard him order men to stop shooting at that bunch of Spaniards the regulars jumped on our side. Those Spaniards were crossing in front of Wood and our boys were mowing them down like ripe wheat, when Wood runs up yelling, 'Don't shoot at retreating men . . . !' Can you imagine Crook or Miles yelling to their boys to lay off winging the Apaches when they had them on the run? Well, it was crazy, Baylen, just crazy."

He growled something to himself, which Fate could not make out. Then he went on.

"Why am I telling you all this, eh, Baylen? Is that what you're thinking? Well, sure it is, and I'm not certain I know just why I am. But I'm going to tell you what I think it is; it's Houck Oatman. And then I'm going to tell you what I want you to do about it, if you will. I want you to get a scout party together. You figure out who you want and I will get them for you. That's regulars or Rough Riders, either one. I don't want a word of it to get to Roosevelt or Wood. That will mean you can't take Fred Herrig. Anybody else, though, and I will see they get detailed to you. What do you say?''

Fate answered carefully. ''Depends,'' he said. ''I got to tell you, Captain, that I love the Colonel.''

Bucky O'Neill laughed his quick, soft laugh. ''Hell, we all love the cocky little feist!'' he said. ''When he gets to baring those teeth and twitching those face muscles of his, the way he always does when he starts working his spiel up on any subject, who's to stand against him? I would follow him into hell for no pay and glad of the chance. You know what he said to us the last night out on the *Yucatan,* standing off Daiquiri out there in the black Cuban night with none of us knowing which would be alive in another twenty-four hours? He lifted up his glass with that mustang chuckle of his and cried out, 'The officers; may the war last until each is killed, wounded, or promoted!' Now, if you can't love a man who thinks like that, you can't love roast sirloin of Arizona steer. Don't talk to me, Baylen, about loving Teddy Roosevelt.''

''No, sir, I'm truly sorry, sir,'' said Fate, feeling his heart swell at this show of loyalty, so like his own. ''What was it you wanted me to do with that scout patrol, Captain?''

''I want you to take it,'' said O'Neill, ''and go out and find me the son of a bitch who killed Houck Oatman and I want you to bring me his head in a sack.''

Fate nodded. ''Anything else?'' he asked.

''Yes,'' said O'Neill. ''I wish I could go with you!''

''All right, Captain,'' said Fate. ''We had better move along now, hadn't we? You look tuckered.''

''No, wait,'' said O'Neill quickly. ''I want to read you something.''

He wore on his belt a small Navy-issue bull's-eye lantern with a storm shield that hid and concentrated its beam into a palm-sized spot. He lit the little lamp now, and focused it upon a rumpled paper which he had drawn from an inner pocket. "This is a copy," he said, "of a field note written by Mr. Marshall, the *Journal* reporter, before he was hurt today. I saw him when the litter bearers were starting off to Siboney with him, and he gave it to me and asked that I see it get to his editors should he fail to last the journey to the base. I meant to turn it over to the Colonel just now but forgot. It's about the way the bullet sings that has your name on it. Listen . . .

" ' . . . I saw many men shot. Everyone went down in a lump without cries, without jumping up in the air, without throwing up hands. They just went down like clods in the grass. It seemed to me that the terrible thud with which they struck the earth was more penetrating than the sound of guns. Some were only wounded; some were dead.

" 'There is much that is awe-inspiring about the death of soldiers on the battlefield. Almost all of us have seen men or women die, but they have died in their carefully arranged beds with doctors daintily hoarding the flickering spark; with loved ones clustered about. . . . On the battlefield there are no delicate scientific problems of strange microbes to be solved. There is no petting, coddling—nothing, nothing, nothing but death. The man lives, he is strong, he is vital, every muscle in him is at its fullest tension when suddenly, "chug," he is dead. That "chug" of the bullets striking flesh is nearly always plainly audible. But bullets which are billeted, so far as I know, do not sing on their way. They go silently, grimly to their mark, and the man is lacerated and torn or dead. I did not hear the bullet shriek that killed Hamilton Fish. I did not hear the bullets shriek which struck the many others who were wounded while I was near them; I did not hear the bullet shriek which struck me. . . . ' "

Bucky O'Neill turned down the light, put away the folded page of Edward Marshall's trust copy of his last report from the field at Guásimas. "I don't know," he said softly to Fate Baylen, "maybe it's nothing; but I wanted to read it to somebody else who was up there this afternoon. What do you think? Did you hear any of them singing to you?"

"Yes, sir," answered Fate, just as quietly. "I heard 'em all; they were all singing, just like Mr. Marshall says."

"It's funny," said Bucky O'Neill, looking off into the night and dropping his voice lower still, "I never heard a damned one."

Chapter Twenty-four

"The Posse," as O'Neill called Fate's scout patrol, did not get out that first night of June 24th. Before the cowboy and the captain got back to A Troop's fires, the order had come through from Young for the Rough Riders to move up. While Wood and Roosevelt sent to check these orders, O'Neill could not implement his hunt for Houck Oatman's killers. Roosevelt himself came to O'Neill, upon his return from seeing General Young and General Joe Wheeler. Fate was luckily present.

Teddy's grin preceded him through the darkness of the meadow wherein they were camped. Fate recognized the squat waddling figure even before he saw the gleam of the teeth. His heart increased its rate and he felt the choke of excitement close in upon his throat. It was the way Teddy Roosevelt affected a man. There was no helping it.

"Well, Captain," said the latter, his squeaky voice hopping with unflagged spirits, "are you all right over here?"

"Sure," said Bucky O'Neill. "How about you, Colonel?"

"All fine." Roosevelt nodded to Fate and, to the cowboy's delight, said, "Good evening, Sergeant. I see you are all of a piece. You've got a good man here, Captain. Church tells me he did more than his three regular orderlies put together."

"Yes sir," said O'Neill carefully. "Baylen is a good man. He had better be. He is replacing the best there was."

"Yes," said Roosevelt, a bit shortly Fate thought. "I was shocked to hear about Oatman. Do you suppose the guerrillas truly are serving the Spaniard?"

Bucky O'Neill looked at him. Fate stirred uncomfortably. They had been over all this with Dr. Church at Roosevelt's tent earlier. Why was the Colonel bringing it up now? Why was he laboring it? He was acting almost as though he had forgotten the previous discussion.

"Colonel," said Bucky, "I haven't changed my mind."

"Oh?" Roosevelt looked at him blankly, the teeth still showing but no longer in the grin. "How was that?"

"What I said earlier. I stand on it."

"Oh yes, yes. Well, you may be right. There's other business just now. Wood and I have been able to persuade General Young to hold off the advance for a day. We want to bury our dead here and get our lightly wounded back to Siboney tonight. We thought we'd have the ceremony for the boys first thing in the morning. Young agreed. As it turned out, it was General Wheeler who wanted to hurry things along." He frowned and added testily, "I do hope Wheeler is not going to be trouble."

"He's already been trouble," snapped Bucky O'Neill. "I personally have little use for old Fighting Joe. Did you hear what he was yelling to General Young's boys this morning? When the Spaniards broke over toward us?''

"No," said Roosevelt, "what was that?"

"The damned old fool ran up on top of a dirt pile in front of our troops, pulled out his sword and hollered, 'After 'em boys! We got the damn yankees on the run . . . !' "

O'Neill paused, scowling angrily, but Roosevelt tossed it off. "Oh, that," he said. "Yes, I heard about it. Now then, about tomorrow, Bucky; will you be ready to go after lunch?"

Fate noted the use of the first name and the man-to-man tone in which it had been used. O'Neill didn't miss it either, but his reactions to it were not as friendly as Fate's.

"Yes, sir," he answered wearily, "I'll be ready."

Roosevelt left with a wave and a flash of the old grin but Bucky O'Neill was scowling openly now. "Sometimes," he growled to Fate, "I wish I didn't love him so. He dodges and ducks like a coyote. Like fluffing off what I just told him about General Wheeler. That doddering old devil could get us all killed with his Civil War charges. Yet Roosevelt says nothing, or makes nothing, of it. For my part, damn it, I wish I had the nerve just for once to speak up and say what I thought to T.R., but I can't. You know what I mean, Baylen?"

"No, sir," said Fate. "But saying what I think is one of my own specialties. It's the main reason I got to be twenty-four years old and never made over forty dollars a month."

Bucky O'Neill laughed his soft laugh and felt better. "You'll do," he said. Then, looking off into the darkness after Roosevelt, "You know why he came over here just now? I mean instead of sending for me, and aside from telling us what he and Wood had gotten out of General Young?"

"No, sir. What? I mean, why?"

"He knew he was wrong this afternoon, when you and

Church braced him with those bullets you took out of Houck. He knew he ought to have stood up to Wood and backed me about a patrol being sent out to get those murdering bushwhackers of Benito Guadaña's. He came over here to let *me* know that *he knew* it. It was his way of apologizing. I mean, apologizing for not showing the sand to buck Wood. Sometimes, Baylen, he just has a mean habit of lying down on you right when the water gets deep and fast. But that's politics for you, as I damned well ought to know from my own experiences.''

"I guess I don't get you, sir," said Fate. "He seemed happy and all just now. As for this afternoon, he was only doing what Wood wanted, and Wood is the commander of the regiment. Ain't that so, Captain?''

O'Neill stared at him a moment, then laughed. "Sure, Baylen," he said, "that's right. Why didn't I think of it?''

Fate blushed. "I didn't aim to be smart, Captain," he muttered. "I reckon you know that.''

Bucky eyed him. He put a big hand on his shoulder and nodded quickly. "Sure, I know that. I didn't aim to be smart either. What's your first name, Baylen?''

"Fate, sir.''

"Well, Fate, you and I are going to ride the river together from here. We'll see and hear a lot we don't care for, things that don't weigh sixteen ounces to the Arizona pound. But we came of our own accord and will stay till the last Spanish fandango is danced. *No es verdad, amigo?*''

"Yes, sir, and thank you, Captain.''

"De nada, hombre," said Bucky O'Neill with a shrug. "Let's turn in and get some rest. Send Lieutenant Greenway up here if you see him, will you? *Hasta la vista. Cuidado.*''

"Sí, Capitán," smiled Fate, trying for a sureness and a spirit he did not feel. *"Hasta luego.''*

171

Chapter Twenty-five

Where the trail crossed the second ridge beyond Las Guásimas, seven of the eight Rough Rider dead were buried.
They were lain in a row, seven sticks marking each man
apart from his fellow. There were no distinct moundings of
the replaced earth, only a general, sad-looking disturbance
of the jungle path, which upset Fate a great deal.

He and the other men who wanted to come stood silently,
heads bared in the morning sun. Chaplain Brown read the
burial service of the Episcopal Church. It was so still that
his low voice carried to the last trooper, well over a hundred
feet from graveside. When he had closed the Bible, Colonel
Roosevelt stepped forward and said he would like for his
men to join him in singing "Rock of Ages." The start of
the old hymn was rough and shaky. The men were not
feeling right. They did not want to sing. But Roosevelt led
them and they would not fail to follow.

When the last notes died away there was an awkward

straining impatience to be gone from that place. Roosevelt was aware of it and, with his always wonderful feeling for such matters, spoke briefly to the restless fellows of those who would fight no more.

Afterward Fate tried to remember what T.R. had said, but he was never sure of the exact words. He thought they were something like this. "Men, let us remember our comrades whom we leave here. But let us not brood over them. And let us not linger over them in sadness. They have not gone far, and will wait for us where the trail bends to meet the river . . ."

Even if he didn't hear it straight, Fate thought it was beautiful. So did the others. They wept openly. But when they left in straggling groups a few minutes later, it was not Roosevelt's farewell which they carried away with them. At least for Fate Baylen it was not. What he remembered was the lonely look of the seventh marker—Houck's marker—and the endless wheeling and dipping in the clear skies above the ridge's summit of the vultures, drawn as always by the smells and signs of death.

It would be good, he thought, to get away from the regiment and be busied with the work, even if risky, of looking for Guadaña. He hurried to find Captain O'Neill. But O'Neill believed they must forego the patrol until the men were moved forward. He said that if Roosevelt got wind of the idea he might rule it out entirely, and that he, O'Neill, meant to carry it on at any price short of insubordination. So they had to go carefully. He said he would send Fate out at the earliest possible moment. Meanwhile, the Arizonan could be thinking of whom he wanted to go with him, and could be making inquiries among the Cuban drifters infesting the flanks of the advance, as to the whereabouts of Guadaña. Here again, however, great caution must be exercised not to let the cat out of the sack. "It's exactly the same," Bucky concluded, "as running down a murderer back home. The local people will likely sympathize with the rascal, and you will get no more help from them than if you were a Yavapai deputy going after a Tonto Rim cow thief. So watch what you say and how you say it. Understand?"

Fate acknowledged the warnings and said that he thought he could handle the inquiries. These Cuban people seemed a great deal like Mexicans and he had always been able to talk to them and get along with them just fine back in Arizona. The fact was, he said, he sometimes preferred Mexicans to Americans. But, at any rate, they were all right and he figured the Cubans were, too.

Bucky O'Neill could not agree and restressed the added danger, in any situation, of thinking that the local natives were the equals, in point of trust, of white men. "I would rather," he said, by way of forceful example, "put my own faith in one of Colonel Baldwin's Tenth Cavalry colored boys than to side with one of these damned insurgents. They are a shiftless lot," said he, "and would as soon knife one of us for our tobacco as not. Sooner, I'd say. Now you remember that, Baylen."

"Yes, sir," said Fate, and promptly forgot it.

The afternoon of the 25th they moved down the far side of the second Guásimas ridge and made camp in a marshy meadow near a sluggish but clear stream of good water. The terrain fell away from the camp toward Santiago and the hills which ringed it. Inland of the city the towering blue peaks of the Sierra Maestra could be clearly seen. The major landmark between the camp and Santiago was a high hill—really a series of hills composing a big ridge very like the two they had just come over from Siboney—which dominated the level plain about the city. Beyond this elevation there would be nothing but an easy, open drive into the city's defenses. The hill, or the ridge complex of which it was the central part, was called San Juan. Going into camp that June afternoon in the landlocked and beautifully green meadow which lay behind its brown-grassed slopes, scarcely a Rough Rider could have been found in the First United States Volunteer Cavalry who would have doubted that the Cuban Campaign was over. All talk was of winning and of going home heroes in a hurry.

Nothing happened the first few days to disturb this refreshing view of the countryside. The enemy lay quiet, wherever he was, and General Shafter was evidently not yet of a mind to stir him up. For the record, General Shafter was scarcely of a mind to stir himself up. He had not appeared on the field at Las Guásimas; he did not appear in the camp which followed. Of the fight and its commander's reluctance to join it; Roosevelt boldly complained:

"Well, whatever comes, I shall feel contented with having left the Navy Department to go into the Army for the war; for our regiment has been in the first fight on land and has done well ... Our regiment furnished over half the men and over half the losses. . . . Young did well. So did Wood. Shafter was not even ashore! The mismanagement has been maddening. We have had very little to eat. But we cared nothing for that as long as we got into the fight. . . ."

That Teddy had the courage to write down such a criticism of the high command while the smell of powder smoke was yet in the air, speaks convincingly of his peculiar position and prerogatives as a lieutenant-colonel.

Not that he was able to do so uncensored. If what Fate and the other staff noncoms heard by way of camp rumor had been accurately repeated, General Lawton had raised hell and put a rock under it. He was supposed to have told Fighting Joe Wheeler to his face that he, Lawton, had been given the command ashore by Shafter; that he was in charge of the advance from Siboney, and the field following Las Guásimas; that he intended to keep that command, if he had to post a guard to keep Wheeler and his self-appointed heroes to the rear. This injunction specifically included the Rough Riders. They were bid, with Wheeler, "very positively," to stay where they were and attempt no more battles on their own.

Fate and those to whom he talked could not agree as to whether the Rough Riders deserved the dressing-down or not. It would appear in some ways that they did. But then again, if the colonel acted like Lawton and the bulk of the Regular Army, they would all still be sweating on the beach at Siboney, or Daiquiri, or along the horrid jungle trail between. Instead, here they were in sight of Santiago, and with the damned Spaniard whipped and sent running. It would look as though Teddy Roosevelt was right, as usual.

The camp was a good one. Some cold rain fell the first night, but the sun dried things up quickly. Some of the men had chills they did not think came from the wet weather, but these, too, were ignored for the time.

Food was scarce for most of the troops. Even the Rough Riders tightened their belts the second day. But by that nightfall Teddy had been to the beach with a string of mules bought out of his own pocket from the Cuban natives, and had, again with his private funds, purchased and packed back to the meadow food for his hungry men as good as that being had in the officer messes of the regulars. As for the enlisted men of the regular forces they ate what they could get, which of course was nowhere near the quality of that secured for his volunteers by the rich volunteer from Oyster Bay. After all, the Army could not afford to keep up with the Roosevelts.

At least, that is what Fate heard from the hard-bitten members of the First and Tenth Cavalry billeted near the regiment. Indeed, he heard more than that of caustic comment in regard to the Colonel and his little private army of college men and cowboys. A tall, twice-wounded Negro cavalryman of the Tenth maintained that the Rough Riders had got ambushed in the Guásimas skirmish and "powerful near ruined everything." The Tenth, the Negro trooper said quietly, had had to come on and save them, at considerable risk to their own position and safety. A white member of the First Cavalry backed him up, but not quietly. Snapped the white trooper angrily, "You all cut and run like whupt dogs. You shot anyways fifteen, twenty of our boys when we was crossing over in front of you. Worser than that, you let them damn garlics get away. We drove them to you and you just stood there. Rough Riders. Jesus, that's good. Anybody but Teddy Roosevelt bossing your show and you would all get court-martialed. You may yet, if General Young don't simmer down. Mister, let me tell you, he is really riled!"

In vain Fate attempted to explain that he and his fellows had not fired at the driven Spaniards on the right, because they, the Spaniards, had called out to them that they were Cubans. On the left, he tried to tell the regulars, Colonel Wood had given orders to hold the fire and not to shoot at retreating men. "How the hell," he asked the angered cavalryman, "you going to know what to do when some garlic hollers out he ain't a garlic, or when your own officers orders you to hold off firing just when you got the Spanish sons square in your sights?''

It was a good question, technically, but the cavalrymen were not technicians.

''All I knows is what I knows,'' said the quiet-voiced Negro. Said his disgusted white companion, ''Me, too. You Rough Riders are a joke. Go to hell and stay put!''

When they had left, Fate and his comrades sat around in the shade of Fate's shelter-half and talked it over. They couldn't get an agreement.

Bear River Smith felt they had done fine in the fight and ought to be proud. Little McGinty tended to side with him, and cited two post-battle cases to show that the spirit of the Rough Riders had not altered subsequently. In one of these a cowboy trooper named Rowland had walked to the base hospital at Siboney with six bullets in him and a hole in his side big enough to hide a calf in. When told by the doctors that he would be sent home on the next boat, if he lived that long, and that the nature and gravity of his wound made his separation from the service an absolute conclusion, Rowland had thanked the medical officers and lain quietly in his bed until dark. Then he had got up, climbed out through a window and marched the whole terrible way back to the front lines beyond Las Guásimas, climbing the two high ridges and using the rough hill trail the whole way, to avoid detection on the main wagon road. The other show of character had been by little Sherman Bell, the ex-Deputy Marshal of Cripple Creek and Wells Fargo shotgun rider. Bell, who had enlisted and come the entire way from Colorado with a serious hernia, had strained himself carrying food packs back from the beach on Roosevelt's first night foray. He had crawled four miles in that night's blinding rain to get back to the front-line camp and stay with the Rough Riders, despite the fact that his tortured groin was reswollen to the size of a football and each least movement a rending agony.

The Colonel, of course, had ordered the right sequel to both these demonstrations of grit and loyalty, countermanding the discharge orders of both men and seeing to it that both got special and continuing attention from Dr. Bob Church.

It was this sort of thing, argued McGinty, that proved his and Bear River's points about the guts and good doings of the Rough Riders to date. And no amount of grousing from any number of small-minded white regulars, or softtalking colored cavalrymen, was going to influence the McGinty statistics on this score. So the hell with it.

Most of the other boys nodded agreement to this. One or two said nothing. Fate scowled and shook his head.

He didn't know. He thought, for his own personal uses, that the Regular Cavalry had carried the brunt of the fight. They had provided the push and kept it going and had done so before the Rough Riders fired a shot. Moreover, when the latter had got up to the Spanish lines, the enemy was already on the run. And, even so, the Spaniards had been able to stop the Rough Riders in their tracks and actually to chew hell out of them with those smokeless Mauser bullets. It did seem to Fate, summing it up now, that the First United States Volunteer Cavalry could be very grateful that the First and Tenth United States Regular Cavalry had been up ahead of them and spoiled what otherwise almost certainly would have been a blind ambush of Fate and his friends.

He still didn't know a thing, really, and neither did any of them. There had been a fight and they had been in it and that was about the extent of it.

"Well," he grinned, "I guess we're all lucky, one way or another. We ain't none of us hurt, nor sick, nor missing and I hear the Colonel has got back from Siboney with three muleloads of potatoes and carrots and a hundred tins of U.S. tomatoes and a entire side of Red Cross beef which he lifted off Miss Clara Barton's boat out in the harbor."

"Yeah," said Little McGinty, "that's right; and you cain't hardly throw rocks at that."

"I heard," said Prayerful James, "that Miss Clara like to shot Old Teddy. She done fired off a telegram to McKinley, they say, demanding that he up and discipline the Colonel, or she would quit."

"She won't, though," said one of the boys, who had been to Siboney for treatment of an arm wound. "She will stay and do her part. Them Red Cross girls are great, I will tell you. And Miss Clara is a fine lady."

"Hell's fire!" said Prayerful. "Nobody is impruning her reputation. Goddammit, why don't you people listen?"

"Speaking of listening," said a neighboring member of B Troop, who had lounged up in time to hear the remark, "listen to this: Buck Dawson just got back with a pack string from Siboney, and he says the word down there is that General Young is dog-sick with the fever and that Wood has moved up to head of the brigade. You got any real quick ideas who that leaves in command of this here regiment?"

For a moment none of the men caught the import of his question. Then it hit them.

"My Gawd!" said Little McGinty. *"Teddy . . . !"*

Chapter Twenty-six

The position of the American encampment was between the mud huts of Sevilla and a commanding hill facing the San Juan Ridge called El Pozo. On the afternoon of the twenty-ninth of June, General Shafter came up and surveyed the field from the safety of some abandoned ranch buildings on top of El Pozo. When Bucky O'Neill heard of this, he sent for Fate Baylen.

Fate responded to the summons with uneasiness, for as reporter Edward Marshall had said, the lowest in the ranks somehow got the "message" when a big move was contemplated. O'Neill confirmed the matter.

"Baylen," he said, "Shafter is up. That can mean but one thing. We are almost ready to go here. For that little exploration you and I talked of, tomorrow may be too late. *Comprehende, hombre?*"

"Sure—I mean, yes, sir," said Fate. "When shall I go?"

"Tonight. Have you talked to your men?"

"No, sir. I was afraid to."

"None of the Cuban scouts, nor our boys either?"

"That's right, Captain."

"Damn, I wish you had done as I told you. Now we haven't a blessed thing to go on, and you don't even have your men picked out, nor prepared, nor a thing done."

"I've been a little busy, Captain," Fate reminded him. "I was on three of them trips to the beach for food with the Colonel and Buck Dawson and the boys. And besides, you told me to shut up. Ain't that so?"

"Yes, yes . . ." O'Neill's voice trailed off beneath his hard frown. Of a sudden, his face lightened. "That's it!" he cried. "I should have thought of it before. Come on, Baylen, let's travel!"

He set off across the encampment at a trot and Fate had to run to catch up with him. "What *is* it?" he panted, leaping a clump of brush in Bucky's wake. "What'd you think of, Captain?"

"The woman!" replied O'Neill, eyes snapping. "You recall the little Cuban guide who was with Houck and the scouts? The one Capron's pickets brought in with the knife in his back? Well, his mother came up to the front two days ago asking where we had put her boy. She wanted to dig him up and tote him back to the beach for reburial. I checked with the Chaplain and found out for her—took her out and showed her the grave. Maybe, just maybe, she can tell where to start looking for this Guadaña snake and his damned guerrillas."

Fate didn't comment, and they cut on through the roughening hill slopes, heading for the wagon road which followed the Little San Juan River back toward the beach and Siboney. Presently they were standing on a rise above the tiny village of Sevilla. Pointing to the sprawl of its wattled adobes, O'Neill said, "The boy's mother told me she was staying with a sister down in Sevilla, yonder. I thought we might be able to catch her before she started back to Siboney with the lad's body."

Fate squinted down the slope toward the town and nodded. "Looks like your hunch hit center, Captain," he announced. "Ain't that a burro cart standing in front of that far *jacal?* And ain't that a pine box laid in its bed?"

O'Neill shaded his eyes and peered below. Scowling, he took out his field glasses and focused them. "You're right as paid-up rent," he muttered. "How in the name of hell did you make that out from all the way up here?"

Fate grinned. "I was a Tonto Rim cow thief, maybe," he said. "Besides, Captain, I never could afford no opery glasses."

"Let's go," nodded O'Neill, and started down the hill.

At the hut in front of which the burro cart waited with its oblong burden, O'Neill stopped and called out in Spanish. Two women came out, fearfully at first, then, the younger, seeing the big American captain and recognizing him, smiled warmly and came forward.

"Capitán!" she greeted him. *"Bienvenida. Qué pasa?"*

O'Neill told her why they had come, expressing the hope that she might be able to furnish them some useful clue as to the probable whereabouts of Benito Guadaña.

The woman—her name was Dolores—at first denied that she possessed such knowledge, and said that she was sorry that she could not help them. O'Neill then said that his reason for making the inquiry did not have to do with American fortunes, but with the honor and memory of her son, who had died so bravely in the cause of freedom. Which cause, as all well knew, was served like a jackal by Benito Guadaña and his killer pack. Now of course, he

183

concluded, if she did not think that much of her courageous son, perhaps she might tell him of some other Cuban in or near Sevilla, who would think enough of the boy's sacrifice to speak of the guerrillas.

At this, Dolores drew up her thin form, black eyes flashing.

"*Señor Capitán,*" she cried out, "you shame my house!"

"I meant to," said O'Neill. "I want to find the killer of your son. I will do it, too. But you must help."

"Yes," she murmured. "I know that."

O'Neill waited. Fate could tell from this action that the big ex-sheriff was *simpático* to these brown people, despite his hard words to the contrary. Presently the woman came closer to them and spoke in a swift flow of Spanish to O'Neill.

She first said that they must behave as though they had come to her hut to purchase firewood of her sister. The sister would bring the wood in tied bundles—all in the area knew this was her livelihood, selling wood—and the *capitán* and his *soldado* must each take a bundle and pay for it, making sure to haggle loudly about the price. The *capitán* would understand that this was necessary, for the guerrillas had eyes and ears everywhere, no less in Sevilla than in Santiago. If the *capitán* would nod, now, that he understood this, then Dolores could call to the sister to bring the wood, and while the latter was doing that, she, Dolores, would tell them where to find Benito Guadaña and his evil ones who had put the death steel to her only son, Hidalgo.

O'Neill assured her that it was a matter of his honor as a soldier, that what she said would never pass his lips, nor the lips of his *sargento*. At this inclusion, and seeing the woman flick anxious eyes in his direction, Fate nodded soberly and said, "*Es verdad, señora;* you may believe it on your life. I was a friend of your Hidalgo. I walked a little with him on the hard trail from Daiquiri. We talked also a little, and he was a true soldier."

Dolores thanked him with a nervous touch of her brown hand on his ragged sleeve and called out for her sister to bring the wood. Then she told them about the traitor, Benito Guadaña.

Chapter Twenty-seven

The patrol halted on the hillside. It was the second night out from Sevilla and the American encampment beyond Guásimas. Fate had lost his way and he and his four men had been forced to lie up in a ratbin of an abandoned sugar mill the whole of the previous day. Tempers were honed, bellies pinched, nerves too finely drawn. It was vastly still up there in the rocky brush above the village of El Soquel. The raw glare of the Cuban moon was small help to their growing apprehensions. Something had to be said.

"I don't suppose," ventured Fate, "that we'd ought to smoke, but the hell with it. The wind's our way."

He brought out the makings and passed them around. His companions, save for Pawnee Pollock, accepted the offering. After a strained moment of spilling the golden flakes, rolling and licking the thin papers, Boone Gaskill said, "Pawnee, how come you ain't got the habit? I never knowed a nigger or redskin wasn't plumb crazy for to-bacco.''

The lean Oklahoman shrugged. "My father was a Christian Indian. He said tobacco was a sin, like trade whiskey."

"Well," grumped Boone resentfully, "I knowed you didn't drink. Leastways not at my bar."

Bear River Smith rumbled deep in his chest. It was either the night air getting to his asthma, or a swallowed laugh. At any rate, he replied good-naturedly to Boone.

"Happen he had been a customer of yours, you Georgia ape, he'd have been a good Injun by now, instead of a crazy one squatting on a hill outside a Spanish town, ten and more miles inside the enemy lines. Ain't that so, Pawnee?"

Pollock laughed softly. Fate was surprised, for he had known very few Indians who laughed with white men; especially with the ones, like Bear River Smith, who were old enough and of evident disposition to have gathered a few red scalp locks in their times. But this was a laugh, and not bitter either.

"My father," explained the dark-skinned trooper, "was a man of unlimited wisdom. Among the many things he taught me was never to argue with a white man—particularly a big white man and one carrying a gun."

Fate, watching his comrades, saw little Blue Calhoun nod silently to what the Plains Indian said. The Tenth Cavalry trooper was the only non-Rough Rider among them. Fate had asked for him only because Houck had said that the small Negro soldier was genuinely good at tracking and at spotting men in the jungle growth. He seemed, Houck had told Fate, to have a "feeling" when somebody was watching from the brush. Studying him now, Fate wondered where he had been when Houck had got it. On an impulse, he reached out and touched Blue Calhoun on the arm.

"Blue," he said, "where was you when Houck Oatman got hit? I mean, did you see him get it?"

A dog barked down below. At once the conversation died. After a moment, the dog barked again, and it was plain from the sound, moving away from them toward the far side of the village, that the mongrel had not challenged them. "Well, suh, Sergeant, to tell you the truth," answered Blue Calhoun, "I didn't see nothing. We was standing there, listening for something I thought I had heard. Sergeant Houck, he just of a sudden slump in the knees, and that was it. I seen the knife buried in his back, as his body fell past me, going down. I took a dive to one side, and the other knife come a whistling past, and got one of them others with us."

The stillness settled in again. All of them were listening now, and watching the little Negro trooper.

"Well," said Fate, "then what? Were you all bunched?"

"Yes, suh. There was Sergeant Houck, Mr. Merrick, Mr. Prewitt, me, and them two other troopers which I didn't know. Them was the two found with Sergeant Houck by Dr. Bob."

"Go on," said Fate.

"Well, suh, when the first of them troopers fell, I got shut of there, like I said. Fast as I moved, though, I still seen the other trooper get it, too. This wasn't a knife, but a hatchet. It went in to the blunt part of the head."

"We found it that way," said Fate carefully. "I carried that one in myself. But we didn't find no knife in Houck."

"Sure you didn't, suh. The guerrillas come out'n the bush after a spell and look at the bodies. The feller what hit Sergeant Houck, he lean down and tooken out his knife. Other two made crosses on they chests, way the garlics do, and didn't want no piece of their weapons, seems."

188

"Houck was shot," said Fate flatly.

"Yes, suh," murmured Blue Calhoun, "three time."

Fate's gray eyes narrowed. "*After* he was knifed?" he asked, unbelievingly.

"Yes, suh. The leader, he laugh and say for the others to get a little target practice. He carry one of them spanking new Lee navy rifles we give them at Daiquiri. You know them small-caliber kind, Sergeant?"

"Yes," said Fate. "Go ahead."

"Leader, he put his gun in Sergeant Houck's belly right smack in the middle and he blow a hole in him big enough to put his hand in. Then two more of them shoot him while he lay there, still alive."

"We got the bullets," said Fate. "All three of them hit ribs or his backbone and stayed in him. We found them. . . ."

There was another spell of silence, this one longer than the first. It was Boone Gaskill, the hill country white man from the red clays of Georgia, who broke it, speaking to Blue.

"And you," he said, slowly drawling it as only a Southern white man can talk to a Negro, "sat there safe in the bushes and watched them do it? With a gun in your hands and plenty of ammunition?"

Blue Calhoun didn't answer. He dropped his head and sat looking at the ground and holding his cigarette in two hands, dangling downward. Fate, in an instant, felt badly about pushing him. He again put his hand on his arm.

"Blue," he said, "we ain't accusing you of nothing. Houck, he was like a brother to me. A father, more likely. I only wanted to know what happened. You're the first one that was on that patrol which I have had a chance to talk to."

189

"Yes, suh," said Blue Calhoun. "Thank you, suh."

"Well," added Boone, "that ain't all I had in *my* mind. We're in a pee-poor situation here, and I reckon we would all like to know who is standing at our right and who at our left. For one, I didn't never cotton to the idee of no nigger being brought along."

"I didn't ask to be tooken with you," said Blue Calhoun softly. "Sergeant Fate, he ask me would I do it, and I say sure I would."

"Don't you talk back to me, you damned coon!" snapped Boone. "I'll peel your black hide right off'n your back!"

"Boone," said Fate quietly, "you call him a coon or a nigger or anything like that, one more time, and you can start peeling on me, you understand that?"

"How's that?" said the Southerner, tensing.

"His name," said Fate, "is Blue Calhoun, and he is a sergeant of Regular Cavalry. That's more than any of us here can say."

"It's all right, suh," said Blue, breaking in diffidently. "Please don't make no fuss. Mr. Boone, he didn't aim to hurt me none."

"Goddammit, don't try to tell me what I aimed and what I didn't aim!" The Georgian was turning ugly now, and Fate got set for trouble. "Either you sat on your blue butt and watched them Cuban monkeys kill Houck Oatman, or you didn't. Now which is it?"

Blue put his chin yet further down upon his thin chest. They could all see his kinky head bob in the moonlight, and his shoulders sag guiltily.

"Yes, suh," he admitted, "I sat there and done what you say, Mr. Boone. I didn't know what else to do, and there wasn't nobody to tell me."

"Wait a minute," said Fate, "what do you mean there wasn't nobody to tell you? What become of Merrick and Post Oak?"

"Oh," said Blue Calhoun, raising his head, "Mr. Merrick, him and Mr. Post Oak, they run off when I first yell out that Sergeant Houck done got it. There wasn't nobody left there with me when them guerrillas come out'n the bresh."

The third silence was heavier yet. It seemed to grow as though it were a yeast of Cuban moon and starlight.

"You hear that, Boone?" asked Fate, talking through his teeth. "Merrick and Prewitt run off." The Georgian said nothing, and Fate went on. "That ain't all. That other boy, the one that got the hatchet in him, he lived long enough to talk to me and Dr. Church. You know how many of them 'Cuban monkeys' there was in that bunch ambushed Houck's patrol? Thirty. Maybe more."

Boone Gaskill angled his lantern jaw at Fate and said defiantly, "What you trying to tell me; that Merrick and Prewitt was yeller? Who wouldn't run? You mean to say you'd of hung around there with Houck and them two others down, and thirty, forty crazy bushwhackers swarming in on you out of the blind brush? In a bull's bung, you would!"

"What I'm telling you," said Fate, still through the teeth, "is that Blue *did* stay. He didn't do anything, but he stayed. He didn't run away, he stayed hoping there might be something he *could* do." His voice rose, the Southwestern aridity of his speech grating like canyon dust. "Now you tell me whether that don't take more guts than you can string on a forty-mile fence!"

Gaskill growled something to himself. It was certainly

not a surrender, but Fate did not get a chance to identify it, nor to challenge it further.

"*Too much talk!*" said Pawnee Pollock. "Shut up."

He bit off the words, and he was right. Down the hill, the dog was barking once more, and this time he was moving toward their side of the walled village.

"Yeah," said Fate. "Sorry, boys. We ain't time for no more social debates."

"Forget it," rumbled Bear River. "I feel better. I reckon we all do. We was all thinking *something* about having Blue along. Boone only said what we was all holding back. You, too, Arizona."

He meant Fate, and the latter nodded. "It's so," he said. "A mean idea is tough to dig out. It's like grubbing mesquite or piñon roots; the more you chop, the more you uncover."

"Be quiet!" ordered Pollock, tensing to peer downward. "Somebody coming up the trail." A moment later he added, "A very small woman, carrying a pack. See?"

Fate squinted hard with the others. Finally they made out the bent figure coming along the hillside track about a hundred yards below them. "Injuns!" snorted Bear River. "Goddammit, they can see in the dark like a varmint!" At his words Pollock's voice hissed in warning. "She heard you!" he accused. "Now there will be trouble."

Fate, watching the woman, shook his head.

"I don't think so," he said. "She's coming right along."

"She is wise to the ways of the night, that's all," denied Pollock. "Probably a guerrilla woman. I saw her pause and turn her head. She heard us."

"Then why don't she take off? Don't look to me like she batted an eye."

"You see where the trail hairpins to come up here?"

"Yes."

"Then, you watch it where it switches back at the top."

"All right, I'm watching it. What am I supposed to see?"

"What *do* you see?"

"Nothing."

"That's what you're supposed to see. The woman will have gone into the brush where the curve in the trail hid her for a dozen steps. We had better scatter and lie separately."

"What?" growled Bear River. "Hide from one little old woman guerrilla? At night? Not this river hoss!"

"Shut up!" said Fate. "Listen . . ."

They cocked heads, straining ears and eyes toward the silent trail below. Nothing moved. There was no sound. Off to their right a wood cuckoo cried out mournfully. Pollock turned to Fate. "That's the guerrilla bird. But it's a forest bird, too. So we know it would not be on this treeless hillside. That's the woman over there. What do we do?"

Fate thought furiously. "Answer it," he decided. "If we can call her in, we'll grab her and see what she can tell us about the town and Benito Guadaña. All right?"

"It's what I was going to suggest," said the Indian. "But we've got to be sure she doesn't cry out. You had better let the best man do it. Let him get out toward her a little way, then we will give the answering call and if she comes to it, our man can get her going by—maybe."

"It's the next shift short of nothing," nodded Fate, "but we ain't no choice. Who can give a good cuckoo?" Before any of the others could reply, Pollock had cupped his hands and answered the guerrilla woman's call perfectly. At once she replied and they could hear her moving toward them. "Now," said Pollock, "that best man has got to go." He didn't move and Bear River rasped, "Well, go on; you're

193

naming yourself best, ain't you?'' Pollock's dark head moved in the negative. ''Our friend, the buffalo soldier,'' he said, ''he's the one. Go on,'' he said to Blue Calhoun, ''show the white brother how it's done.''

The little Negro cavalryman grinned. They all saw his teeth flash, and that is about all they saw. The next moment they were looking at nothing where Blue Calhoun had been sitting an instant before. He had simply evaporated like a puff of smoke.

''He is better than any Indian,'' nodded Pawnee Pollock, low-voiced. ''Better even than my father. Possibly even than my grandfather, who was the greatest warrior the *Panani* ever knew.''

''The 'Pan-anny?' '' said Boone Gaskill. ''Who the hell brought them up? Sounds like something what would be growed in the jungle, or ett by monkeys.''

''He means the Pawnee,'' explained Bear River. ''His people. They translate it 'pony stealers.' ''

''That's right,'' said Pollock.

''Hoss thieves, you mean!'' said Boone, superior not merely to Negroes. But Pollock had not been reared in the South.

''The finest the world has ever known,'' he answered Boone. ''Easily the equal in their skills and daring to any white whiskey peddler. Shut your damned mouth, Gaskill.''

There would have been war on the hillside right then had not Fate, alert to the whispered exchange, hit Boone in the ribs with his elbow. It was a blow hard enough to fracture a fence post, and the lanky Southerner gasped in pained surprise. Before he could recover himself, the call of the wood cuckoo sounded much more closely to them and Pollock answered it immediately. In the pause of stillness which followed, all the patrol waited with held breaths.

A barely audible scuffle ensued, some fifty feet away on the hillside. Then another silence. Then the unmuffled sounds of Blue Calhoun making his way back to them. Directly, they saw him coming, bent nearly double beneath the burden of the captive guerrilla woman. It was not precisely the job of work which might have been brought off by just any man, and Pollock said proudly, "Welcome back, Blue; your medicine is plenty strong!"

"Thank you," said Blue Calhoun. "It wasn't nothing much. Here you are, suh," he added, to Fate. "It ain't no little old woman, it's a little old gal. Careful. I got her head wrop in her shawl. She likely holler, you hand her the chance. Watch them teeth now, she bite like a weasel."

"You keep her!" ordered Fate, alarmed. "Good Lord! A little girl. Now what the hell do we do?"

"Open up a orphan asyllium," suggested Bear River.

"Hold a raffle," sneered Boone Gaskill, "and sell all the tickets to the Tenth Calvary."

"Boone," said Fate, on edge, "lay off Blue, you hear? You got a hard nose. We get out of this, I'm going to soften it up for you."

"You got a mouth to go with the rest of you," grated the Georgia moonshiner, "big."

"Sergeant," said Pawnee Pollock quietly, "why don't you try your Spanish on the kid? Tell her we're friends, *yanquis*, out scouting the Spanish lines. Tell her we'd like to talk to her, if she won't cry out. And tell her if she does cry out, we'll slit her tongue."

"Jesus!" shuddered Bear River. "I'm glad you ain't a Sioux; you'd want to slit her throat, I suppose."

"Throat, tongue, what's the difference?" asked Pollock. "I'm not making jokes. We're ten miles behind the Spanish lines. Is that funny?" To Fate he repeated, hard-eyed, "Tell her what I said, Sergeant. Unless you'd rather it was our necks got sliced.''

Fate nodded. Like Bear River, he could not get used to hearing Pollock talk so much like a white man one minute and then, without any warning at all, revert to a red Indian. But he could appreciate the educated Pawnee trooper's logic.

He reached out and put his hand gently on the small bundle which Blue Calhoun held so closely.

''*Niña,*'' he said in Spanish, ''we are your friends. We do not mean to harm you. We want to talk with you. *Comprende,* little one? *Qué dice, hija?* What do you say? Will you be quiet?''

There was a responsive and lively stirring of the bundle, as Blue Calhoun eased his grip upon the wrapped shawl to permit the captive to reply. This she did with a burst of Cuban invective which made Fate Baylen gasp.

''Well,'' demanded Bear River irritably, ''what did she say?''

Fate, surprise given way to a wry Arizona grin, shook his shaggy head.

''Put charitable,'' he replied, ''she raised the doubt as to any of us ever making the grade as herd bulls.''

Bear River considered the slander for a moment, then said cheerfully, ''Well, hell, even a steer can try.''

''That's so,'' agreed Fate. ''I'll keep going.''

The child, it proved, was bluffing. She had thought they were guerrillas. Convinced they were actually the *americanos* come to set her people free, she talked an entirely different line—commencing with a profuse apology for her previous language. Her concern over being mistaken for something less than a lady struck Fate and his friends as intriguing. Considering her age, ''just nine this day,'' they were impressed. Better yet, they were entirely taken into camp by the charms of "Cuba Libre," as her patriot mother had named the child. Her family name she would not divulge, but this was not important. Within five minutes of Blue Calhoun relinquishing her, she had the Benito Guadaña posse chasing her rather than the celebrated guerrilla chief.

Fate, taking a chance he knew he must, presently asked her if she personally knew Benito Guadaña. She looked at him as though he were of simple mind and replied that everyone knew Benito Guadaña. He was a big man. This was his village, as it was hers. What did the *yanqui soldados* seek to know about Benito?

"*Niña*," Fate said, "I am going to put my faith in your honor as a Spanish lady. I am going to ask you a question that will give you great power over my life. The safety of myself and my four friends will lie in your hands. What do you say?"

"What do you expect me to say?" asked the girl. "You have called me a lady. Command me."

Plunging the rest of the way, Fate then told her of the patrol's mission, ending, "It's just like this, *niña*. If we catch Benito we are going to kill him. If you tell us where we can find him, you are helping to destroy him. Do you understand that?"

"Certainly," said the child calmly. "Do I look like a fool?"

"You can help us then?" said Fate. "Tell us if Benito is in the village? Perhaps a way that we can get in and out with some chance of our lives? Eh? *Es verdad, niña?*"

"No," said the girl, "*no es verdad*. I can show you the way, yes. And I can tell you if Benito is there. But I can give you no chance for your lives. *Es impossible, patrón.*

If you go in, you will not come out. Unless . . ."

Fate leaned forward. "Unless what, *niña?*"

The little Cuban girl's face grew angry. Fate could see her dark eyes flash in the moonlight. "Let me tell you a story, *patrón,*" she said. "It is not long."

Fate nodded, and she spoke quickly.

"My mother was the prettiest woman in El Soquel. My father went away to fight with General García when the trouble began again three years ago. I was but six then. Benito Guadaña was a friend of my father's. He went away to fight for Cuba, too. But he did not stay. He came back. I heard him tell my mother it was because of her; that he had come back to make her his woman. He said my father had been killed in Pinar del Rio. My mother knew that he lied. When he tried to make love to her, she put a knife in his ribs. He got over it and went away. We did not see him for a long time."

When she paused, the American troopers could see the tears glisten in her eyes, and none of them said anything. They could not understand her words, but the American soldier who could not understand a little child's tears had not yet enlisted in his country's service. "Go on," urged Fate gently. "We know it is a difficult thing to tell." Cuba Libre nodded and continued.

"This spring Benito came back. He had many men with him. They called themselves Cubans, but we had heard they were being paid by the Spaniards. We also knew by this time that it was Benito who had killed my father, and not in Pinar del Rio fighting for freedom. He had followed him out of El Soquel and killed him on the trail where we stand this moment." She pointed down the hill. "My father died down there, not fifty paces, a knife in his back from Benito

Guadaña, his best friend.'' Again the pause, this time shorter.

''When word came that the *yanquis* were landing at Daiquiri, the Spanish troops in our village were called in to defend Santiago by General José Toral, the brave commandant in that city. Benito Guadaña said that he was in command of El Soquel. Some of our village men said that he was a lying dog and a Spanish killer. Those men were gone the next day and no one has seen them since. From that time Benito has been the headman of El Soquel. He and his guerrillas have hidden there in our village.''

The child paused, firming her lips.

''I have not told you the most evil thing. When the Spanish soldiers departed, Benito took my mother and carried her off. Padre Espada, the Spanish priest who had our church in El Soquel and who stayed bravely after the soldiers had gone, he thinks Benito took my mother to Santiago. As for me, *patrón,* I do not know where my mother is, but I live my life only to find her and to take the old grandmother to her so that we may all three live happily as we did before Benito Guadaña came back to El Soquel.

''What? The old grandmother? I have not mentioned her before? *Pues,* well *patrón,* it is her to whom I go with this food and these few warm things of clothing. She lives in a cave over the hill, hiding there while I am held in El Soquel by Benito. You ask why I stay, *patrón?* Why I do not run away when it is plain that I am able to slip out into the night like this? Very simple, *hombre.* Benito has said that if I flee, he will kill my mother. He has told her the same thing. If she tries to come back to El Soquel, he will kill me. You see, *patrón,* Benito is the Devil, as Padre Espada has said. The padre has told me to obey Benito because of this evilness which is his. Meanwhile, the padre helps me steal out of the village by night, back again before daylight by a secret way." The small Cuban patriot sighed with the weight of the memory, but concluded with spirit. "Now you must know why all good Cubans hate Benito Guadaña, and also why I myself have reasons beyond most of my countrymen for despising him. Yes, *patrón,* I will help you to find Benito Guadaña. But the real question is: Will you dare to go with me?"

Fate talked it over with his companions. To the man they were silenced by the girl's history. Yet each, when he found his voice, swore wickedly and voted to go get Benito Guadaña and the hell with whether they got out alive afterward. Or, at least, the hell with worrying about it right then. But when Fate turned to Cuba Libre and told her, "*Niña,* my men say their hearts go out to you and they want to help you; they will gladly go with you," he was straightened up by her quiet reply that while she was grateful she could not accept. Only one man could go with her. It was impossible that as many as five men could go by the risky route she used in and out of El Soquel. They would all be discovered and have their hearts cut out. But if only one had the courage to go with her, his companions waiting upon the hill for him to kill Benito and return—if he *were* to return— why, then, it might be done. That is, if Padre Espada would help, it might.

"Now, then, *patrón,*" she said, "it remains as I have said. What do you say? What do your men say? Will they have the *intestinos* for it? To stay here on the hill and wait for you?"

"Well," Fate began, but was cut off immediately.

"Come, come!" chirped the girl. "Don't take my time if you are doubtful. Are you all old women, or do you stand up to make water like *hombres?*"

Fate shook his head, suppressing the laugh which wanted to break through. "*Niña,*" he managed with proper gravity, "that is a remarkably good question; *por favor,* allow my friends and me a moment to dwell upon it."

Chapter Twenty-eight

Fate had to grin. Not so much at following a nine-year-old Cuban girl on hands and knees through a dank tunnel in the blind darkness, but more at the whole idea of the thing. Naturally he had been unable to avoid nominating himself for the honor which now had him creeping through this fox burrow under the fortified walls and entrenchments of the village of El Soquel. Blue and Pawnee and Bear River, yes, and the butt-headed Boone Gaskill, too, had all wanted to draw straws for the chance, but what the hell? Fate was the leader. Moreover, he had not wanted to let Cuba Libre get any wrong notions about him. So he had gone.

Now, though, the long silence was beginning to wear thin, and so was the skin on his bony knees.

"Niña!" he whispered. "How much farther?"

"We are there," she replied. "Light a match."

Fate felt for and found his shell-case matchbox, and scratched a sulphur-tipped light. The sight which met his squinting gaze was not precisely what he had envisioned as tunnel's end, nor was it exactly what he needed by way of reassurance at the moment.

"Holy smokes," he murmured, "it's the Roman catchy-combs!"

"It is the Portavale family crypt," said Cuba Libre. "See, there on the shelf by your shoulder, the skull with the large eye sockets and the broken bone in the forehead? That is old Gaspar Nuñez y Portavale, the head of the line. He came to Cuba with Pedro Alvarez and Cortez himself, or so they say. The very small *nicho* which you see by my elbow, here, these are the remains of my own little friend, Serena Portavale. She was but a child, having eight summers only. She died this spring. Padre Espada said it was weakness from the scant food. He said Benito Guadaña killed her. That is why he believes that Benito must die. He is evil, Padre Espada says. He says the Holy Book decrees that a man shall not serve two masters."

"Whew!" said Fate, scanning the walls of the crypt, "this is creepy. There must be about fifty skulls niched in this cyclone cellar!"

"Fifty-one," corrected Cuba. "There was fifty before Serena."

"Ouch!" gritted Fate, and dropped the match which had burned his fingers.

"Light another," ordered his small guide. "There is a candle in the hole behind Don Gaspar's broken head bone."

"You mean *in* the skull?" asked Fate.

"Of course. Even in a tomb, one must be careful these days. Reach in and get it. Don Gaspar will not bite. He had eighty-seven years when he died, and but three teeth."

Again Fate's grin broke the taut lines of his face. *"Ay*

de mí,'' he said admiringly, ''you are a wonder, little one!''
Then, belatedly, and realizing they had both been talking
English and Spanish, mixed, for the past moments, he grew
stern. ''You didn't say to me that you understood and could
speak my language,'' he said. ''You let me believe you
used only *español.*''

''You let yourself believe it, *patrón,*'' the girl said with
a shrug. ''Besides, does a lady tell all she knows?''

''Never!'' said the tall cowboy. ''Lead on.''

But after she was gone, having assured him he would
need to wait no longer than ten minutes for her return with
Padre Espada, he was not so certain of himself nor of his
guide. It wasn't the sort of thing a nine-year-old girl would
naturally do, that business of talking only Spanish back
there on the hillside and not once letting on she understood
or spoke English. In uncomfortable fact, she had waited
until she had him in the box canyon of this burial vault,
God alone knew where, before revealing her ability to comprehend and speak *''yanqui.''* Why?

Of a sudden, Fate Baylen felt ill at ease. It occurred to
him that it was a little late at night to be getting second
ideas about this pretty little Cuban kid's relationships with
Benito Guadaña.

It grew in his slow ranch boy's mind that he might be
sitting there holding that damned stupid candle to light Benito Guadaña's way to him, and that Padre Espada might
be nothing but a shred of the girl's imagination, or, worse
yet, another nickname for Benito. *Espada.* In Spanish, that
came out ''the sword.'' And was ''the sword'' very far
from ''the scythe'' in a careless translation?

Fate decided that it was not. With a curse he blew out
the candle.

Chapter Twenty-nine

But Padre Espada was not an invention of Cuba Libre's imagination. Nor was the little girl in league with the guerrilla devil, Benito Guadaña.

Espada was a moor-dark Spaniard, intense and vibrant as the blade for which he was named. He was a man of Houck Oatman's age, somewhere in the indeterminate middle years, and there was something about his sinewy figure and graceful, quick carriage which reminded Fate very much of the Payson deputy.

"*Señor*," said the priest softly, entering the darkness of the Portavale crypt while the smoke of the blown-out candle was still greasing the stale air, "it is I, Espada. The child is with me. All is well."

"*Padre*," replied Fate, putting down the marble bust of Anastasia Portavale y Gomez, which he had picked up to introduce himself to Benito Guadaña, should it prove to be the guerrilla chief with the child, "you cannot imagine what sensations of delight this information brings me. *Bienvenida!*"

"*Mil gracias,*" said the priest. "And now to work . . ."

Bidding Cuba Libre to stand guard outside the closed door of the vault, he came swiftly to the point with Fate Baylen.

"There is no real need for the child to watch outside," he said. "Save that I do not wish her to hear all of what I must tell you. Why should the innocent suffer the cares and evils of this world sooner than they must?"

"Agreed," nodded Fate. "Go on."

"I will help you," said Espada. "Benito is here, in El Soquel. He came back yesterday. He had mules, American Army mules, and much of military supplies stolen from your troops. He boasts that he takes from the living, as well as from the dead. He says the *yanquis* are women and worse, that they are stupid and soft of head and heart and have no idea of what war is, or how to fight."

"I'm not prepared to argue that, *padre,*" put in Fate glumly. "So far we have not covered ourselves with honor or great deeds."

"It is no matter, my son. How the Americans fight does not concern me. I am Spanish and Cuban, the one by birth, the other by deep wish of adoption. I do not welcome your soldiers. But I welcome less the devil who is Benito Guadaña."

"I am waiting," said Fate. "*Hágame un favor, padre.* Hurry along. I am not what you might call nervous, but I do have reasons for desiring to remove myself from El Soquel at the earliest opportunity consistent with good manners and the dispensations of Mother Church. Do I offend you, or take advantage of your charity?"

"*No por cierto,* not at all," replied the lean priest. "I

understand your apprehension even more than you do. You see, I know Benito better than you can possibly know him.''

''*Gracias,*'' gulped Fate dryly.

''*De nada,*'' shrugged the other. ''Will you now listen rather than to talk?''

''It ain't my long suit,'' grinned Fate in English, ''but I'll give it a whirl. Shoot.''

Espada did not understand the words, but clearly got their general sense and went on with an answering smile of his own.

''Benito is in the barracks abandoned by our troops when Toral called them in to Santiago,'' he said. ''There are perhaps twenty men with him. I have here a map of El Soquel, which I will give you and which may be of use to your commanders in case of your escape. I shall be required to ask you not to do that, not to give this map to them. Destroy it, should you carry out your mission here. Do I have your word?''

''Yes,'' said Fate unhesitatingly, taking the map.

''Good. Now, here is what you must do, my son, and why you must do it. . . .''

He told Fate that Benito had secreted Cuba's mother, an extremely handsome young woman, in the guerrilla headquarters within Santiago. This was, he said, a place of low and vicious reputation to go with the likes of Benito Guadaña and his wolf pack. It was called *La Mala Mujer, The Bad Woman,* and for reasons obvious to all. Cuba's mother was held there both by physical restraint and the shame of her defilement by Benito. She was known as his woman and a member of his band. Fate must see that the child, Cuba, found her mother in Santiago. And see that the Americans sent word, with Cuba, through the Spanish lines

that their guerrilla, Benito Guadaña, was a traitor to both
Spain and the Cuban Insurgents and was fighting in the war
only to enrich himself. Also it must be made clear that the
mother of Cuba Libre living at *La Mala Mujer* in Santiago
was *not* a traitor but a loyal Spanish woman of the True
Faith, and that Padre Estabán Espada of El Soquel was
authority for her innocence, as well as the guilt of that dog,
Benito Guadaña.

If Fate were to succeed in his own grim mission to kill
Guadaña and secure his head there in El Soquel, then he
must take from that head the right ear, the one in which
Benito wore the golden earring which was his evil identification from Oriente to Pinar del Rio Provinces.

Then Fate was to send the ear, by Cuba Libre, to Santiago so that General José Toral, who commanded there,
might know his trusted friend Estabán Espada spoke the
truth as to the death of Benito Guadaña in Soquel.

Should Fate now agree to these conditions, Espada would
tell him how the rest of the plan would work—would tell
him how he would be taken to Benito Guadaña, and by
whom. What did the American sergeant say? Did Espada
have his word as a gentleman and soldier that all which
had passed between them should be inviolate?

Fate looked around at the guttering candle, the rows of
Spanish skulls on their inset shelves, the masonry walls of
the Portavale crypt. Lastly, he brought his gaze back to the
lean, black-robed figure of Father Estabán Espada. He
dwelled particularly upon the padre's dark, gaunt face, and
upon the peculiar, two-foot-long silver cross which he wore
suspended by a golden chain from his neck. The Arizonan's
mind dug hard to find some firm ground upon which to
stand for a moment. All of this intrigue and infiltration,
tunnels, secret tombs, nine-year-old Cuban girls and mid-

dle-aged Spanish priests who fought together against the common evil—well, it was a few too many for Fate Baylen, he decided, and it gave him the devil's own time trying to come up with an answer to Espada's question.

As far as the hillside where he had left his companions, risky and unauthorized as Captain Bucky O'Neill's sending of them to that point was, the thing had made some sense. But from the moment of capturing Cuba Libre, it went all to pot. Why had he followed the kid? Why had he believed her about Espada and Benito Guadaña? Why was he standing here now, still believing her? How did he know she was standing outside that tomb door? What was to stop her from having gone for Benito the minute Espada told her to wait outside? Damn! The things a fellow could get himself into when he didn't have normal brain powers!

"If you are wondering whether to trust me," said Espada softly, "what other choice have you left yourself by now?"

"A fine point," grinned Fate wryly. "Go on, *padre,* you have my word."

Espada told him quickly, then, that he must take Cuba Libre with him as his guide through the back ways of the village to the barracks. The girl would leave him there and would return to be waiting with Espada at the church when his business was completed. Espada would then see about getting him back out of El Soquel.

To this meager plan Fate agreed. Within five minutes he and the little Cuban girl were stealing up the dust of an alley directly behind the Spanish barracks. In another five minutes Cuba had led the way up onto the low-tiled roof of the place and was pointing to a barred grille in the ridge-peak cupola, whispering that this gave a view down into the main *sala* of the building. Fate nodded, and they crept upward to the barred opening and peered down through it.

The sight below was sobering.

At the head of a long wooden mess table covered with half-empty wine bottles and past-century Spanish silver cups lolled Benito Guadaña. With him were Villalobos, his chief lieutenant, and eight followers. Their faces were flushed, their talk loud. And there were women present and the quality of the talk was not for the ears of nine-year-old girls. Fate pushed Cuba down with his left hand, forcing her head below the frame of the grilled window. He whispered to her, "*Callate*," the imperative order to be quiet, then returned his own glance to the activity below. The scene in the smoky *sala* had not changed for the better. The yellow gold of the ring in Benito's ear caught the light of the oil lamps which lit the dim room. It vied in its glittering with the whiteness of Benito's teeth, bared now in leering smiles at the low jests and gestures of the nearly nude Afro woman sprawling with her buttocks athwart his lap and her parted, heavy lips teasing the bandit chief's ear which bore the golden amulet.

On the roof above, Fate Baylen held his breath and wondered what in God's good name he was doing there. And, more to the point of his orders from Bucky to bring back Benito's head, how in that same God's sweet grace he was going to get at the wearer of that evil earring.

Well, for one thing, he had to get Cuba started back to the church. That was the first move. Then he could go it from there the best way the luck of the ignorant might send him. He waited for a particularly noisy outburst from the drunken diners below, then leaned and whispered to Cuba Libre, "Come on, *niña*, we're getting away from this place *muy pronto*." The little girl nodded and smiled that she understood this, and that it was agreeable to her. Both she and the big American cowboy eased to their feet and began the treacherous descent of the sloping roof. It was on the third step that Fate's boot hit a split tile and broke it with a resounding crack which sent its shards clattering downward like a handful of thrown rocks. In the quick twist to recover his balance and keep from falling, his foot went on through the rotting boards beneath the tiles and plunged through the ceiling of the room below. The now-familiar Rough Rider brown legging drew a cry of recognition from the startled guerrillas, which chilled Fate's bones to the marrow.

"*¡Mire!*" snarled Benito Guadaña. "*Vamos, amigos!*"

"*Sí, Jefe,*" replied Villalobos, reaching for his cartridge belt, "as you have said, *vamos*. Let us go."

Go, they did, and with their savage jungle cries shattering the night and Fate Baylen's nerves. He leaped from the roof to the ground, Cuba in his long arms, and sprinted awkwardly down the darkened alley. He was not only running for his own life, he realized with dread, but for the little girl's, too. He must not let the guerrillas see the child with him, no matter what.

"Listen," he ordered her, "I am going to put you down when we turn that corner into the square. You run for the church. If you get there, tell Padre Espada how it went for us, and that I will do my best not to give him away. Do you understand, *muchacha?*"

"Surely," said Cuba quickly. "You are very clumsy, *patrón,* but I will do as you say. Here we are. Put me down."

Fate dropped her to her feet and snapped at her to go on and run, but instead she seized his hand and held him fast. "But of course," she grinned up at him. "Precisely as you say, *patrón.* Only we will run together or not at all. How is that for your plans? Do *you* understand now?"

"Oh, Lord!" groaned Fate in English, and galloped off at her heels.

But the delay had given the guerrillas full sight of them together. The moon was bright and there could be no doubt the devils would identify Cuba Libre. In Fate's heart as he lumbered desperately to keep up with the village sprite, who ran like a prairie coyote cub, was the ugly thought that with his bumbling stupidity he had drawn the mark of death to a helpless and innocent child. If it were the last gasp of his miserable life, he must get her to Padre Espada and the possible sanctuary of the church. Their religion had a powerful hold on these people, he knew, and there was no other chance.

Throwing a wall-eyed glance over his shoulder, his new hope sank. From the closeness of the pursuit, he and the girl were going to lose the race for the church doors by a wide margin. He groaned again and the sound drew a laugh and some sharp advice on out-legging guerrillas from his tiny companion. "Come on, *patrón*," she cried, eyes dancing in the moonlight, "do not give up as yet! Let me show you how to gain a little ground on those *perros* back there!"

The mechanism for the reprieve, she explained on the giggling run, had to do with a certain brood sow and litter of very new piglets, about which Cuba knew and the guerrillas of Benito Guadaña did not. If the *patrón* would now follow her sharply to the left, just ahead, they would find themselves in a narrow lane which went between the village *jacals,* its houses of mud and thatch, to this pigsty which was built in such a way as to close off the lane. Now, she called to Fate, great care must be taken that they did not put so much as the small toe into that sty with that determined and unfriendly mother pig and her new babies. But if they made a good jump from the top of the fence, they could get to the roof of the sty house and, going over that, exit on the far side of the enclosure and be running free for the church again. Now, if the guerrillas did as they should, simply jumped over the fence and into the pen with the mother pig, Cuba would guarantee the *patrón* that he would never again hear such Spanish language. If nothing more, Benito and his fellows would be mired in a foot of swine dung and reeking mud. But it was almost a certainty that they would receive more blessings than that from the mother pig. "Here! Here!" she cried suddenly to Fate. The turn was at this very spot. *Izquierdo! Izquierdo!* Now— run!

They swung left, down the lane, and over the pigsty by way of its broodhouse roof. As they cleared the far fence, the first of the guerrillas burst into the lane behind them.

Moments later wild Cuban yells were intermingling with Spanish curses and the wicked squealings of the old sow. Above the piercing screams of the unhappy ones whose limbs were opened up by the she-pig's tushes, Fate could hear the glopp-slopping of the fetid mud as the raging and spurious heroes of Cuban independence fell from the fence, or slipped farther into the slime in their galvanic attempts to elude the aroused mother pig. Rewarding as the uproar was, Fate did not linger to enjoy it. He and Cuba never slacked stride in their race for the church doors.

Padre Espada, brought running by the outcry at the pigsty, ushered them through his unlit church and out a side exit into the cemetery. They were at the tunnel tomb of the Portavale family within seconds, but there was some heart-stopping delay when the bronze door of the crypt would not open to the priest's touch. Shortly he got it to swing back. But now, the guerrillas had broken through the church and out into the grave-yard.

"*Alli!*" yelled Villalobos, "there they are!"

"*Padre,*" said Fate Baylen, drawing his old .45 long Colt, "do you know any good prayers for such an occasion?"

"No," said the lean priest, clutching his slim silver cross to his breast. "But with the devil you do not pray."

"How's that?" inquired Fate, eyeing him.

"You *fight,*" said the other, and removing its golden chain from about his neck, he gripped the head of the silver cross in his dark hand.

Chapter Thirty

"I'll remember it," said Fate, "to my dying day."

"I reckon," said Bear River. "It must of really shook you. I mean, him being a priest and all."

They were going along the hill trail, around the ridge, away from El Soquel. The moon was down a little now, and they had the help of some taller growth on the ocean side of the elevation. It was about four o'clock. They had been moving since three, when Fate had come up from the village and told them, "Let's go; let's get the hell shut of this place."

Blue Calhoun, leading the way because of his better nose for the night wind, called back softly to Fate, next in line behind him. "Then what? Go on, Sergeant. Leave him tell it, suh," he said to Bear River. "I wants to hear what come of the little gal."

"Sure, sure," nodded the huge Wyoming hunter, "go ahead, Baylen, like the little feller says."

215

Fate nodded in turn. "Well," he resumed, "there they came, that damned Villalobos, the one they call 'Wolf,' and Benito Guadaña. Back of them is the others, mebbe five, six of them. Espada, he lays aholt of that big cross, like I told. Benito, he is first up to him, and Espada steps out in front of me and the kid, and holds up the cross and yells out for them to halt in the name of *Dios*. Well, they do it. Sort of force of habit, I reckon. You know how them kind is about their religion. They go it whole hawg."

"That's right," said Pawnee Pollock. "I knew one down in the Panhandle who cut his throat because the priest told him he had done a bad thing and ought to deprive himself of something important in penance. He figured he didn't have anything more important than his life."

"You Injuns," growled Boone Gaskill, "is about as cheerful as a dose of the itch. Jesus, I wisht I had a drink."

"Well," said Fate, going ahead quickly, "the Padre he stops them a minute with his cross, but Benito, he don't believe on that cross near so hard as most. Fact is, he says to Wolf, 'You and the rest get ready. Don't hurt the *padre* but grab Cuba and keep her out of the way. I am going to cut the heart out of the big *Gringo*.' To this, naturally, I ain't in favor. So I says to him, talking around the *padre*, 'Benito, you want a piece of me, you come get it. It won't cost you nothing but a bullet hole twixt your eyes. And one each for the next five behind you.'

"But, damn him, he was smart. All the time the other one, that Wolf sonofabitch, he is inching around to grab the kid. And, *whish*, he does it, before me or the *padre* can move. Then, Wolf, he's got his knife at her neck, and Benito is telling me, 'All right, *Gringo*, here I come. Remember that the first bullet fired means the knife will slip.'

"I thought that was the end, but this Padre Espada was

holding the case ace. As Benito moves past him to get at me, Espada whips the head off of that silver cross and I see the gleam and flash of the blade in the moonlight and, so help me Gawd, it's a sword cross, and before Benito, or Wolf, or any of them can see it, he puts that eighteen inches of Toledo steel through Benito Guadaña, and six inches of it sticking out of his back. Benito don't see it. Wolf don't see it. None of them see it. Only me, who was standing behind the padre and had a better chance with the moon at my back, and not shining in my eyes, as it was them guerrillas.

"Well, Benito, he stops and stands there. Espada slips the blade out of him and back into the cross scabbard so smooth and quick them others never knew what happened. All they saw was Benito stiffen up and fall, and that cussed padre astanding there holding that silver cross over his dead body. They must have thought it was some kind of a miracle. Espada, he said something to Wolf in that Latin they pray with in their churches. Wolf bobbed his head and crossed himself and took one more look at Benito laying there staring up at the moon. Then he mutters *'Madre de Dios!'* and gets the hell out of there. The others turn and stampede after him and the padre stoops down and takes Benito's knife and makes a quick slice with it. Then he says to me, 'Here, *hijo,* give this to the Spanish when you have taken Cuba Libre to their lines.' Well, without thinking, I reached out and took it. It felt like a dried apple slice, only it was hot and wet and had stiff hairs on it. It was Benito Guadaña's ear; the one with the golden earring in it."

"Jesus," said Bear River, shuddering.

"That's what I said," nodded Fate. "But I managed to hang onto it and to grab little Cuba with the other hand and

217

to get through that tomb door into the tunnel in about two jumps. Believe me, I plumb forgot about getting Benito's head for Bucky, or a damn thing else. Last glance I took back, I seen Espada standing there over Benito with his hands folded and his head down, praying. I reckon that's the last any man alive will see of that padre, too, happen those guerrillas tumble to what stabbed old Benito. I never see a man with more pure nerve.''

"Yeah," drawled Boone Gaskill. "Good thing he's a loyal Spanyerd and not a El Soquel guerrilla. A few like him with them and those murdering bush-monkeys might run us clean back to Tampa Bay."

"Good man," said Pollock in his deep voice. "Strong medicine."

"Christ!" complained Bear River. "Onct a Injun, always a Injun!"

"Suh," said Blue Calhoun to Fate, pausing at a drop off in the trail, "you ain't said yet about the little gal."

"No," replied Fate, "I ain't. It's because I'm right shamed about her, I reckon. But she was too cute for me. When we come out'n the tunnel, down there in the gully below the town, she asked me to give her the ear, as we might possibly get separated in the dark and then she would have no way to get through the Spanish lines to find her mother. Like a damn fool I handed it over to her without thinking. Minute she had it, she piped up and says to me, squeezing my hand and planting a big kiss on it, *'Vaya con Dios, patrón!'* She run off in the brush a ways, then calls back, quick, 'I will go alone, *patrón.* I do not want to draw the guerrillas down upon you. God bless the *yanqui* soldiers! *Viva Cuba!'* and that was the last I seen or heard of her.''

"She such a little old thing," said Blue Calhoun. "I

hope she doan get hurt. I hope God give her a hand.''

"Hell, we all do," rumbled Bear River. "But I reckon we'd best say *adios* to her and this whole section about as fast as we can cut it. My backbones are beginning to ache me. That's a mean bad sign for certain.''

"What the hell have your backbones got to do with it?'' asked Boone Gaskill. "Personally, I'm tuckered. I'm gonna set a spell and roll me a smoke.''

"*No smoke*," said Pawnee Pollock. "*Bear River is right.*"

"Goddammit, what you mean he's right?''

It was not the Indian, Pollock, who answered the Georgian's irritable question, but the homely little soft-voiced sergeant of Tenth Cavalry, Blue Calhoun.

"*He mean he right, Mr. Boone,*" repeated the Negro trooper. "*We got company on the trail, afore and ahint us.*"

Fate felt his mouth go dry.

The immediate and continuing thing was silence. Absolute stillness. After enough of that had been endured, Fate crawled over to Pawnee Pollock for a whispered consultation. The two then crawled up to Blue Calhoun, where another round of whispers was shared. Directly, Blue slid over the lip of the trail and glided down the steep slope in front. At the same time, Pollock disappeared soundlessly to the rear, along the way they had just come. Fate crept back to join Boone Gaskill and Bear River Smith.

"*Shhh!*" he warned them. "Pawnee and Blue are gonna try and see how many we got to contend with.''

Neither the Georgian nor the Wyoming giant said anything. By this time it was clearly understood, all of them being hunters and trackers, that they were not yet home.

After what seemed two hours and was not over thirty

minutes, Blue came back. There were eight men laid out in some rocks half a mile down the hill, he said. They were smoking and talking, and did not seem to realize their quarry was so near. There could be no doubt, however, as to the reason for their presence. They were waiting for someone to come along the trail. At a little before five o'clock in the morning, out on a lonely hillside in the Cuban bush, not far from the front lines of the Spanish-American war, it was not likely that it would be their sweethearts for whom they lingered with cocked Lee-Enfield rifles.

So spoke long-boned Fate Baylen when the little Negro trooper had finished his report. Bear River agreed. Boone Gaskill said nothing. The four sat in the dark, waiting. Pollock, returning shortly, told of ten men camped on the back trail. If the original reported number of guerrillas in El Soquel with Benito Guadaña—twenty—were correct, the arithmetic was adding up. Benito subtracted would leave nineteen. Allow one for a messenger presently en route from one of the ambushing parties to the other, and the remainder would be eighteen, exactly the number found by Blue and Pawnee.

"I think," muttered Fate, in uneasy admission, "that it's Villalobos and the boys from El Soquel." To this opinion, Pollock grunted eloquently. "No need to think; we can count on it. I smelled strong pig smell back there. Some of those little apes were the ones you led into the sow's wallow."

"Fine," said Fate. "Thanks a lot. It is always nice to be sure. Blue, did you smell any sow gumbo up front?"

"No, suh."

No one said anything then, and all sat there feeling the

minutes crawl past. Finally Fate asked unhappily, "Any suggestions?"

"Sure," said Bear River, the group optimist. "We'd ought to have deserted in San Antonia."

"If you'd saved it like you'd ought to have," groused Boone Gaskill, "we could show 'em Benito's ear. That might impress 'em. Villalobos might have wanted it for his watch fob."

Pollock stared at him. "I always thought you missed your calling," he said. "You should have been an undertaker."

"By God!" said Bear River enthusiastically, "that's a gospel fact. You look just like a goddam body-snatcher."

"When we get back," grated the moonshiner, "I am going to take you on, one by one. Bare knuckles, barrel staves, broken beer bottles, or any way you want it."

"*If* we get back," said Fate quickly. "Somehow it don't strike me humorous to have eighteen guerrillas squatting on our trail, fore and aft. I'll ask it again. Any suggestions?"

"The thing to consider," said Pollock soberly, "is that we can't make any noise. We can't be more than two miles from the Spanish lines on San Juan Ridge."

"That's right," said Blue Calhoun. "The Spanyerd trenches and bob wire start long 'bout two mile fum here."

"That's so." Fate nodded, frowning harder. "But I ain't yet heard what I want."

"Well," said Boone, sniffing down his long nose, "if you'd let somebody besides niggers and Injuns do your scouting, maybe you'd get some answers you could use."

Pollock, the fullblood Pawnee horse Indian, placed a restraining hand on Fate Baylen's drawn back fist. "No need to hit him," he said. "If he doesn't cotton to the scout work of niggers and Indians, he doesn't have to take part in the proceeds thereof." The slender Pawnee stood up, his handsome face lit with a rare smile. "You wait here, Sergeant," he said softly. "I'll go and get you something which I found by Injun-scouting while I was out just now."

He was gone before any of them could say a word, and back almost as quickly. Over his shoulder he carried the bound and gagged figure of an El Soquel guerrilla. When he dumped the white-clad body in the midst of his companions, he only said, "*Good medicine,*" deliberately grunting it like a tipi brave, and standing back with arms folded and head stiffly held to await their reaction.

"What the hell?" growled Bear River, leading the common motion to crouch and peer closely at the captive.

"A little luck," smiled Pollock. "Such a thing as will come by pure fortune to a poor dumb redskin on the scout. I caught him standing guard fifty feet from his friends. The rest was very simple, for an Indian."

There was a long pause, and then Fate said wonderingly, "Lord A'mighty, it's Villalobos!"

"I recognized him from your story," shrugged Pollock. "He was standing against the sky, and I could see his hunched shoulders and sharp face and the way he paced like a wolf, with bent knees and shuffling feet. It was easy."

"So you said," muttered Boone Gaskill, impressed at last. "I surrender on the Injun insult. Let's go."

There seemed nothing else for it, considering the light beginning to grow in the east. They set out single file, Fate and Pollock immediately behind the prisoner Villalobos made no trouble, having understood from Fate that Pollock was a savage and would kill him instantly should he make an outcry, or try any Cuban trick.

A hundred yards uptrail from the staked-out guerrillas,

Fate called in Spanish that they were the *yanquis* from El Soquel, and not to fire as they were going to come down peaceably. A coarse laugh answered this comment, and a gravel-voiced bandit suggested they come ahead. Fate replied that they would now do so, but that the guerrillas were to examine carefully the face and way of walking of their native guide, who claimed to be from El Soquel and a great friend of their late chief, Benito Guadaña.

Benito's name brought a curse from the guerrillas. In the following moment the Rough Rider patrol turned the bend of trail which hid the ambuscade, and the cursers got a good look at Villalobos in the first bright ray of the morning sun to slide past the ragged crest of San Juan Ridge.

"Jesús María!" roared the same heavy voice which had laughed at them before.

"No," said Fate patiently. *"No es Jesús María. Es Pedro Villalobos."*

"Hijo!" cried the broad-chested one. "Not alone do we get outsmarted, but insulted with poor *yanqui* jokes, as well! What a fate! How did you let it happen, *compadre?"*

Villalobos elevated his shoulders. *"¿Quién sabe?"* he replied. "What are you talking about?"

"What do you mean, what does it matter?" said the other.

"Here I am," answered Villalobos. "They have me and they have my word. We are going through in peace."

"Aha! So they have your word, do they? How about mine?"

"Your word, Gaspar?" The disdain of Villalobos was classic. "What does it matter? I am *Jefe* now."

"Oh?" laughed the squat guerrilla. "That is very funny."

Villalobos turned his head slightly and spoke over his

shoulder to Fate. "Shoot him," he said.

Fate started to remonstrate, to explain the niceties of the suggestion to an Arizona cowboy's view, but Pollock, who comprehended such things more clearly, nodded to Villalobos and took his Krag carbine out of the latter's back and, firing from the hip, blew out the hairy belly of Gaspar, the heavy-set guerrilla. The fellow stood a moment, staring blankly, then slid forward into the hillside. "How funny is that, Gaspar?" called Villalobos. Then, ignoring the dying man, he said quietly to the others, "*Amigos,* perhaps you did not hear what I said to Gaspar. I am *Jefe* now. That is what I told him. What do you say, men? Do you also have bad ears?"

A swarthy villain with the kinked hair and flat nose of the negroid Cuban, grinned like a bush dog smelling dead meat. "For one," he said, "I hear like a cat with a mouse in the wall. We will follow at a safe distance, Pedro, and see they do not harm you. We owe it to cousin Benito to see the *yanquis* back to their lines. *No es verdad, Jefe?*"

"Very true," agreed Villalobos. "Stand away and let us pass, Elfego. If you have the opportunity to do so, you will kill all of these *yanqui bastardos* with me." He jerked his head over his shoulder, indicating Fate Baylen and his four friends. "The Spanish will pay double for each head of those who cut off the ear of Benito Guadaña."

"Let's go!" said Fate, jabbing Villalobos with his long-barreled Colt. "We stand here much longer we'll get a sunburn."

It was true. The sun was rapidly clearing the tops of the main ridge heights. They must get on and find some cover. It was too late to worry about a thing except to run for it. As if to cement the thought, Blue Calhoun moved up to

Fate's side and said quickly, "Company on the right flank, Sergeant. We best light out."

Fate glanced back. The other guerrillas, Villalobos' bunch, drawn by the deep, distinctive bark of the Krag which had killed Gaspar, were just topping the hill behind them. Fate swung about and rattled a short burst of Spanish at the negroid cousin of Benito Guadaña. The latter comprehended the instruction and called up to his newly arrived companions to hold their fire, and come on down the hill. The moment they acquiesced, and were out of sight in the hillside brush, Fate led his followers on the run through the rocks, past the lower skirt of the hill, and into the heavy growth which hid the small stream bed below. Benito Guadaña's cousin Elfego and his men stood silently aside and let them go. Only when the creek brush had closed behind Boone Gaskill—the rear guard because deadliest shot of the patrol—did they make a move or a sound. Then it was only to laugh.

Fate and his friend heard them, but could not halt to learn the reason. They were committed now and must push on down the tiny vale at full speed if they were to make the American lines before the Spanish lines should be entirely awake. It was then about 6:30 A.M.

After another thirty minutes of tough going, the country began to open out a bit and they could see ahead. Fate stopped his patrol and studied the way ahead through the field glasses which Bucky O'Neill had lent him. The vista looked peaceful. Beneath the still clinging mists of the highland night, touched now by the first rose of day, the land was almost lovely. If it had not been for the Spaniard, who must be out there somewhere, it could have been a pastoral scene to delight American travelers.

"What stream is this small one we have been following

downward out of the hills?'' Fate asked Villalobos. ''Does it run into the San Juan River?''

''*Buaro* is the name of the stream,'' said the guerrilla lieutenant, ''Buzzard Creek. Yes, it goes into the San Juan.'' He pointed to a distant height. It was some two miles south and east. Atop its balding, grass-covered eminence a white-walled Spanish blockhouse gleamed like an exposed fang in the drawn back green gums of the Cuban rock and brushlands. ''That is El Caney,'' said Villalobos, ''a strong place of the Spaniard. *Buaro* comes into the San Juan about there.''

''*Gracias,*'' nodded Fate. ''And where is El Pozo?''

He watched the guerrilla carefully. El Pozo, Bucky O'Neill had told him, was the highest hill on the American side overlooking the valley of the San Juan. Undoubtedly, the Prescott mayor had added, it would be the U.S. command post. It would have to be. It gave view over all else, even San Juan Ridge, and the plains and the Bay of Santiago beyond. Bucky had told Fate that he had gone up there with Teddy Roosevelt and Micah Jenkins the night of June 28th, and seen clearly the street lights of the Spanish city. Now, as he watched Villalobos, the latter shrugged and nodded.

''Can you see that other elevation due south of El Caney?''

Fate focused the glasses. ''Yes,'' he said, ''I see it.''

''Do you see also upon its very top a group of buildings? A sugar mill? Cane-crushing wheel? The juice vats?''

''Yes, yes, that's right.''

''That is El Pozo,'' said Pedro Villalobos, ''the Big Hill.''

Fate Baylen put down the glasses. ''Blue, Pollock, Bear River,'' he said, ''come over here. Boone, keep a gun on

Villalobos.'' He moved away from the guerrilla chief. The others followed him. He handed the glasses to Pollock. "You've got hawk eyes," he said. "Tell me what you see up on that hill besides sugar buildings."

The Pawnee took the glasses, focused them. Fate, watching his dark face, could see the bronzed features tense. Pollock handed the glasses in wordless turn to Blue Calhoun. The little Negro took them and raised them quickly. "Man, man!" he murmured excitedly. "That sure is some busy sugar mill!"

Fate took back the glasses. "No need for you to look, Bear River," he said, his own excitement lighting up his gray eyes. "Up on that hill are more damned American soldiers than you ever saw. Hundreds and hundreds and hundreds of 'em. They ain't up there for drill, neither. They're ready to go. Them's fighting troops up there, and a swarm of them. They must be going to attack the Spanyerds!"

"My Gawd!" muttered Bear River. "That damn hill is a good four miles from here! Boys, we've got to hurry if we aim to get back to our lines in time for the main shoot!"

"We'll never make it, Mr. Bear River, suh," said Blue Calhoun. "It must be near seven o'clock in the morning. If they's going to attack this day, it ain't going to be no more'n another few minutes afore they jump."

"Damn!" complained Fate. "We're still way inside the Spanish lines. We got either to gamble and cut straight through them down the San Juan River, or circle clean out around El Caney, yonder, to come in the safe way back of our lines. I don't know which to tell you, boys."

"Why tell us either?" asked Pollock.

"What you mean?" Fate was worried, sensing trouble.

"Take a vote," said the Indian trooper. "Long straw we

run for it down the river, short straw we circle El Caney and play it safe. It's simple. Either we want to fight or we don't. Nobody but us will ever know what we did."

"That's so, suh," said Blue Calhoun. "Let's get the straws." He took off his issue hat. "We kin put 'em here under my neckcloth. Secret ballot, suh."

"All right." Fate stooped and picked a handful of the tough hill grass. "I'll break five long and five short stems," he said. "Each man will get two stems. Go fetch Boone."

When the Georgian herded Villalobos over to them, Fate took him aside and quickly explained the situation. Boone only gave a nodding grunt and asked for his two straws.

Fate held the hat. He kept Blue's Tenth Cavalry kerchief carefully spread over it. Each man closed his fist and put it under the kerchief before depositing his straw. Fate was last. When he withdrew his hand, he grinned and said, "Well, here is where the heroes get separated from the decent, self-respecting cowards. . . ." He whipped off the kerchief and peered into the hat. A frown crossed his face and he looked up and held the hat out toward his companions. "Hell, we all lied," he said. "Five longs."

As he spoke, and far closer than El Pozo Hill, a cotton-white cloud of gunsmoke blossomed above the tangled woodland of the San Juan Valley.

Whoosh! Whoosh! Whoosh! Whoosh! The artillery fired in rhythmic cadence, whistling almost directly overhead. They could feel the quake of the disturbed air and distinctly hear the *"whoomphs"* with which the American shells bit into the Spanish breastworks.

"Kee-rist, boys!" said Boone Gaskill, "you are great artillery spotters. El Pozo, you say? Them goddam cannon is just yonder behint El Caney!"

"It's a battery of four light guns," said Blue Calhoun.

"Mus' be Gen'ril Lawton and the infantry. We got only Cap'n Grimes and his old museum artillery in the cavalry."

"It's our side, anyways!" roared Bear River, tiny eyes snapping. "Sweet Jesus! listen to our little old Krags boom, too!"

"Our little old Krags, hell!" rasped Boone. "Listen to them high whining lousy goddam Spanish Mausers! Don't worry about our Krags, boys, cain't you hear them smoke-less Mausers? By God, they're outfiring our riflemen by ten-to-one. Come on! We got to get over there and help our boys out!"

"Hold up!" yelled Fate. "We'll go when I say."

Boone wheeled on him. "You better say quick, then," he warned, "or you'll be standing here giving orders to yourse'f. Them Mausers is murdering our boys."

Fate nodded. He jabbed his revolver at Villalobos, who was grinning happily at the apparent *yanqui* dissension.

"*Hombre,*" barked Fate, "how far down to the river following this creek we're on? Two miles?"

"*Sí, patrón,* but there is a shorter way. I was about to suggest it. It goes straight as my pointing finger into the thick growth you see below us here. It's a goat path but Villalobos knows it like his woman's—"

"All right, all right," said Fate. "How much closer is it?"

"As you can see, *patrón,* the river is but half a mile from us as the bird flies, through the air. By my little trail it is scarcely any longer."

Fate turned to his companions and told them of the short cut and Boone Gaskill said, "Well, I'll take a piece of that track. Who's coming with me?" All seemed of a like mind and Fate nodded his acquiescence. "Boone," he said, "I'll take over Villalobos. You hang back and cover the rear.

Blue, you take the lead. Everybody move quick. The sooner we get down to them river trees, the better.''

"That's very true,'' grinned Pedro Villalobos. "Come on, *amigos,* let's go.''

Five minutes later, following their still-grinning guide, they had got down the steep hillside and into the first of the river trees and were soon trotting along a brushy path on the right bank of the San Juan. It was perhaps five more minutes when they stumbled into the ambush set along the trail for them by Benito's cousin Elfego and the same guerrilla friends of Villalobos who had laughed good-bye to them not two hours gone on the trail out of El Soquel. It was only the overeagerness of the guerrillas to begin shooting at the *yanqui* fools, whom they had outwitted by coming a shorter way to this special path of Pedro Villalobos, that gave Fate and his friends any chance at all. As it was, when the guerrilla rifles roared prematurely, Fate and the patrol went into the brush like flushed prairie chickens. They were into the long jungle grass and behind the trees faster than Cousin Elfego's hidden riflemen could rebolt their guns for second shots. Of the first guerrilla fusillade, only two bullets went home. One winged Blue Calhoun in the upper arm, the other scraped Pawnee Pollock's high red cheekbone. The most startling aspect of the trap, to both sides, was the nerve-curdling war cry with which the full-blooded American Indian took his wound and went rolling into the tangled cover.

Villalobos, left alone in the middle of the trail, did not instantly respond to his freedom. His mind was not nearly as swift as the trained hunter's reflexes of Bear River Smith. The Wyoming giant fired from the ground, the heavy Krag bullet striking Villalobos in the spine just above the buttocks. It broke his back and came out through his bladder in front. He took three crazy steps, jerking his arms like a puppet, then went down and lay thrashing in the leaves and twigs of the jungle trail. "*He's* anchored!" bellowed Bear River. "Let's get us some monkey scalps, boys! They'll sure be in style, time we get back to the regiment!"

His shout drew a hail of guerrilla fire and the hidden Rough Riders went to work.

Fate shot one of the enemy running between two trees with his Colt. Boone shot two more, hitting small pieces of their heads where his hillman's eye-sight caught the exposures. Bear River shot another by the simple expedient of crashing straight ahead through the brush until he stepped on the rascal. With four of their number dead, the guerrillas held their fire and seemed to be in some doubt as to continuing the ambush on the *yanqui* terms. This hesitation was presently resolved.

The signal was a frightful guerrilla scream from the thicket some thirty feet to Fate's right. The Arizona cowboy fired at the sound and his shot was greeted by a second war whoop from the spot, together with an admonition from Pawnee Pollock to ease off. Fate bolted in another round and waited.

There was a stir in the jungle midway between the two forces. Out of the bushes, flopping and bouncing, flew the body of an El Soquel guerrilla. It was a familiar body, yet not familiar. Then Fate saw what it was that was missing for identification. That was Benito Guadaña's kinky-haired cousin Elfego lying out there in the trail. Only he wasn't kinky-haired any more. He was bald.

It was in that moment of discovery that Pawnee Pollock waved the long stick above the brush clump which hid him. On the stick was the missing scalp lock of Cousin Elfego.

The only sounds which broke the ensuing silence were those made by the terrified exodus of the Guadaña guerrillas from the presence of a demented enemy who not only wantonly attacked and killed brave Cuban patriots but skinned them out on the spot!

There was only one other small thing, before Fate and his patrol left the four dead guerrillas and went on. It concerned Villalobos.

When the Rough Riders came out of the brush and gathered in the trail, listening to make sure their ambushers had indeed fled, they saw that Benito's one-time lieutenant was still alive. He was trying to raise his head, looking up at Fate, trying to say something. The tall cowboy knelt beside him. He uncorked his canteen and held it to the graying lips. Villalobos drank a little and moved his head in seeming gratitude. Fate thought he saw the traces of a smile. Then the guerrilla's hand moved to his breast, fumbling weakly for the shirt pocket, beneath the heavy cartridge bandoleer. He managed to retrieve something from the pocket and held it up toward Fate. Fate reached and took it. "For you, *patrón*," murmured Pedro Villalobos. "I thought you would like to have it. Something to remember me by . . ." This time there was no doubt about the smile. Weak and flickering, as life itself, it was still unmistakably a smile. Whatever it was he had handed over to Fate Baylen, Benito's lieutenant had thought it was funny. By now, the Arizonan knew a little something of the guerrilla sense of humor. Belatedly, he felt of the token in his hand. And recognized it. His comrades, watching, saw his face harden. He looked up at them and held out the hand.

In it lay the golden-ringed ear of Benito Guadaña.

The American soldiers said nothing. They moved out on the trot, carbines at the ready, Blue Calhoun in the lead.

Behind them, in the little open place of the trail, Pedro Villalobos was still smiling. But above Pedro the black shadows of the Cuban vultures were already floating. The patrol ran on, panting, stumbling, not wanting to look back. But its members could not leave behind them the picture which had come into the mind of each man when Fate Baylen had held out in his hand the bloodied shard of Benito Guadaña's ear. That picture was not of Benito Guadaña. Nor of his ear. Nor of Villalobos, his grinning, glazing-eyed lieutenant. Nor of the vultures which wheeled above the latter and would not wait until his flesh was cool before tearing it from him. That picture was of Cuba Libre, the little patriot girl of El Soquel.

Had the child betrayed them to Villalobos? Had she given him the ear? Is that what Villalobos meant by giving the ear, in turn, to Fate Baylen? Or had the girl been loyal, and had the murderous guerrillas of "the Wolf" caught her sometime after her voluntary separation from Fate? The silent American soldiers did not know the truth. They could not know it. They could only know what they so greatly feared, and what their sickened hearts told them, that their cheerful little Cuban comrade was loyal—and dead.

Chapter Thirty-one

It took them an hour to get as far down the river as El Caney. All the while there was a hot fire going forward on the far side of that hilltop fortress. That would be to their left, as they faced south looking down the valley of the San Juan. Repeatedly they were forced to lie up and hide from Spanish soldiers moving to and from the contested height. The enemy troopers looked to be well trained, well equipped and not in any way disorganized by the American attack. Compared to the native Cuban Insurgents with their wolfish looks and conduct, the "minions of the Pope" seemed to be clean and decent men. "If it wasn't that the rest of you is watching," said Boone Gaskill, "I'd be a mind to surrender to General Toral's boys. They look more like white men than we do." To this, little Blue Calhoun said, "Yes, suh, Mr. Boone, than some of us, they sure does," and everybody had a good chuckle and felt better.

As they started on, the trail rose a little and for a few

yards traversed an open knob. At the edge of this overlook they paused, as men will always pause, to see over unfamiliar terrain.

El Pozo lay ahead on their left, appearing to be more like three than two miles beyond El Caney. Facing it, across the river valley, were the high and tumbled folds of San Juan Ridge, with its two major heights, San Juan and Kettle Hills standing on the watchers' right. Kettle Hill, the nearer of the two, was little more than a mile off. It, like San Juan Hill, and the remainder of the ridge, waited silently in the morning sun.

Fate shook his head and unslung the field glasses. He studied El Pozo and said, "Our troops are still milling around up there. Don't look to me like there's any forming-up going on, though. Those fellers I can see, appear to be standing around scratching their noses. I can make out a few of our officers glassing the enemy ridge, that's all."

He swung to the Spanish side and cursed at once. "Boys," he said, lowering the glasses, "we got to get to the Colonel in a hurry. Them garlics is dug in along San Juan and Kettle like they was aiming to spend the winter. They'll slaughter our boys. Here, look . . ."

Pollock took the glasses, then passed them around. Boone, last in turn, gave them back to Fate. "I dunno," he said. "What the hell? Don't you reckon our side can see the wire and trenches and blockhouses, same as you and us? Hell, they're close to 'em as we are. What we gonna tell 'em they cain't see for themse'ves? I'd sooner swing around El Caney and give a hand there."

"Sure, they can *see*," replied Fate, "but not the same as us. Angle's different. We look down their diggings, long ways, from here. Over yonder on El Pozo, Colonel can't do nothing but look abreast into them. You can't see nothing thataway but them piles of dirt they got flang out in front of them. No, sir, we got to get to the Colonel.''

"Well, goddammit," stormed Boone, "that's great! But how the hell we know where he is? You know Teddy. Christ, he could be anywheres. Including back down to Siboney stealing canned tomatoes from Miss Clara and the Red Cross.''

"You got him wrong," insisted Fate. "Lots of people has. When there's a fight in view, that's where he'll be.''

"Jesus Murphy! I ain't said he didn't have no sand! Dig out your ears, Baylen. All I allowed was that you ain't no way of knowing even where the goddam cavalry division is, let alone our outfit and the Colonel.''

"Well, suh," put in Sergeant Blue Calhoun, "we *is* got some idee. We knows it's Gen'ril Lawton and the infantry yonder at El Caney. If they taking this end the line, cavalry got to be taking the other.''

"What you mean we *know?* We don't know a goddam thing, only what you told us. To me, that's the same as nothing. Leastways, I ain't heard of them appointing no nigger generals yet.''

"No, suh, Mr. Boone, you ain't. I didn't mean to anger you. It's only that I knows them guns.''

"Yes," said Fate quietly, "and he knows a hell of a lot more, too. Where you think our cavalry boys are, Blue? Yonder on El Pozo? This way of it? Still over to Sevilla? What?''

"No, suh, they ain't still back to Sevilla, they up all right. Ev'rything up. I reckon that's us on El Pozo. Yes, suh, both the Rough Rider and the Tenth regiments up there. For sure, that the command post. Got to be, with that position.''

"Goddammit—" began Boone again, but was cut short.

Whoompf! Whoompf! The guns went off, and this time they did feel the impact—or hear it—as the shells hit into the Spanish hillside not a mile off. They all saw the dirt fly, and all saw the black-powder smoke roll up from the top of El Pozo.

Fate handed the glasses to Blue Calhoun.

"See if we're moving!" he cried. "See if them was our division's guns."

Blue's smile was that beatific one of the old professional soldier at the sound of the artillery opening.

"Sergeant, suh," he said, "I don't need no glasses to call them guns for you. They pukes up more smoke than a barnfire. They goes off like a boiler explosion on the Robert E. Lee. Them's Captain Grimes' guns, Sergeant! We got us our war agoing at las'!"

"Looks like it!" grinned Fate excitedly. "Come on . . . !"

He ran forward, out across the open knob and down its far side toward the river again. He was yelling like a madman. The others followed him, their own cries as wild and wordless as his. All weariness was at once gone, all doubt dissolved. The smell of gunsmoke and the flash of cannon fire filled the air of the valley below. Like the unnumbered multitude of men before and since, the sight and sound and fury of the battle joined erased all else of sense and sanity save the primal impulse to kill or to be killed.

History had set a good stage for the opportunity. First Sergeant Blue Calhoun, Tenth U.S. Cavalry, Reg., had been correct in his professional calling of the El Pozo battery. It was that of Captain Grimes, in support of the dismounted Second Brigade, General Samuel Sumner commanding in relief of Joe Wheeler. And three minutes after Grimes' ancient cannon opened, the Spanish artillery, zeroing on the billowing clouds of black-powder smoke from the obsolescent American guns, landed a salvo of four rounds of mixed solid and shrapnel shot among the carelessly massed U.S. troops on the command-post hill.

The casualties were severe. Heaviest hit were the Rough Riders of Lieutenant-Colonel Theodore Roosevelt, who himself took a raking piece of lead across the back of his right hand, and who was already fuming with impatience at his orders which directed him explicitly to hold his independent army of college men and cowboys in reserve, precisely where they were, behind the crown of El Pozo Hill, and presumably out of the way of the Regular Army.

It was 8:05 A.M., Friday, July 1, 1898, when Teddy cursed the shell fragment which had struck him and whinnied to Jenkins and O'Neill standing with him drinking coffee, ''The devil with these orders! we're not missing this fight . . . !''

It was within the same minute that Bucky O'Neill lifted his cup and laughed. ''The officers—may we all get killed, wounded, or promoted!''

The three officers clinked their tin cups, drank, tossed the tins away, ran for their horses.

The Keeper of the Record watched them go. He nodded silently and opened the book.

''*San Juan Hill,*'' he wrote, ''*the Battle of . . .*''

Chapter Thirty-two

The heat was stifling. Shafter was sick from it. He was so sick he could not sit up, and had to be propped at a slant upon a requisitioned barn door that he might, from his headquarters telephone tent behind El Pozo, direct the development of the battle.

What he had achieved by ten o'clock in the morning, in the face of galling Spanish small arms and artillery fire, was an incipient disaster.

The valley of the San Juan River ran slantingly southwest by northwest. The Santiago-Siboney wagon road traversed the valley in a similarly askew easterly and westerly line from El Pozo to the city outskirts. Across the river from the American lines were the enemy breast and wire works upon Kettle and San Juan Hills. Directly between the forces the floor of the valley lay level and thickly choked with tree growth. Only here and there could be seen the occasional savannas, or open breaks of grassland, such as had been encountered at Guásimas. At the very foot of the San Juan Ridge the forest thinned and an open, climbing meadow began. This ground, otherwise the only space available for maneuver and a return of the enemy's fire, was completely entangled with barbed wire.

Threading the jungle behind the wired, open land, and leading up to it from El Pozo, was the only known artery of travel, the main Santiago road. Off to its right ran the secondary lateral of the Caney mule track. Both of these lines of advance, particularly and principally the Santiago road, were jammed with American troops, supply vehicles, pack strings and artillery teams, all fighting to use, at the same time, the one and miserable "hole" through which they might crawl to reach the open country which footed the ridge and gave access to the Spanish positions. Of these latter, Kettle Hill had been given to Sumner and the cavalry, including the Rough Riders, while San Juan Hill had been allotted to Kent and the infantry. The assault was to be undertaken "as soon as contact with Lawton might be made upon the right."

Now, three hours after opening with his battery at seven, Lawton had not won an inch up the slope at Caney. He had been granted two hours to take the hill, turn the enemy flank, and join up with Kent and Sumner in the middle. Instead, he was presently sending to Shafter to know if it might not be wise to break off until some more obvious avenues might be explored for turning the right.

To this query, Colonel McClernand, Shafter's adjutant who was directing the action from El Pozo until his superior might summon the will to order his enormous hulk borne up the hill upon his barn door from the telephone tent far back near Sevilla, responded brusquely: "Keep trying, we shall press more vigorously here. . . ."

By pressing more vigorously he meant along the directions he forthwith sent Kent and Sumner to advance along the Santiago road where their troops were already lying, helpless to move, because of the jammed-up traffic. Also frustrating the American troops were a near total lack of proper orders, officership, information on the terrain ahead, and knowledge of the enemy dispositions. As one of Colonel Roosevelt's inelegant cowboys put it, "Shafter wasn't furnishing us a damn thing of decent help excepting a gas-bag artillery balloon that was bobbing around above the brush at columnhead and doing such an outstanding job of spotting the enemy that it drawed down on us every goddam piece of Spanyerd cannon what would chamber and fire."

The official view of Shafter differed somewhat both in language and content from that of the disgusted Rough Rider.

"At this time the cavalry division under General Sumner, which was lying concealed in the vicinity of the El Pozo house, was ordered forward with directions to cross the San Juan River and deploy to the right on the Santiago side, while Kent's division was to follow closely in its rear and deploy to the left."

"These troops moved forward in compliance with the orders, but the road was so narrow as to render it impracticable to retain the columns of fours formation at all points, while the undergrowth on either side was so dense as to preclude the possibility of deploying skirmishers. It naturally resulted that the progress made was slow, and the long-range fire of the enemy killed and wounded a number of our men.

"At this time Generals Kent and Sumner were ordered to push forward with all possible haste and place their troops in position to engage the enemy.

"A few hundred yards before reaching the San Juan the road forks, a fact that was discovered by Lieutenant-Colonel Derby, of my staff, who had approached well to the front in a war balloon. This information he furnished to the troops, resulting in Sumner moving on 1the right-hand road while Kent was enabled to utilize the road to the left."

By twelve noon the stalled advance had lain along the suffocating dust of the Santiago road for more than two hours. Casualties had become severe.

At the Santiago road crossing of the San Juan, the American field hospital was a shambles. There was no estimate of the dead and injured at this time. They simply lay in mixed lots, the medical orderlies stirring them with a probing foot to select those who moved in response for the "next in line" to go to the operating tables. After the first hour, as at Las Guásimas, no abdominal wounds were accepted for surgery, and for the same grim reason. All the men so injured died under the knife and time would not permit such luxury to the frantic doctors. Overhead, held away only by the intensity of the Spanish rifle fire, the island vultures already swung in countless numbers.

The thousands of men trapped on the road neared panic beneath the increasing enemy fusillade. Individual commanders threatened to move without orders. Among these latter was Lieutenant-Colonel Theodore Roosevelt, now in command of the First United States Volunteer Cavalry.

Teddy was beside himself. There seemed to remain to him, as he later admitted, but a sole course beyond the terrible halt at Bloody Bend. It was outright insubordination, and the devil with the risk of court-martial. Men were dying, who had no reason to die, with no chance to see or to fire back at the foe who was pouring upon the Santiago road and the field dressing station a molten hail of Mauser and artillery fire.

It was while he rode Little Texas, his small bay war horse, up and down the bogged column in search of Sumner, who had ordered and was personally responsible for the deadly halt, that a ragged figure in torn and fouled brown duck broke from the jungle and staggered forward to catch at Roosevelt's stirrup.

The exhausted trooper was dripping green water and slime from his fording of the San Juan. His eyes were wide and wild with march fatigue and battle fever. He was more a blood-caked scarecrow of a Rough Rider than a real-life one, and Roosevelt saw enough of his condition in a glance to halt his mount and inquire down as to his mission.

"Well, sir," he said to the soldier, "you have found me extremely busy, but you do not appear to have been idle yourself. What is it you want?"

The trooper could not speak. He sagged against the horse to keep from falling. At once, Roosevelt was on the ground. In the same motion he uncorked his canteen and held it to the man's mouth. Then he was calling, broadcast, for a medical orderly. And, without pausing to hear his request honored, he was peering more closely at the reeling trooper and barking at him in his reedy voice, "Here, don't I know you? Of course I do, you're O'Neill's man. Is he in trouble? Did he send you to find me? My God, you're wet as well as bloody! Has that crazy Irishman crossed the river? Here! Don't faint on me, man! I'm talking to you!"

"Yes, sir," gasped Fate, bracing himself. "I got to find Captain O'Neill, Colonel."

"Be quiet," said Roosevelt, "you're badly hurt."

"No, sir, I ain't. That ain't my blood, Colonel. It's a friend's."

"Shut up, man. Orderly! Over here!"

"Colonel, if you please, sir, I got to find . . ."

"Be still, sir!" snapped Roosevelt. "Get on this horse."

"Your horse, Colonel?"

"You damned fool! Do you see any other horse?"

Fate managed to crawl up on the little mustang and collapse in its saddle. Roosevelt started off leading the animal and still shouting, "Orderly! Orderly! Damn it all, where are the pills around here? Come over at once, somebody, and get this man! That's an order. *Or-der-leee!*"

It was incongruous and wonderful. Fate never forgot it. In the middle of that fearful whine of Mausers and Spanish shrapnel Teddy Roosevelt still had time to surrender his horse to an ordinary soldier of the ranks. Maybe that didn't make him a great man. Maybe it was only politics as usual. Maybe it was just playing it up big for the newspapers back home. But Fate Baylen didn't think so. In all that filthy, stenchful and fetid trough of Cuban jungle there beyond the Bloody Bend dressing station, in that particular moment of time and space in the Santiago campaign, Fate could not see a solitary newspaper reporter present to write up the event, and brave troopers were dying and crying out in pain and agony upon every side. What was Teddy doing? He was stomping along through it all with his blunt jaw set, his eyeglasses blinking in the fierce sun, his face muscles twitching as he cursed and called for orderlies who were not there, and as he kept right on leading that little old Texas mustang carrying that nobody of an Arizona cowboy unmindfully through shot and shell toward whatever aid and safety and comfort he might find for him. By God! That wasn't politics, it was Teddy Roosevelt!

The proud thought was Fate's last of the morning.

He fell heavily forward across the horn of the saddle and remembered no more until he awoke to see above him the homely face of O'Toole, the little Jewish medical orderly.

"Well," smiled Fate wanly, "looks like the Colonel found his pill, after all."

It was the Regular Army's name for the hospital corpsmen and O'Toole nodded to it noncommittally. "Yeah. So what else?"

Fate sat up.

He was lying on the bare, hot ground in the full sun. The heat was enormous. O'Toole was still busy tying off the sling bandage which encased his left chest, shoulder and arm. Fate glanced down at the bandage and at the new red blood already seeping through it. Evidently the gore caked on him before was not *all* Bear River Smith's. Funny. He had not felt nor heard the bullet which got him. He thought of Bucky O'Neill and of their conversation in the dark that night about the sound of bullets. And he remembered reporter Edward Marshall's description of getting hit, which Bucky had read to him. He recalled having argued with his troop leader about that description, and he thought that if he had the argument to make over again, he would side with the Captain and with Mr. Marshall, for a man surely did *not* hear the bullet which had his name on it, nor did he even feel it.

He looked over O'Toole's shoulder. Many other wounded lay about on the ground, untended. There were rows of them, and jumbled piles, too. O'Toole, watching Fate and seeing him blanch, spoke tersely. "The ones in the rows are the good risks. The heaped-up ones ain't going

245

to make it." Fate shivered and felt ill. "I didn't feel the damn bullet hit me," he complained. "Ain't that peculiar?" "No," said O'Toole, finishing the tie and standing up, "not a goddam bit. Lay back and shut up."

Fate shook his head and tried to rise. O'Toole squatted down and talked fast to him. "Listen, you big boob, it looks like you got a main artery nicked in the apex of that left lung. You play it careful, you'll get to go back to the damn beach and get decent care and hot food. Otherwise, *poo-oof!*"

This time, Fate made it to one knee, but his nurse had no time for heroic cowhands. He shoved him back down, hard, collapsing him into the row with the other white-faced victims. "Look, simple!" he cried. "If you don't stay down, you'll hemorrhage. Maybe quick, maybe slow. *But absolutely sure.* Now, I'm trying to do you a favor. Quit pushing!"

He got up, with the warning, and started away toward the surgical station. Fate struggled up again, calling desperately after him, "O'Toole! O'Toole! Don't you remember me? I'm the boy that helped you at Guásimas . . . !"

The Jewish orderly stopped and came back. He looked closely at Fate, then shrugged. "*Ih!* So it's you. Sure, I remember. You know it ain't easy telling you birds apart with the dung and dirt and the dysentery, plastered down with blood and a ten-day beard. What you want? A two-week pass?"

"I want help, O'Toole," pleaded Fate. "I got to get out of here, back up front. I got to find Captain O'Neill."

"Back up front you want to go? You're crazy. You got it all downhill from here. You're safe. You might even get a medal. Never minding a hot meal, and clean underdrawers. I won't do it. Not even to a Gentile!"

They argued another minute or two, then O'Toole gave in and told Fate to lie where he was until he could get back to him. Fate agreed and began counting the seconds. To his surprise, he found he could not remember getting past fifteen or twenty. While he was still trying, O'Toole returned. Fate asked him how long he had been gone and the orderly said, "Half an hour or so. I got caught over there and had to help hold the arms down on a bird who was losing his leg to Dr. Church's bone saw. Hope I didn't keep you from nothing you'd planned?"

Fate shook his head and asked, "Is he all right?"

"Who?" said O'Toole, digging in his pocket for the pills he had brought.

"The feller lost the leg?"

"Hell no. He died on the table. Shock. Here's two kinds of pills. One fer pain, the greens. The other for dizzy spells, the yellows. Now beat it. No, say, hang around a minute. You said A Troop? Captain O'Neill?"

"Yep."

"You might be Sergeant Baylen maybe?"

"That's me. Yes, sir. Why?"

O'Toole shrugged as though it was less than nothing, but his words did not match the camouflage. "There's a little colored trooper over by the river—all shot to hell—says he's Tenth Cavalry, Regular. I tied his belly together and asked him if there was anything I could do for him and he said, yes, if I found Sergeant Baylen of Troop A to tell him Blue Calhoun made it through all right and would like to see him sometime if it wasn't too much trouble."

"Oh Lord," said Fate, "that's just wonderful. Old Blue, he made it!"

"Well, if you can call being shot in the stomach 'making it,' yeah. You want to see him, Baylen?"

"Certain sure I do. Where is he at?"

O'Toole pointed hurriedly.

"You see where Dr. Church is down there? No, to the left under that tent fly, by that packing box with the one-legged stiff on it. Yeah, yeah, that's it. Well, you go past there and follow the riverbed to your left. We got thirty or forty shock cases laying in the shallow water along the bank. Helps to keep the heat from killing them before we get the chance to. Here, easy, stand still a minute and breathe deep and slow. Slow, that's it. Calhoun will keep. He ain't going nowhere. Not nowhere."

Fate steadied himself against the tough little orderly. When the giddy feeling has passed, he said, "O'Toole, God bless you till you find better work. I will see you in church." The other grinned and waved derisively. "Not in my church, you won't," he said. "They wouldn't let you near the joint. Keep your nose clean, cowboy."

Fate waved back and started on. He heard the shriek of the Spanish shell pass over him and heard the bite and shake and *bal-looomphf* of it, as it smashed into the dressing-station area he had just left.

He huddled where he was until the shower of clods, tree limbs, rocks and the larger general debris of an artillery shell landing, pointblank, had settled out of the air about him. When he turned, the dust was still hanging and the smaller solid particles were still raining down out of the sky. A pack of orderlies, led by Dr. Bob Church, ran by him toward the burst. Beyond them he saw the pock hole of the shell and saw its grisly perimeter of mushroomed earth and torn whole bodies and shattered parts of whole bodies which had composed the row of "good risks" from which his friend O'Toole had just released him.

"God damn them," he heard Dr. Church say, "they got O'Toole!"

Fate turned away, confused and benumbed. He stumbled toward the river. When he went through the operating area he stared at the ammunition boxes and pack-mule panniers which lay at the foot of the tables. They were filled with amputated limbs thrown as callously into them as cordwood. He remembered the stink of death and the hordes of blow flies which clouded everything in sight. His feet scuffed at the ankle-deep litter of bloody clothing and cut-off shoes which surrounded the packing-box operating slabs. It was like a scene from Hell.

As he left the deserted surgery, he felt the rush of wind-brushed air come in behind him. He turned in time to see one of the Cuban vultures settling to the ground not fifteen feet from him. The bloated creature struggled to rise again with the trophy it had retrieved from one of the limb boxes. It lurched upward, passing low over Fate, still laboring to climb. But it did not have a good grip on its grisly prize, and it could not hold onto it. The object fell, striking the blank-faced soldier below, bounding off him to land in the dirt at his feet. Fate looked down at it, hypnotically. It was the intact left hand of a man, with the wedding ring and wrist and six inches of hairy forearm still attached to it.

When Fate had vomited and regained his breath, he saw Dr. Church and two of the orderlies coming back with the first of the wounded. They were shouting and cursing to drive off the other vultures which had dropped to the refuse heaps and meat boxes. They did not notice Fate. He was glad for that, and forced his wobbly legs to carry him on toward the river before they should see him and detain him.

Once safely into the brush, he bore to the left as O'Toole had instructed him. It was only after a timeless and difficult trial of thorny bushes, shoulder-high grass and noisome slough mud that he found Blue Calhoun and the other shock cases lying in the San Juan shallows.

The little colored trooper cried when the tall Arizonan lifted him in his arms and carried him to a shaded and dry place higher up on the bank. It was not a good place, but it was the best Fate could find. The heat of the riverbed was that of the Santiago road multiplied. The smell and humid vapors of the water and the terrible odor of the poor torn devils who waited in its murky, steaming current were nearly beyond endurance. Fate was ill again before he could gather the intelligence and physical strength to speak to Blue Calhoun. Then it was all he could do merely to order the latter to take two of O'Toole's pain pills, and two of the ones for dizziness, together with some canteen water. Fate took some of the pills for himself, too. He didn't remember how many, or of which color, they were.

Presently he and Calhoun were sufficiently recovered to exchange nods and wordless pats of the hand on knee and shoulder. The wizened Negro cavalryman even summoned up a grateful smile.

"Sergeant, suh," he told Fate, "that ain't bad stuff you got in the canteen. Where at in the world you get it?"

Fate frowned, puzzled. He opened the canteen and tasted it. It was the first he realized that he even had the canteen with him, much less that it was the one Roosevelt had given him and that it contained something other than brackish camp water. "Why, it's the Colonel's," he announced, wonderingly. "It's got to be. I reckon he must of left it with me at the dressing station when he brung me in."

"*The* Colonel, suh? You all mean Teddy Roosevelt?"

"Sure, Blue. Sure I do."

"Colonel Teddy Roosevelt, he leave you a canteen wid

drinking brandy in it? Naw!''

"Well, doggone it, he must have, Blue. Where else would I garner it? It sure wasn't give me by them hospital folks.''

"Well, mebbe. Say, that hospital talk, that remind me, suh. You seen that little Jewish feller up there? He find you and tell you what I say fer him to say? 'Bout me and you?''

"Yep, he sure did, Blue. Wasn't he a stout little fellow, though?''

"Yes, suh.''

They fell still, looking at the river and fighting to get their breath and not to faint or get sick again.

"Blue,'' said Fate after a moment, ''what happened to you and Boone Gaskill after we got split up? Last I seen of you two, you and him was diving back of that downed log. Me and Pollock and Bear River had to get shut of there so swift we didn't get a chance to say good-bye. That surely was foul luck stepping square into that Spanish rifle nest, like that. Jesus, boy, they run us for near a mile down the stream. They got four rounds through Bear River, and him and me had to hole up and fight them off from under the bank for two hours and more.''

"Yes, suh, I allow it were fierce. Mr. Bear River, he gwine make it, you suppose?''

"Nope. I left him under the bank.''

"Daid, suh?''

"No. He couldn't walk and he wouldn't have me staying with him for nothing. He knowed he wasn't leaving that hole and didn't see no reason for the both of us to share it.''

"And Pawnee, suh. How about him? He make it?''

"I think he did, Blue. Last I seen of him he was running clean. I don't believe he even took one hit.''

"Yes, suh, he's a Injun, hard to kill, same as a nigger, suh. He gwine make it."

"Sure he will, Blue." Fate paused, then said carefully, "Blue, how bad you hit?"

"Fair bad, suh. But I gwine live, the Jewish boy tell me. He say I gwine make it easy as throwing snake eyes."

"Sure. Who's your company officer, Blue?" Fate asked it, knowing that O'Toole had lied. "I want to tell him where you are, so's he can send somebody to pick you up and to see you get the right care, and all."

"That sure right good of you, suh. You been a mighty good friend. You make a man proud."

"Oh, hell I have. You're the one, Blue. You're a Regular. You done everything like a soldier ought. We was *all* proud of *you*."

The little colored trooper bobbed his head and Fate saw again the shine of the tears on the dark cheek.

"Thank you, suh," he said. Then, with patent difficulty, "I got to tell you something, Sergeant. You gonna say it cain't be, but I learn better. You know, Mr. Boone, suh?"

He waited, and Fate said, yes, that he did know the mean-eyed Georgia moonshiner, but that Blue should not put too much blame on the latter for his behavior, as he was only doing what he had been taught to do in his part of the country. "It ain't that he rightly hates niggers, Blue," he said. "It's only that he's been *told* he does."

Blue's head moved again. "That jus' what he learn me," he said softly.

"How do you mean?" frowned Fate. "You trying to tell me you and Boone made it up to one another back of that damn log?"

"No, suh, it mus' have been later on than that."

"Later? What the hell you saying, Blue? You're tough

as Pollock to talk to. You go around in circles stomping out your own tracks.''

"Yes, suh. It like I say. Us niggers and Injuns is much alike.''

"Damn it, we wasn't talking about niggers and Indians. We was talking about Boone Gaskill.''

"Yes, suh. Well, Mr. Boone, he laying next me back of the log. *Whanggg!* Hyar come this bullet and go clean th'ough me. Mr. Boone, he say, 'Goddam it, nigger! Cain't you even hide ahint a log without messing things up? By Christ, I'd ought to kill you myse'f and get it done with!' It was right then, suh, the minute he say that, when along come the one with he name on it. *Bloompps!* That bullet smack him square th'ough the rib. I hearn him go, *'Gurntt,'* same as a pig whop on the head wid the hammer. It got the guts, suh. Deep.''

"Go ahead, go ahead.''

"Well, I don't know nothing for a spell. I flicks out cold. I come back, there the little Jewish pill abending 'bove me. I say to him, 'Suh, what happen?' And he say back to me, 'I dunno, Sambo. You was brung in by a big longjaw hillbilly and he don't tell us nothing, neither, on account he die-up on us five minute arter he dump you on the ground and yell, *Hyar! Take care this little old coon!*'' He paused, head moving in slow doubt. "I dunno what you gwine call it, Sergeant, but me, I figures Mr. Boone he show he don't truly hate a nigger, arter all.''

There was the final moment, then, during which neither man could, nor cared to, say more. Then Fate Baylen handed over to his comrade the Teddy Roosevelt canteen of brandied water. He patted him on the shoulder and stood up at a considerable cost of stiffened pain.

"We all learn something every day, Blue," was all he said. "Rest easy."

"Good-bye, suh," said the colored cavalryman, but Fate had already started on. He did not look back and he never saw Sergeant Blue Calhoun again.

Chapter Thirty-three

"General Wheeler, the permanent commander of the cavalry division who had been ill, came forward during the morning, and later returned to duty and rendered most gallant and efficient service during the remainder of the day.

"After crossing the stream the cavalry moved to the right, with a view of connecting with Lawton's left when he could come up, and with their own left resting near the Santiago road.

"In the meantime, Kent's division, with the exception of two regiments of Hawkins's brigade, being thus uncovered, moved rapidly to the front from the forks in the road previously mentioned, utilizing both trails, but more especially the one to the left, and crossing the creek to form for attack in front of San Juan Hill. During this formation, the Second Brigade suffered severely. While personally superintending this movement, its gallant commander, Colonel Wikoff, was killed. The command of the brigade then devolved upon Lieutenant-Colonel Worth, Thirteenth Infantry, who was soon severely wounded, and next upon Lieutenant-Colonel Liscum, Twenty-fourth Infantry, who five minutes later also fell under the terrible fire of the enemy, and the command of the brigade then devolved upon Lieutenant-Colonel Ewers, Ninth Infantry.

"While the formation thus described was taking place, General Kent took measures to hurry forward his rear brigade. The Tenth and Second Infantry were ordered to follow Wikoff's brigade, while the Twenty-first was sent on the right-hand road to support the First Brigade, under General Hawkins, who had crossed the stream and formed on the right of the division. The Second and Tenth . . . moved forward on the left . . . and drove the enemy back toward his trenches.

"After completing their formation under a destructive fire, both divisions found in their front a wide bottom, in which had been placed a barbed wire entanglement, and beyond which there was a high hill, along the crest of which the enemy was strongly posted."

William R. Shafter
Major-General, United States Army

The volume of fire, as Fate neared the San Juan crossing, had neither risen nor fallen from its earlier drumming pace. But at the forks of the roads he was in time to witness a strange happening which *did* affect and alter the terrible intensity of the Spanish fusillade.

As he came along, stumbling and peering ahead to see his way past and through the jam of troops which was everywhere, he saw a clearing, near the forks, and, just beyond it toward El Pozo and the American lines, the gas-bag observation balloon of Colonel George McC. Derby hovering monstrously above the treetops. Fate shook his head and tottered on, convinced that he did not appreciate higher military strategy. It was equally certain that he did not appreciate military history in the making, either, for as he watched Colonel Derby the latter had just made his discovery of the famed left-hand branch road at Bloody Bend, and the Arizona cowboy's only reaction was to mutter to himself that it would be a Christian mercy if Captain Grimes would turn his El Pozo battery on the observation balloon and blast it to smithereens before it could draw any more Spanish artillery fire onto those poor boys jammed along the main road.

It was a real blessing, Fate told himself, starting on, that Colonel Teddy had earlier been able to get the regiment out from under that damned balloon. A soldier of whom he had asked directions had told him that Roosevelt had warned General Sumner that he was going to take the Rough Riders right on by him, with or without Sumner's permission, and that Sumner had not given Roosevelt the permission and that inside of ten minutes the Rough Riders *were* moving up past the stalled regular cavalry of Sumner, and going on over the river into the far-side safety of the Santiago road where Derby and his balloon *were not*. Fate grinned to himself with the thought and said aloud to no one, *"By God, that's him, that's Teddy!"* and plodded on with renewed determination.

Once again Old Teddy had shown them. He had worked his "go-as-you-please" plan, just as he had right along, and this time it had saved the Rough Riders from getting shot to bits, with no chance of shooting back, in that stifling slot in the jungle under that miserable gasbag.

The recurrent thought of Colonel Derby's conveyance caused him to stop and peer back at the balloon's mooring. As he did, a tremendous cheer went up from the American troops and he saw the balloon gracefully descending through the treetops, holed at last by a burst of Spanish shrapnel.

Fate watched long enough to see a natty officer step out of the basket, unscratched, then to listen with glad relief at the almost instantaneous slackening of the enemy fire which accompanied the downing of the gasbag. After that he pushed on for the river again. Something about the balloon and the forks of the road and the matter of the familiarity of the entire happening still disturbed him. But his memory was not working well, and he was feeling weak and sick again and he knew that the important thing was to find Captain O'Neill and report to him on the Benito Guadaña patrol. He went on. He had a lot of trouble getting through the San Juan at the crossing. It seemed to take him twenty minutes to wade the thirty feet of waist-deep sluggish water. Of course, he knew it wasn't anything like that long. More like two minutes, probably. And it wasn't more than another five minutes after he got across, he was sure, that he saw ahead of him the familiar brown duck uniform of a Rough Rider trooper stationed at the roadside directing the cavalry traffic to turn to the right.

The sight of that trooper was better than a shot of pure rye. The latter's new sergeant's chevrons and company police armband did not fool Fate Baylen for a minute. He knew that boy and he limped up to him with an Arizona grin a yard wide, and said to him, "Well, Pete, how do I smell now . . . ?"

The other man peered at him, startled, then dropped his Krag and threw both arms about him and cried, "Lofty! Welcome home! Say, cowboy, you smell better than that redhead at the Tampa House. Naturally, in a different way."

After the greeting, Van Schuyler told him some things which were not so pleasant to hear. A runner from Shafter had just gone through looking for Sumner. Lawton, with his 5,000 men, had not made ten feet up the hill against the few hundred Spaniards at El Caney. Shafter had dispatched to him all of his reserves. The only advice which went to Lawton with the new troops had been frightening. Said the fat commander-in-chief, safely behind El Pozo Hill and entirely out of sight and touch with his dying troops on Santiago road and El Caney Hill: "I would not bother with little blockhouses. They cannot harm us. You should move on the city. . . ."

As for the troops on the San Juan and Kettle Hill end of the battle line, there had been no reserves for them. And, worse yet, no new orders and no possibility of new orders until the headquarters runner found Sumner and told him Shafter wished to see him, or to hear from him, in the matter of determining the situation in his sector.

"My God," said Fate, "that's pretty lean bacon. I've just seen that 'little blockhouse' up to Caney, and it's a bearcat. I don't think they will ever take it, reserves or no reserves. Ain't you a bit sick, Pete? I mean, to think that an officer like General Shafter has got the say over you, when he ain't even been up to the lines all day?"

"Sick?" said Van Schuyler. "I guess so! Especially when I take sober pause to consider the fact that it's two o'clock in the afternoon and General Lawton was supposed to take Caney and join up with General Sumner—that's us, boy—not later than ten this morning! You might say that 'sick' is a polite way to spell it, Lofty.''

"Two o'clock?" said Fate, stunned. "That's impossible, Pete! I just come acrost the river at a little past noon.''

Young Van Schuyler patted him on the shoulder. "Don't worry about it," he said. "Nobody bothers about time in a mess like this. Things get all turned around. A man's mind jumps back and forth like a damned goalie in a hockey game. We do nutty things. You just now sat on that log down by the river—after you got across—for at least forty-five minutes before you got up and came on up here. I kept watching you, thinking I had seen you somewhere and not able to say where. I'll bet you didn't even know you sat down. Or, if you did, that you thought it was only for a minute or two. Am I right?''

Fate shook his head. "That's pretty bad," he said. "I don't remember nothing except seeing you up here and coming toward you. I knowed you right off, though, Pete.''

He frowned, trying to think, to straighten things out. It *was* bad when you couldn't remember things. Maybe that cussed bullet in his chest—no, hell, that had nothing to do with it. It was only a scratch. But, then . . .

"Pete," he said, "do you know when that feller in the balloon got shot down?''

"Sure," said the other, "right around noon sometime.''

"You remember what time it was that he discovered the left-hand trail from up there in his basket?''

"Yeah, about ten or eleven this morning. Why? What's it matter?''

"Oh, it don't, I guess," said Fate. "It's sort of spooky, though. Somewheres back there, just now, I lost three

260

hours. I thought I seen Colonel Derby yell down about the road and then get the bag of his balloon punctured by the Spanish artillery and then me get on over here to you, all in about ten, fifteen minutes. Pete, I don't feel so good."

"They are not going to hand you any first prizes for looking good, either," replied Van Schuyler. "You had better find yourself a sitting log and preempt it until my relief gets here. Then I'll take you up to Troop A myself. What do you say, cowboy?"

Fate nodded weakly.

He slumped down upon a shell-snapped acacia trunk beside the road and waved with a wan grin. "You talked me into it, Pete; ignorance still ain't no match for education."

The New York youth returned the grin.

"And you're still not whipped, are you, Lofty?" he said.

Fate frowned, considering it.

"I reckon not," he said at last. "I'm still breathing."

Chapter Thirty-four

Now, where they were lain up in the scrub bush bordering
the meadow which faced San Juan Ridge, Fate saw the men
of the dismounted Ninth (Negro) and Sixth (white) Regular
Cavalry. They were largely exposed and were taking a
heavy fire. As for their return fire, which was the first any
of the American troops had actually enjoyed, Fate noted
that it was spirited but useless. The upward angle of fire
and the high embankments of Spanish trenches made any
effectiveness impossible.

"Damn," shouted Fate to his slender blond guide,
"them poor devils is getting murdered out there! Why in
God's name don't they pull back here in the trees?"

"Because," Van Schuyler yelled back, "the damned
trees are already full of our own brave lads. The volunteers,
cowboy. Careful you don't step on one and injure his dig-
nity. Our heroes are on their bellies so thick around here
that the poor damned regulars couldn't pull back ten feet

if McKinley made it an Executive Order. Oh, I must say this is not the day of the noble citizen soldier. I think you and I are the only enlisted Rough Riders standing up on this side of the river. Thank God for the regulars!''

"You saying our boys have turnt yeller?" panted Fate. He was getting faint again. The heat was enormous at river level. He fought to stay upright. "That don't sound like Teddy's Terriers to me. Say, where is Colonel Teddy? God, he ain't been hit, has he?''

"Not unless it was by one of our own dashing grenadiers!" laughed the Eastern boy. "But that's not impossible either. There are more of us behind the line than on it. Look for yourself, Lofty."

It was true. Fate could not deny it.

For some time he had been conscious of the heavy increase in the traffic of wounded toward the rear. This stream of shattered men, both ambulatory and litter cases, had been but a trickle when he and Van Schuyler left the Santiago road only minutes before.

At the beginning the casualties and the unwounded men helping them to the rear had been nearly all from the Negro outfits, both from the Ninth, out in the meadow, and the Tenth, which Van Schuyler said was in the trees next to their own regiment. But the boys coming yonder now, the injured ones, were wearing Rough Rider brown duck, Fate noted with a glad pride that the Negro troopers of the Tenth, through whose position he and Van Schuyler were presently moving, were showing the quickest, most gentle sympathy, not only for their own wounded but for those of the Rough Riders, as well. Yet when he commented happily to Van Schuyler on this plain evidence of stout loyalty, his companion said sharply, "Shut up and save your strength for ducking Mauser bullets, Lofty. You can't sell me on the martial virtues of the Smoked Yankee.''

Fate didn't try to answer him. He knew what the New York boy implied by his short reply. Van Schuyler suspected the colored soldiers were helping the Rough Riders only so that they, themselves, might get to the rear. Fate did not agree, yet what could he say to his white companion that would, in view of all the mean stories spread against the Negroes, possibly convince him otherwise? Fate didn't know. What he *did* know was that those stories were a lot of straight horse manure. He had personally *seen* these same colored boys of the Tenth come up and save Bucky O'Neill's and Micah Jenkins' right flank at Guásimas, when a breakthrough would have meant at least the court-martial of Colonel Theodore Roosevelt, if not of Joe Wheeler and the whole works. And in that case it had not been the Negroes who were running, but the tough and hard-shooting Spaniards who had been on the verge of driving the Rough Riders clear back to Siboney. And the colored boys had done their driving of the enemy without any hoopla whatever. They and their white fellows of the First Cavalry had fought like tigers. And they had done a hell of a lot better, either outfit of them, than had Fate and Pete and Teddy Roosevelt and the rest of the Volunteer Cavalry.

But he knew that didn't make any difference in the favor of the poor colored boys. The white boys still would say, and still said, that the Negroes wouldn't fight a lick, that the Spaniards on the O'Neill-Jenkins front were already running when the Tenth lit out after them, and that the colored boys were only hound-dogging the tracks of game that had been jumped by the white troops.

Fate wondered, angrily, where Pete Van Schuyler had been in that Guásimas battle. His K Troop had been in the thick of it and the New York boy ought to have seen just what Fate Baylen and A Troop saw. But it was clear that he had not.

Fate still didn't argue it. He knew it was hopeless with a man whose mind was made up before he opened his mouth. The only thing which really bothered him was that Pete was a Northern boy. He could have understood such smallness from Boone, or Post Oak, or the other Southerners, but that a nice New York fellow would swallow such hogwash troubled him.

"Cowboy," said Van Schuyler suddenly, "there's your bunch."

"What?" asked Fate, his thoughts fuzzed.

"There's A Troop," said Van Schuyler. "Straight ahead, there. You see Captain O'Neill standing on the parapet?"

"Standing on the what?" Fate asked. His mind was still not working as it should. He had been having difficulty holding a thought line since the big shell had killed O'Toole back at Bloody Bend, and since being forced to leave lonely little Blue Calhoun to die, unhelped, by the riverbank.

"The piled-up dirt in front of that trench up there!" snapped Van Schuyler impatiently. "You see where Henry Bardshar is nosed in, don't you?"

"Old Henry, sure I see him. Who couldn't? He's bigger than a shorthorn bull."

"Yeah, well that's O'Neill standing above where 'Old Henry' is warming his belly. You just keep heading for them, I've got to turn off. Troop K is just to the left here."

"All right, Pete, thank you very much. And, Pete—"

"Yeah, Lofty?"

"It's good we're friends again."

"Sure, cowboy, you bet. Stay low now. Those Mausers

are really buzzing through here. For God's sake don't stand up in the open.''

"I won't, Pete. So long.''

"Yeah, Lofty, 'remember the Maine!' '' The New York youth grinned and ran, doubled over and dodgingly, for K Troop's position on A's left flank. Fate waited to see that he made it safely through the opened tree growth. Then gritting his teeth to subdue the pain and faintness induced by his wound and the fearsome heat, he too bent over and ran forward. Miraculously none of the .30 caliber Mausers did more than hole the dirty cloth of his brown duck trousers, yet Fate heard and felt them going by and, he swore, could see them as well. He leaped two dead bodies in the distance to O'Neill's side. One was a trooper of the Tenth, the other a Rough Rider. The latter was on his back, pale face staring up from the tawny cane. His eyes were open and his teeth bared in a snarl like that of a rabid dog. It was a frightening, terrible look, the more so because, in the very leap which took Fate over its silent owner, the Arizonan recognized the dead man.

It was the small, quiet, gentle little man called ''Hell Roaring Jones.''

"Hell Roaring" had never harmed a flea in his life and had enlisted only because he was from Montana and felt it his bounden duty to go and fight for the cause of his country. Up to this minute he had been a Rough Rider only by virtue of being embarrassed into it by his frontier friends. Now he had won the honor on the field. Now he was a real soldier.

Fate staggered on, weak and sick and wanting to drop and never get up again. But he did not quit and he reached the trees on the far side of the intervening opening, still alive and fighting to stay conscious and upright. He seized the stem of a palm sapling to keep from falling, and stood gasping for the breath to make the last few feet up to O'Neill and Bardshar and the forward salient of A Troop's line.

In the moment of this respite, the volume of the Spanish fire seemed to double. Fate shook his head to clear his vision and his thinking. The enemy had the Rough Rider and regular positions ranged to the yard. His own short dash across the open had shown that. Any time an individual soldier drew volley fire, it was getting the bead down about as fine as it could be held. A man did not have to be General Shafter to figure out what was going to happen here. The enemy trenches were only 600 yards away. The ground in between was wide open and literally spider-webbed with barbedwire entanglements. The Spanish firing points were all well above those of the Americans, allowing the blue-and white-clad regulars of General Toral's and General Linares's Santiago defenders to shoot down into the trapped Fifth Army Corps' dismounted cavalry division and to cut it to bits and pieces where it lay. It was not going to be a battle, it was going to be an execution. The Rough Riders were to be allowed to die but not to fight.

The men of A Troop, all about Fate, were dug into the red island dirt and burrowed beneath the yellow, heat-seared grass like fever ticks welting the hide of a steer. They didn't even move when they were stepped on. It was lie low or get shot—stay down or never get up. Only the officers were on their feet and only some of them. Even Acting Sergeant Henry Bardshar, the giant hardrock gold miner from Cañada del Oro and Canyon Creek, a man who Fate knew would wrestle a boar grizzly and give him the first hand-hold, was hugging the Cuban earth as though it assayed four hundred dollars an ounce and couldn't be filed on until the spring thaw.

But if Sergeant Bardshar's body was anchored, his voice was not. Fate could hear him hoarsely pleading with Bucky O'Neill to get down, as he, Fate, ran the last few feet up to the front trench and plunged into it alongside the huge miner. But Bucky would not heed the warning.

Not deigning even to turn, the ex-sheriff of Yavapai laughed and took a deep drag upon his ever-present cigarette. "Sergeant," he said to Bardshar, "the Spanish bullet isn't made that will kill me."

"Get down, Captain!" repeated Bardshar. "For God's sake, sir, get down or one of them is sure to hit you!"

"Nonsense," replied O'Neill, spinning his cigarette away, "they're firing wild."

He was wrong, and forever wrong.

Over upon the high ridge frowning above San Juan as the other ridge had frowned above Las Guásimas, a Spanish soldier of the auxiliary Guarda Civil gave a hitch to his carelessly slung cartridge bandoleer and selected from its captive number the round nestled in the second loop above his left breast. He did not look down at the cartridge, nor would he have recognized the name it bore upon its blunt bullet, had he done so. What did some crazy *yanqui capitán* mean to Juan Fernandez of the Santiago Civil Guard? How little could a man feel for such a thing? In this life a bullet waited for everyone. If not for Juan Fernandez, then for the *yanqui capitán. ¿Que diferencia?*

The Spanish soldier single-loaded the .45 caliber shell into the old Remington, drew back the heavy hammer, sighted briefly.

On the parapet fronting A Troop, 543 yards away, Captain William O. "Bucky" O'Neill was discussing with a

268

neighboring white officer of Tenth Cavalry the principal direction of the Spanish fire. He started to turn from this conversation to reply to a shout from his line sergeant, Henry Bardshar, informing him that Sergeant Fate Baylen, the leader of the El Soquel patrol, had just reported in.

The bullet struck O'Neill in the mouth. It shed its jagged coating of brass in the explosive rupture of its lead core, vaporized the skull at point of exit, blew back at Fate and Henry Bardshar the jellied content of the brain.

One thought limned itself before Fate's mind. The bullet was not a Mauser and it did not sing when it came for Bucky O'Neill. But it came for him. And the newspaperman at Guásimas was right. You never heard the one that carried your name.

Chapter Thirty-five

O'Neill's lieutenants, Greenway, Frantz and Carter were occupied elsewhere in the line at the moment he was killed. His regular First Sergeant, W. W. Greenwood, was back in the wooded area getting up the men. Bardshar and Fate Baylen were alone for the opening seconds but the former was an old hand at easing out of tight spots and quickly said to Fate, "Come on, boy, this ain't no place for us with Bucky gone." He started to crawl along the trench and Fate called, "Wait, you cain't leave, you're a noncommissioned officer!" The big miner laughed. "I am like hell," he said. "I was only filling in for Greenwood. You don't see no stripes on me, do you?" Fate was instantly mad. "Only that one big yeller one down your back!" he yelled. Bardshar came rolling back at him, balled up like a giant tumblebug to keep below the sheet of Mauser fire pouring overhead. "Listen, you dumb saddle tramp," he shouted, "don't be calling me no names, you hear? You want to stay, fine. Yonder comes Lieutenant Greenway, report to him." He pointed and, following the aim of his knotty finger, Fate could see the long-legged youth sprinting over from the right. "He's a good boy," said Henry Bardshar, "but I know where to find me a better one, and, I'm off to find him. Now, you coming or staying?"

"Where you going?"

"Where the excitement's at. Over to Teddy's side."

"I dunno," said Fate.

"Yeah, well you write me a letter when you make up your mind. Me, I'm gone."

Bardshar started off again. Fate, after a last glance at the flying Greenway, ducked down and went after Bardshar. The big miner was right. They didn't need Henry Bardshar and Fate Baylen to run A Troop, and where the Colonel was, that was where Fate wanted to be. Besides, the regiments and companies and squadrons and troops and, hell, even brigades, were all snarled up on this side of the river. Shafter and Sumner themselves didn't know where one outfit started and another stopped. In such an overlapped mess, there couldn't be any real reason not to go find Teddy. Yes, and not only to find him, but to stick to him like a burr under a bucking rig, once you did find him.

With that Spanish fire murdering the men it looked as though the whole damned thing was going to blow wide open inside of five or ten minutes. If a man could judge one thing, just one single damned thing, about this crazy army of theirs, it was that when trouble loomed and everybody else was standing around scratching his backside, Teddy Roosevelt would be off and winging.

Midway over to K Troop's position, where Roosevelt was stationed with Micah Jenkins and Woodbury Kane, Bardshar and Fate met Sergeant Tiffany. Tiffany was running a message to O'Neill to pull over and join up with K. Teddy had decided to go it on his own and retreat, full flight, *toward* the Spanish entrenchments on San Juan Ridge.

Fate could have cried, he was that proud of the little Colonel. He knew it! God damn it, he knew it! The rest of them could all go to hell, but Teddy wouldn't let his boys lie there and get chewed to bits by those miserable garlics! Not Teddy!

They told Tiffany of O'Neill's death. Fate volunteered to go back to A Troop with Tiffany, making sure by the two of them going that one would get through with Roosevelt's vital order. Tiffany said, yes, that was a good idea but that it would be Bardshar, not Fate, who went with him.

"You're not up to it, cowboy," he told Fate, putting an unexpectedly gentle hand on the tall Arizonan's arm. "I think you had better go on along and let Pete Van Schuyler take you to our dressing station. You're the color of cold grease."

"Thank you, Tiffany," said Fate. "I believe I will do it. Bardshar is stronger and I would only worry you."

When the other two had set off, running, toward Greenway and the forward trench, he started on to K Troop's better hidden position on the left, directly behind the Ninth Cavalry. There he found Pete Van Schuyler, but he found him with Teddy Roosevelt and a hastily summoned fragment of his staff, and all thoughts of the dressing station and of easement to the rear fled. If he died in the next ten steps, Fate decided, he would do it following the Colonel and not tottering back toward Bloody Bend and Dr. Bob Church. Out in front, the meadow beckoned bright and clean. Beyond it, the ridge of San Juan stood clear and brilliant in the afternoon sun. That was the place to go. Not back there where the flies and the dried blood and the buzzards and the cut-off arms and legs and the groans of the dying and the awful stink of the dead were all that would make a man's last memories. No, out there in the dry grass and the cleansing wash of the sunshine. Out there, where it looked so like home, with its harsh-cut hills, its tawny, heat-shimmered range grass, its raw blue sky and cottonboll clouds and its still, windless, silence, that was the place.

Recovering himself, Fate shook his head to clear his mind, then went forward to report the death of Bucky O'Neill to Colonel Roosevelt and the staff. When he had done so, Roosevelt wheeled like a caged lion on the others and cried out, high voice squeaking with unmanaged anger, "There! God damn it! What did I say? Bucky gone for nothing, and we shall be next! I won't have it! I won't have it!"

He whirled about. "Captain Mills," he said to his aide, "prepare an order."

Fate, with the others, drew in, sensing the moment.

In the half-breath that they waited for Roosevelt to go on, they saw another of the dramatic alterations of the man which he could effect as no other. From the high-voiced, petulant attitude of childish anger, he went, on the instant, to the tense, completely determined mien of commander and leader of men. His blunt jaw was set like a rock. His broad teeth and owlish eyeglasses glinted. The muscles of his nervously afflicted face jumped and fluttered with independent life. And now, far from the rageful frustration of the moment and the hours past, he was smiling. The famous Roosevelt grin was spread beneath the bristling sweep of the straw-colored mustache as it had not been since the gay and untaught days of Camp San Antonio. This was Teddy Roosevelt.

"Mills," he said, "we are going to march toward the guns. I have sent messenger after messenger to try to find General Sumner or General Wood and get permission to advance. We cannot seem to find any sort of an arrangement which will get us out of this devilish mess, and I am presently determined to remove my men from it."

He hesitated, very definitely aware that he was speaking for the record.

"If we go forward here," he said, "I know that General Hawkins will come on with the infantry on our left. He has had his men ready to go all the while, and I have seen him walking their front over there, in full view of the enemy, for the past thirty minutes. If something is not done, he will go the way of brave Bucky O'Neill, and after him, the rest of us. This fight will be lost simply for our lying here and letting it be lost. Someone has got to take the risk. The regulars will not do it. Hawkins will follow but he cannot lead off. It's up to us. The Rough Riders have got to do it. And they will do it."

The last pause was for effect, not theatrical effect, but the necessary effect of absolute understanding.

"Make that into an order, Mills," he said, and turned to move toward Little Texas, being held outside the staff circle by newly promoted Orderly-Sergeant P. W. B. Van Schuyler IV.

Before he could swing up on his war pony, a courier dashed up on horseback. It was Lieutenant-Colonel Dorst. He was standing in his stirrups and shouting for attention of the Rough Riders' commander, even though the Mauser bullets were whipping about him in a blizzard of aimed fire. "All right, Colonel," he yelled to Roosevelt, "go ahead! Sumner has authority from Shafter, via Miley. The order is to move forward and support the regulars in the assault on the hills in front. Understood, sir . . . ?''

It was understood. Teddy Roosevelt was already on his Texas pony. Fate always remembered and treasured that fleeting picture of him, in his brown uniform and blue polkadot bandanna, his hat again pinned up in the flaring Custer-style of San Antonio, famed teeth and steel-rimmed spectacles aglint as he faced the Spaniard at San Juan. And he forever remembered and treasured what he said there, and the wonderful subdued way in which he said it.

"Let's go, men," was all that Teddy told them. "Follow me."

As to that "following," the versions were limited only by the eyesight, imagination, cupidity, honor, rascality and political ambitions of the observer. The variations upon the theme were endless, as they always are with national heroism under military fire. At San Juan they went full swing. Shafter was restrained, as befitted a commander-in-chief who was not there:

"In this fierce encounter words fail to do justice to the gallant regimental commanders and their heroic men, for, while the generals indicated the formations and the points of attack, it was, after all, the intrepid bravery of the subordinate officers and men that planted our colors on the crest of San Juan Hill and drove the enemy from his trenches and block-houses, thus gaining a position which sealed the fate of Santiago. . . .

"My own health was impaired by over-exertion in the sun and intense heat of the day before, which prevented me from participating as actively in the battle as I desired. . . ."

Roosevelt's account, which the irrepressible Mr. Dooley called *Alone in Cubia,* used a prose rather less restrained than Shafter's. Said Teddy: "The instant I received the order I sprang on my horse and then my 'crowded hour' began. . . . I formed my men in column of troops, each troop extended in open skirmishing order, the right resting on the wire fences which bordered the sunken lane. . . . I started in the rear of the regiment, the position in which the colonel should theoretically stay. . . . [but] . . . I soon found that I could get that line, behind which I personally was, faster forward than the one immediately in front of it, with the result that the two rearmost lines of the regiment began to crowd together; so I rode through them both, the better to move on the one in front. This happened with every line in succession, until I found myself at the head of the regiment.''

The other versions, those of the enlisted soldiers who also ran and fell that day, but who did not enjoy the second chance of the published word to set the battle straight, were neither so carefully correct nor so unabashedly assumptive as those of the generals and the colonels. One of the soldiers who ran and fell that day was Fate Baylen. This is what he saw.

Chapter Thirty-six

The charge up San Juan Hill was not a charge, it was a labored climb. And for the Rough Riders, it was not even up San Juan but up Kettle Hill, a much less fortified, lower and altogether simpler height than San Juan. It lay nearer the river and to the American right of the main elevation. Between the two high points a spur of the Santiago road ran up to El Caney. This rutted track, more a mule trail than a formal road, was sunken below the level of the surrounding terrain and channeled by wire fencing on either side. The Rough Riders had to get down this wire and cross this road about midway of their approach to the ranch buildings and trenches topping Kettle Hill. Here they took their first casualties and here, due to the fact the Negro troops had no wire cutters among them, the Ninth piled up momentarily and caused the first of Roosevelt's singular opportunities of the day.

Fate, running with Henry Bardshar, Pete Van Schuyler,

Tiffany and Lieutenant Woodbury Kane, as hard as they could follow upon the flying heels of Little Texas and Colonel Teddy—Micah Jenkins had not the speed afoot for such pursuit—was in time to witness the affair. It concerned the Ninth, whose dark members, for some peculiar reason of refraction in the Cuban sun, Colonel Roosevelt was unable to see clearly, either then or later. Most of his men, Southwesterners in the main and heir to the identical weakness, suffered the same stroke of color blindness on the hill that day. Some very few of them did not, and Fate was of the latter number.

He saw what he saw. He did not add to it nor take away from it for reason of skin tone or regional disdain. And he heard what he heard.

The first speaker was Teddy Roosevelt raging at a nameless captain of regular cavalry as to the delay at the wire and inquiring in four-letter words as to what possible excuse the colored troops had for "lying down" before the advance was well begun.

The white officer of the Ninth was polite and calm. His superior, Lieutenant-Colonel Hamilton, had ordered the halt while he sent to the rear for directions from this point, because he believed he saw a better way to go. This was by way of the sunken road to a less steep part of the hill, which would permit better access to the fortified buildings on its top.

"Well, sir," shouted Teddy, "who is your colonel's colonel?" The captain told him and Roosevelt snapped, "I know him; he won't tell Hamilton a damned thing. Since I am the ranking officer here—" The captain interrupted him, saying quietly, "Beg pardon, Colonel, but I have my orders and I will hold to them." Roosevelt recoiled, literally yelling at him, "Damn it, Captain, we are being shot up standing here. If you will not get your men up to go forward, for God's sake get them up so that they may move aside and let my men through.''

The stout captain, Regular Army and not doing one thing to violate express orders, shook his head.

''Sorry, Colonel Roosevelt,'' he said, ''I have my instructions to hold where I am. I can't move the men for you.''

''Then, by God,'' stormed Roosevelt, ''I will show you how to do it!''

And he did.

He spurred Little Texas right in among the startled Negroes, nearly running down the white captain and trampling two or three of the men before they could scramble to their feet and vacate their ''holes.''

Fate could not help joining the shout of laughter which went up from the Rough Riders, and, to be truthful, from many of the colored soldiers themselves. The college men and cowboys followed their stubby leader through the Ninth Cavalry on the double. Before they had passed half their number through the colored troops, the latter were beginning to join in the yelling for Teddy and by the time Roosevelt had reached the actual wiring of the road, it was half a dozen Negro cavalrymen who rushed forward and beat down the wire with their carbine butts. Then they lay upon it with their unprotected bodies to hold it down while Little Texas took his rider through and out upon the sunken road which circled the foot of Kettle Hill.

Fate was yipping and running with the others. Inside of five minutes both regiments, regular colored and volunteer white, were through the wire and across the road, following the spurring, shouting, arm-waving Colonel of the Rough

Riders up the now opened flank of Kettle Hill. The rest seemed easy.

In the entire attack, but one American trooper, John Foster of B Troop, Rough Riders, came close enough to touch a Spaniard. The Arizona soldier killed a brave defender who refused to run, by clubbing him to death with his rifle butt. Fate saw this incident and it didn't make him proud, it made him sick.

He saw other things, too, which remained in his memory. Roosevelt, somewhere in the rush upward, had got a scratch on one hand. It was bleeding somewhat freely and in passing a really badly hurt Rough Rider who was being helped to cover by two medical corpsmen, he waved his own "wound" and called, "Here, there, I've got it, too; you needn't look so damned proud!"

He meant it as something to hearten the man and to assure and amuse the others about him who had hesitated at the sight of their shattered comrade. But the wounded man did not smile and neither did the others.

Captains McBlain, Taylor and C. J. Stevens of the Ninth Cavalry were officers who led their colored men up Kettle Hill in separate rushes which were easily abreast of the leading Rough Riders and, over on the right, at the last moment, Fate saw Sergeant George Berry of the Tenth Cavalry carrying two regimental standards, his own and that of the Third Cavalry. His repeated deep-voiced calls to "Dress on the colors, boys, dress on the colors!" together with his calm advance upward, unarmed save for the two guidons, was as brave a thing as any on the hill and, moreover, he had his Negro troopers *ahead* of the Rough Riders in the last drive past the final barbed-wire of the slope.

Here it was that, forty yards from the top, Roosevelt jumped off of Little Texas to go the rest of the way on foot, and here it was that Fate, gasping to come up with the dismounted colonel and his foot-shadow Henry Bardshar, saw the latter steady his Krag carbine across a standing fence post and shoot down the last two Spanish soldiers to leave the trench behind the wire. It was like taking a brace to hold steady for knocking over a jackrabbit or coyote, far out, and to Fate it did not seem real. He stood and watched Bardshar kill the two men, his own carbine in his hand, his own Colt in his belt, both forgotten, both untouched. From sunken road to summit, he had run, stumbled, fallen, scrambled up again and gone on, just to follow the Colonel. He had not thought of killing Spaniards, but only of not being killed by them. Now, seeing the enemy close up, seeing him in his clean light blue and white uniform, his odd shiny straw hat and crossed cartridge bandoleers, with his handlebar black mustache, dark sun-dyed skin and long shiny Mauser rifle, he could still not bring himself to shoot one of them. Down in the grass, or the jungle trees, it was different. There you shot back at a flash of clothing, or a movement of the bush, or the sound of a rifle bark. Even in the ambushes with the enemy guerrillas, it was a general thing, mixed up, both sides firing free and wild. In the real long-range work, like lying down below in the river growth and blasting up the hill at the Spanish trenches, it was, again, a matter of company firing. No one was picking targets and drawing down on them. Each man was just cursing and working his bolt and blazing away in great style and doing no damned harm at all. If a bullet of his found an enemy mark up the hill, it was no personal fault of his. The same with an enemy bullet finding him. He didn't figure it was one particular man taking a bead on him. It was just one of those things. It was war.

But Henry Bardshar throwing down on those two toy

soldiers just now, that wasn't war. Henry could have let them get away. They weren't firing back. They were running for their lives. They had been brave. They had stayed as long as any man would dare. They had fought a good fight and now they wanted only to get away. Fate would have let them go. There were several others of the Rough Riders of A Troop, immediately behind Roosevelt and Bardshar and himself, who could have shot themselves a Spaniard, too. But they did not. Neither did the Colonel. But Henry had. And he had not simply whanged away at his target, which was all that his duty required. No. He had deliberately taken a brace so that he could kill himself a couple of garlics. It was a strange thing. Some men would shoot to kill and others would not. The Rough Riders had had it drilled into them at San Antonio and Tampa that they were not to worry about shooting the enemy—when the enemy began to shoot at you, you would find the necessary moral guidance to shoot back in one hell of a hurry. This was not so, and Fate wondered how the big thinkers in the army business could be that wrong about something so central to their success. He had not been conscious on the long struggle up the hill that he wasn't firing. But now that he did think about it, he realized that *most* of the men around him had not been firing either. They had all, as had he, been yelling and shouting and raising the war whoop something fearful. But most of them had not been firing their Krags at all. It was a very strange thing; something to remember and think about.

The only other stray fact about the final sweep of the "charge" over the crest of Kettle Hill, which stayed with Fate long afterward, was another case of the Colonel's pen hand being quicker than the Sergeant's seeing eye. This was the matter of who took Kettle Hill. To Fate Baylen it was clear. When he and Bardshar and the first of the Rough Riders of A Troop followed Roosevelt toward the ranch buildings, they thought they were the winners. They could see no one but a bunch of their own boys—some of the New Mexico troops—coming over the rise behind them. But when they drew near the forted-up buildings, expecting momentarily to be met with a blast of enemy fire, they were met, instead, by a battery of broad grins and good-natured, ragging shouts from no less than half a troop of fellow American soldiers. The only trouble was they were regulars. Regulars, and the wrong color.

Roosevelt wrote: "The first guidons planted there [on Kettle Hill] were those of the three New Mexican troops, G, E, and F, of my regiment, under their captains, Llewellen, Luna, and Muller."

This was undeniably true. Fate saw it. Those Rough Rider guidons of the New Mexico boys were the first ones planted on the hill. But the Negro troopers of the Ninth Regular U.S. Cavalry had no guidons to plant. All they had done was to get up the hill first, and quietly, and knock the Spaniards out of those buildings so that the Arizona and New Mexico heroes could get their guidons up there to plant. Just a little "history" which somehow managed to escape Teddy in the heat and excitement of the battle.

Fate always hoped it was his eyeglasses.

Chapter Thirty-seven

The sound of the Mausers spanging off the sides of the big black iron sugar kettle was vastly unreal. Fate, keeping behind the shelter of the rusted container's bulging sides, was not of a mind to leave such good cover. It made the sound of the bullets almost pretty. Rather like rain on a tin roof. Or hail against an oil-paper window. That old kettle gave a man more confidence than anything he had hidden behind since Houck Oatman. With him behind the ten-foot diameter of the refining vessel which gave the hill its name were eight other men. The various buildings sheltered the rest, and those who could not find solid cover lay down on the ground and tried to look like Cuban rocks. It was not too humorous a situation presently.

The Spanish fire from San Juan, the higher hill to the west, was far hotter than anything they had faced coming up the hill. The range was not over 400 yards to the first trench of the enemy—the trench which they soon enough determined was the one they must take—and its occupants were in the light blue and white uniforms of the regulars and they could shoot. The Rough Riders, in fact, were being shot to hell. In the five minutes since they had reached the top of Kettle Hill, Colonel Hamilton, commanding the gallant Ninth Negroes, had been killed; Colonel Carroll, commander of the First Brigade had been seriously wounded; Captain Mills, Roosevelt's aide, had been shot through the head, and the motley mixture of First, Third, Tenth, and Ninth Cavalry and Rough Riders pinned down on the bald knob of the lower hill, was in immediate risk of being destroyed or driven back over the height they had just won.

The morale began to crack as soon as word spread that Hamilton was gone. He, the officer whom Roosevelt had cursed in the sunken road below, and whose cool-headed study of Kettle Hill had shown the proper way to assault it with but twelve resulting casualties in Roosevelt's own troops, had been senior on Kettle until his bullet found him. He had kept the men in iron order despite the galling fire. But when he went down, and then Carroll fell, the command in that part of the field went to Teddy Roosevelt, and Teddy Roosevelt did not have the military experience to handle so many mixed troops. To lead his own college men and cowboys was one thing. To lead the remnants of an entire brigade, after seeing the brigade commander shot, then his senior colonel killed, then to lose his own, and only remaining, aide in the same number of withering minutes was enough to shake any soldier.

Fate and the others, plastering themselves to Mother Cuba and looking to Teddy to get them unpeeled, as he had never failed previously to do, began to grow fearful when they could see that their leader was not doing a thing.

The rain and rattle of the Mausers off the iron kettle and

the wood and adobe flanks of the ranch buildings was suddenly no longer musical. To it now was added another note. Two Spanish guns opened on the crest of Kettle Hill from their point-blank emplacements on San Juan. They were fired with time fuses set to blow about ten or fifteen feet over the American position, and the first rounds exploded precisely in order. They were shrapnel-loaded and the casualties were severe.

In the same instant, over on the face of San Juan, up which the infantry of Kent, under Hawkins, had been storming with such courageous success, a terrifying sight was beheld. The American artillery, all day long the bane of the U.S. soldiers it was designed to protect, opened in reply to the Spanish battery which was exterminating the Rough Riders and regulars on Kettle Hill. Their fire, too low to harm the enemy pieces, was perfectly placed to land in the faces of Kent's and Hawkins's American infantrymen going up the last steep rise of San Juan. The brave troops were first stunned, then completely demoralized by the stupidity and incredibility of this blunder, and the assault wave recoiled upon itself and fell back down the hill in broken, streaming rivulets of cursing, raging U.S. riflemen who had had the enemy beaten only to be cut away from him and driven back by their own artillery fire.

Fate, who still had Bucky O'Neill's field glasses, saw this action magnified eight times, and still could not accept its reality. He could, however, as could the others on Kettle Hill, understand what the retreat of the infantry on San Juan would mean to them, and to the entire operation, if it were allowed to stand unchallenged. Instinctively the harried men looked to the dashing amateur colonel of the Rough Riders for leadership and succor, but Roosevelt seemed spellbound by the enormity of the action going forward on the other hill, and by the volume of fire being directed his own way from the nearer Spanish trenches.

If he were momentarily awed, however, General Samuel Sumner was not. Fate saw the general coming up Kettle Hill on his white horse as calmly as if he were riding on parade at Tampa. He was letting the horse go his own gait and pick his own path up the slope, and he was riding completely alone. The sight of a high general officer displaying such behavior under a fire which had them stinking with the sweat of fear, worked a miracle on the mixed command of cavalry then dying atop Kettle Hill. The men actually leaped to their feet in greeting, ignoring the fire which but a moment before had their noses in the enemy dirt.

The arrival of the brigade commander had an equally salutary effect on Teddy Roosevelt. He instantly began to run up and down his ragged lines exhorting them to steady down and fire in volleys. The troopers, giving him the battle courtesy which they claimed for themselves—the privilege of being scared stiff—replied with a good will and resumed work with their Krags, as Sumner rode up.

The cavalry commander brought no good news. "You must go forward here," he told Roosevelt, "and I will send some help in behind you, as soon as I am able."

That was all. Just that. *Go on now and get killed, and I will come in then and walk over to San Juan on your bodies.* He turned his white horse about and rode back down the hill without another word. Oh, yes, there was one other word: *good-bye, Teddy, and good luck!*

Roosevelt did not argue his orders. Neither did he obey them—at once.

His Rough Riders and the regulars with them were volley-firing in good order now and, until that situation over

287

on San Juan was straightened out, it would be murder to lead men down the saddle between Kettle and the parent hill. Unless the infantry rallied and came on over there, the Rough Riders had gone as far as they were going that day. "Live heroes, fine; but dead heroes don't vote." That's what one of the small-minded rascals with Fate's group growled about the delay, but Fate Baylen was there also and saw what he saw, and he didn't feel that the Colonel could have done a thing but what he did do, or what he didn't do. Maybe crusty old Joe Wheeler or General Hawkins would have charged the Spaniards from Kettle Hill when the American infantry fell back on San Juan. Sure, maybe they would, and maybe the regulars were right when they claimed such a charge would have saved the day. But Teddy thought of his men. That's what made him different from the Army officers. It was what made his men love him. And be ready to follow him, win or lose, live or die.

Besides, in his blustery, bluff and bulldoggy way, Colonel Roosevelt had a feel for things the others didn't have. And he had the guts to do what that feel told him to do. He was always a man who did, in the end, what his conscience and his hard, tough head told him to do. In this case it was to stay right where he was on Kettle Hill until something broke to give him his next opening. And he was right again.

Fate had no sooner told his companions behind the black kettle—six of the eight were regulars—to leave off the mean words for Colonel Roosevelt, because he would get them out of there and do it better than any damned West Pointer on a white horse, when a weird and ominous new sound of fire arose from the direction of San Juan Hill. The moment was the most fateful in the balance of the battle, and Roosevelt sensed it.

"Suddenly," said he, "above the cracking of the carbines, rose a peculiar drumming sound, and some of the
men cried, 'The Spanish machine-guns!' Listening, I made
out that it came from the flat ground to the left, and jumped
to my feet, smiting my hand on my thigh and shouting
aloud with exultation, 'It's the Gatlings, men, our Gatlings!' Lieutenant Parker was bringing his four Gatlings
into action, and shoving them nearer and nearer the front.
Now and then the drumming ceased for a moment; then it
would resound again, always closer to San Juan Hill, which
Parker, like ourselves, was hammering to assist the infantry
attack. Our men cheered lustily. We saw much of Parker
after that, and there was never a more welcome sound than
his Gatlings as they opened. It was the only sound which
I ever heard my men cheer in battle.

"The infantry got nearer and nearer the crest of the hill.
At last we could see the Spaniards running from the rifle
pits as the Americans came on in their final rush. Then I
stopped my men [from firing] for fear they should injure
their comrades, and called to them to charge the next line
of trenches, on the hills in our front, from which we had
been undergoing a good deal of punishment."

The scene which followed Teddy's command to attack
the rifle pits across the grassy meadow of the saddle between Kettle and San Juan was another failure of fact to
support the variant fancies of the observers.

What Fate and the other near-at-hand Rough Riders saw
was Teddy Roosevelt, followed by five men, jump up suddenly with a yell and a wave of his arm, then run down
the slope toward the meadow, leaping a low wire fence at
its base and starting out across the flat. Not another enlisted
man of the regiment, nor of the several score regular cavalrymen who witnessed the strange dash, made a move to
follow its bandy-legged leader. The lack of officers with an

inclination to join in the six-man rush at the Spanish entrenchments on San Juan was equally unanimous. No regular or volunteer rank holder, lieutenant, captain, major or light colonel, shifted a boot to get up and go after the gallant little regimental commander of the First U.S.V.C.

Many reasons for this peculiar behavior were to be assigned. Among them, Roosevelt's own apologia was a classic of elastic retrospect.

"Thinking that the men would all come," he said, "I jumped over the wire fence in front of us and started at the double; but, as a matter of fact, the troopers were so excited, what with shooting and being shot, and shouting and cheering, that they did not hear, or did not heed me; and after running about a hundred yards I found I had only five men along with me. Bullets were ripping the grass all around us . . . Clay Green was mortally wounded . . . Winslow Clark was shot first in the leg and then through the body. . . . There was no use going on with the remaining three men, and I bade them stay where they were while I went back and brought up the rest of the brigade. . . .

". . . I ran back . . . filled with anger against the troopers . . . for not having accompanied me. They, of course, were quite innocent of wrong-doing; and even while I taunted them bitterly for not having followed me, it was all I could do not to smile at the look of injury and surprise that came over their faces, while they cried out, 'We didn't hear you, we didn't see you go, Colonel; lead on now, we'll sure follow you.' "

Fate and the eight troopers cowering with him behind the black iron sugar kettle had a slightly different view of it. They clearly heard Colonel Roosevelt yell for his brave fighters to follow him. As plainly, they saw his skidding stop out in mid-field, at the sudden realization that he had charged the enemy without his troops. They also saw Green and Clark get hit and go down, and Teddy turn and scramble back home, after ordering the other three men with him to dive for the cover of the tall meadow grass and stay there.

Subsequently they were ear-scorched witnesses to T.R.'s furious return slide to safety, his recovery and striking of the memorable pose, upright and unmindful of the Spanish lead, and the high-voiced, indignant shriek with which he exhorted his bellied-down army of college men and cowboys to get up on their feet and fight.

Fate and his two Rough Rider and six Regular Cavalry comrades saw more. They saw a few of the challenged soldiers come skulking to their feet. Some issued from the ranch buildings. Some crept out from behind the nearby rise of the hill. Some appeared sheepishly from the nearer tall grass and scant brush. Fate and half the regulars with him came out from behind the rendering kettle. A handful of others came from nowhere, seemingly, and perhaps fifty hangdog heroes, in all, came cringing to heel at Teddy's rightfully angry curses. It was a poor and tawdry moment for the Rough Riders and would have been worse had not General Samuel Sumner returned just then to inquire after the delay in carrying out his order to assault San Juan in support of the infantry of Kent and Hawkins, once more desperately attacking behind support of Parker's Gatlings.

Here again, in a trying situation, official memory and enlisted recollection would not jibe. Said Roosevelt: "I wanted the other regiments to come too, so I ran down to where General Sumner was and asked him if I might make the charge; and he told me to go and that he would see that the men followed. By this time everybody had his attention attracted, and when I leaped over the fence again, with Major Jenkins beside me, the men of the various regiments which were already on the hill came with a rush, and we started across the wide valley which lay between us and the Spanish intrenchments.''

Fate and the men with him never believed that such officers as Micah Jenkins, Woodbury Kane, Greenway, Llewellen, Luna or Muller had heard and refused Roosevelt's original order to go forward. Indeed, it would have been humanly impossible for all of the Rough Riders on muster that day, as well as for many of the scattered units of regulars temporarily with Teddy, to have even seen, much less heard, the Colonel start down the hill.

Naturally, by the time he and the five soldiers had reached the meadow and begun getting shot up, nearly *all* the troops in the vicinity, as Roosevelt said, ''had their attention attracted.''

Yet that was another matter, and well understood and agreed upon by most viewers. What Fate saw, and what the other Rough Riders saw, and what the regular cavalrymen saw, was that *some* of the officers and *some* of the men *did* funk out. Neither was their number low. Their leader's kindness to the contrary, the greater part of those who *did* hear Teddy Roosevelt yell, and who *did* see him take off on the fly toward the enemy, failed to heed his order or to follow his example.

Fate and his eight behind the kettle were with this guilty majority in the first place, and they were now with the hangdog minority, which came out of its hiding places in reply to Roosevelt's violent language upon his return from No Man's Land.

It was this ''loyal'' group which surrounded Colonel Teddy upon General Sumner's arrival, and which heard what the brigadier told his regimental colonel of volunteer cavalry.

It was not the sort of language, form or content, which a man cares to remember. Not if he were as guilty as the men standing with Theodore Roosevelt upon Kettle Hill that day. Fate did his best to forget it and to remember only Teddy's response to the wicked whipping which the general officer delivered, and which, in the personal sense, was as utterly unfair to Teddy, as it was deserved in full by those of his "Terrors" who had refused to follow him over the fence in his six-man charge of the Spanish position on San Juan.

Roosevelt, for the record, said not one word about the misconduct of his men. He accepted Sumner's raw-hiding. He took it like the man he was, and when he had done so he merely turned to Kane and Jenkins and the two score shamefaced troopers with them, and said, "All right, men, get back to your positions and get ready to go."

Less than two minutes later the Rough Riders went over the wire fence and across the flat of the saddle meadow in the historic charge of San Juan Hill.

Their impetus took with them the cheering, shouting remnants of Regular Cavalry, particularly the Ninth Negro, which had been caught with them atop Kettle Hill. Timed with the crucial arrival of Lieutenant Parker and the Gatling Battery to save the infantry on San Juan, and to spearhead its resurgent drive back up the hill, the flanking attack of Teddy Roosevelt and his dismounted, disobedient, ragtag and near-rebellious "Rocky Mountain Rustlers" carried the Spanish trenches, the heights beyond, the blockhouses crowning them, and the day, for the Fifth Army Corps in Cuba.

Chapter Thirty-eight

There was some close work, and not easy, at the very last. It came almost to hand-to-hand in the final series of trenches at the blockhouses. The enemy, in some of the laterals, held until the Americans were leaping into their "holes" with them. Fate, being of the long-legged ones like Lieutenant Greenway and Henry Bardshar of A Troop, swept past the bulk of the other troops and past Teddy, too, with his short, churning strides. In this position Fate was able to observe the only true contact with the enemy in the campaign. It consisted of about five minutes' hot firing and pursuit and dodging snapshooting at the overly brave individuals of the Spanish regulars who stayed until the point of honor was reached, and passed, before jumping out of the entrenchments and running around the now-empty blockhouses, and beyond them, down the long slope of San Juan Ridge, inland, toward the bay and Santiago.

Fate saw—that is to say that he remembered seeing—

two Spaniards killed and one American officer shot down. The first Spaniard fell to the revolver of a fellow sergeant, First Sergeant Clarence Gould of the First (Reg.) Cavalry, who blew away the left ribcage of an enemy corporal who was in the act of shooting Fate from a blind, quarter-rear angle. The other Spanish infantryman was also taken by a revolver shot, but his case was far more celebrated than that of the luckless trooper who almost killed Fate Baylen.

This was the incident about which Roosevelt said, "I was with Henry Bardshar, running at the double, and two Spaniards leaped from the trenches and fired at us, not ten yards away. As they turned to run I closed in and fired twice, missing the first and killing the second."

Many were the times to come when this cool claim of the myopic, spectacle-wearing volunteer colonel was to be denigrated and, for that matter, outrightly challenged by his detractors. But there were a dozen soldiers of A and K Troops, beside Henry Bardshar and Fate Baylen, who saw the shot and who, ever after, stoutly defended their colonel's right to its dubious credit.

The latter, however, was as far above defending his minor triumphs as he was incapable of admitting his major blunders. Said Teddy airily of his "soldier" at San Juan: "My revolver was from the sunken battleship *Maine,* and had been given me by my brother-in-law, Captain W. S. Cowles, of the Navy. At the time I did not know of Gould's exploit, and supposed my feat to be unique; and although Gould had killed his Spaniard in the trenches, not very far from me, I never learned of it until weeks after."

Then, in what surely must rank with the all-time masterpieces of aplomb: "It is astonishing what a limited area of vision and experience one has in the hurly-burly of a battle."

As always, though, there was in Teddy's opinion and expression a kernel of truth; the situation at the top of San Juan Hill was a bee swarm of confusion in which white regulars, colored regulars and Rough Riders were hopelessly intermixed and in which regular officers led volunteer troops and volunteer officers headed regular units and no officer and no man knew where his command began or ended.

It was precisely in such a welter of doubt and colliding orders that the inventor of the "go-as-you-please" plan functioned to his highest efficiency, and in his own greatest interests. Knowing the importance of the opportunity before him, Roosevelt acted while the regular officers were still getting their troops regrouped and steadied from the hard climb up San Juan from the front. Shouting to Major Jenkins to pass the command and follow him with all available troops, he at once set off in personal pursuit of the Spaniards who had, so far as visible fact went, already vacated the heights. With him, in that historic rush past the deserted blockhouses, went Henry Bardshar and Fate Baylen, his two tall Arizona shadows, and perhaps a full troop of mixed-company Rough Riders—not over fifty men in their total strength, including the two present lieutenants, Goodrich and Carr.

Fate, heated and wound-sick as he was, felt new power flow through him for that last effort. Somehow he sensed, as the others with Teddy in that valiant honor guard, the finality of their sweep across the waving brown grasses of San Juan. In among and out through the various ranch and blockhouses before them, they ran, and then on to the graceful line of palms which delineated the fall-away of the Santiago slope. When they came, stumbling and shouting hoarsely through this stand of tropic sentinels, and could see from their lacy shade the glinting of the late sun upon the silver waters of the harbor and the white, red-tiled houses of the city of Santiago de Cuba, they knew what they had done and where they stood in that hushed, hard-panting moment.

It was the end of the slapdash, crazy trail that had begun at Whipple Barracks, in Prescott's mile-high saucer of pines and red-gray granite rocks.

A few more guns would go off, a few more men would get killed. The enemy would likely bluff a time or two, and the god-awful heat of the days and chill dews of the nights and the fever and the bad food and the blundering of the Fifth Corps' higher command as to all sorts of supplies and access to the base at Siboney would go right along, as usual. But the big fight was behind them. Parker's Gatling guns and Teddy Roosevelt's Rough Riders had taken San Juan Ridge. And when the history books came to write about it, it would be even simpler than that. It was plain as the bow in Little McGinty's legs. Even a dumb cowboy from Bell Rock, a butthead hardrock miner from Camp Condon, or an illiterate bear hunter out of Wind River, Wyoming could see the lie of that land sloping from San Juan to the shores of Santiago Harbor.

Fate knew it, they all knew it. There wouldn't be any headlines written about Lieutenant John Henry Parker taking San Juan Hill. The war with Spain was as good as over. And Teddy Roosevelt had won it.

Chapter Thirty-nine

After a while the position atop San Juan became less certain. The enemy had not deserted the field, as was first assumed, but merely retired to a secondary ridge behind San Juan, where they occupied prepared trenching and breastworks from which a good line of fire could be had to halt any further advance of the Americans. Indeed, before the Rough Riders got their wind back and Colonel Roosevelt was able to organize his mixed command, the effect of the Spanish resistance was such that he had to order his men to retire to cover on the hither face of San Juan.

At this point some doubt was in the air. Directly, however, Captain Robert Howze, an aide of General Sumner, dashed up with a message from the General to "halt where you are, advancing no farther, but holding the hill at all hazards." At the same time a similar message was being delivered by a second aide, Lieutenant Andrews, to Captain Beck, who had his Tenth Cavalry regulars on the Rough

Rider left and who was leading the Negro troops as an independent command. Also, the order went to the right flank, being then held by the Ninth Cavalry.

A consultation of the various officers involved, called by Roosevelt, who once again found himself ranking officer in the area, resulted in a group agreement to stay where they were. Later, rumors began to haunt the line that some of the officers along the ridgetop were asking to be allowed to "retire to stronger positions farther back." The idea of any retreat outraged the Rough Rider Colonel but he was prevented additional worry over the possibility of giving ground at the moment of victory when old "Fighting Joe" Wheeler, returning to the field from his sickbed in the afternoon, took command at the front and laid into the rumor makers as only an ex-Confederate General of Cavalry could do.

"Fighting Joe" had just ridden up to see that all was well with Teddy and the Rough Riders in the center of his battle line atop San Juan Ridge, and was complimenting the Colonel on the manner in which he had led his mixed command of volunteers and regulars, when a hapless aide to a nearby commander rode over to inquire after the feasibility of "falling back" a bit that evening.

The tongue lashing which followed nearly flayed the startled young officer alive. "Fighting Joe's" extemporaneous remarks on the idiocies of retreat were awe-inspiring. None of the Rough Riders had ever heard the English language flown so high before. Nor so hot.

Listening to the white-haired old soldier "gnaw apart" the timid neighboring commander's terrified aide, and watching Colonel Teddy's face muscles twitch and jump and his blond mustache bristle, his smudgy eyeglasses gleam and blink in the downing sun, and his famous teeth

299

bare themselves in the sheer physical joy of the Teddy Roosevelt grin at what the old devil was saying, Fate and the others were restored past all measure of their own uncertainty. From the moment of Fighting Joe Wheeler's "speech" on the subject of precipitate retirement with the enemy "already whupt and sent askinning," there was no further instance of indecision among the remnants of the six cavalry regiments which from that moment until next daylight formed the command of Colonel Theodore Roosevelt upon San Juan Ridge.

Any shred of question which may have remained in the minds of the U.S. command at any point of the extended lines that July first sunset was dispelled when the delayed news came that General Lawton, at 4:30 P.M., had stormed and taken El Caney, and driven in the Spanish left flank. By dawn he would have his infantry regrouped and added to the American right center. With sunrise of July 2, the Spanish could throw the whole 11,000-man Santiago garrison into the fight and still not make a dent in the U.S. line. Not even the rumor, earlier received, of General Calixto García's failure to prevent the entry into Santiago of several thousand reinforcements from outlying garrisons, could depress the rearoused spirit of the Americans.

Throughout the night, hungry, hurt, exhausted, they cheerfully trenched in all along the ridge. At 3:00 A.M. there was a bluff by Spanish pickets, quickly driven in by the Rough Rider outposts. After that, there was only the quiet and the chill and the white blazing stars of the Cuban dawn.

With shooting light the Spaniard resumed firing, both of rifle and artillery, with a vigor which hinted that he did not comprehend the hopelessness of his position.

Daylight brought other hesitations to the American esprit. Night had come on too quickly the previous sunset for

the full extent of the casualties to be appreciated. Many of
the wounded were not found until daylight of the second
disclosed their falling places. Of the dead, a number were
yet unaccounted for even by sundown of the second. But
by that time the casualty list had grown to exceed 1400
officers and men. The second day was one of sweltering
heat, little water and no food in the American lines, and
was climaxed, not by a rumor of retreat, but by the certain
knowledge that General Shafter had wired Washington for
permission to pull back his entire line five miles to safer
ground.

This report severely affected the men on the line. If the
corps commander was afraid, everything was apt to go by
the boards. Something must have gone wrong which was
not apparent to the Rough Rider rank and file.

Worse news was coming. General Joe Wheeler was said
to be suffering second thoughts. Evidently his closer in-
spection of the U.S. lines, subsequent to his rousing speech
to T.R. and his regiment, had altered his definitions of
"whupt" and "skinned." To Shafter he forwarded a dubious plea and doleful prediction:

"A number of officers have appealed to me to have the line
withdrawn and take up a strong position farther back, and I
expect they will appeal to you. I have positively discounte-
nanced this, as it would cost us much prestige. The lines are
now very thin, as so many men have gone to the rear with
wounded and so many are exhausted, but I hope these men
can be got up tonight . . . We ought to hold tomorrow, but I
fear it will be a severe day."

For Fate Baylen, who had suffered through the long, hot
hell of July 2 on nerve and pride, Fighting Joe's concern

proved prophetic. With darkness came the protection from discovery of the friendly night. Iron will and mesquite-tough muscles would obey no more. The weary Arizonan put down his Krag carbine, laid aside his trenching shovel, unslung and placed with the gun Bucky O'Neill's field glasses. Then he sank upon the hillside beside them and sat staring at the distant gleaming lights of Santiago.

About him on the hill lay or crouched the semivisible forms of his fellows. Some talked quietly, some smoked in silence, some, like Fate, waited apart from the others, knowing it was better to meet the last enemy where friends and comrades could not see. A man, a prideful man, knowing he was weak, knowing he could fight no more, would be grateful for that privacy. Fate was grateful.

He had wanted it to be in the sunshine. Out in the golden meadow at the climbing of the land from the river. But now he knew the night was better, and that he was lucky. If he could only manage to be brave, as well . . .

He was not so ill now. And his mind was sharp as glass. The pain had eased, too. The new bleeding seemed to have done that. There were strange blessings to be found in a war. When the wound had broken open again, just at sunset, he had been frightened. He had thought of what O'Toole had told him, and his heart had beat like a bird against his ribs. But then, the hurting in his whole body had faded, being replaced by a calm steadiness of thought, a welcome slowing of all fears and all feelings. It had been wonderful, and not until this moment had he guessed what it was. That was a blessing. A man had to call that a blessing.

He was aware of the shrouded night sounds of the Army about him, yet he kept his gaze outward over the starlit harbor below; outward and away and beyond the harbor north and west and homeward those two thousand and more vaulting miles to the Tonto Rim and the sun-washed stillness of Oak Creek Canyon: *home,* he thought, the word that says it all.

The tears ran silently then, coursing down his dirty, bearded cheeks, cutting pale rivulets through the powder grime and filth which overlay the once-bronzed and windburned face. He put his head down, ashamed, and smiled self-consciously and tried to think when was the last time he had caught Fate Baylen crying. He couldn't recall it, had a little laugh at himself for his foolishness, and raised his head again. Hell, it wasn't any crime to get homesick, and lonesome, and scared to death. He wondered what his father was doing. He hoped somehow that way over there in the dark, he was thinking of his boy, Fate, as his boy Fate was thinking of him. Home, oh, my God, what a man wouldn't give to be home.

Fate was still sitting there in the dark, still staring out over the valley, when Sergeant Tiffany, brevetted a lieutenant for gallantry the day before, came looking for him about eight o'clock.

Tiffany's news, in lieu of a cup of hot, black coffee, a cigarette, a mouthful of sustaining food, or even a cooling draft of clean water, placed in the scale the final unbearable grain. Pete Van Schuyler was dead.

A Spanish sniper's bullet had taken him through the lungs. He had been found, and the buzzards fought off his body, only at sunset. Apparently he had fallen in the first charge yesterday, and lain since then dying and spoiling in the fearsome Cuban heat. There was a bit of good news, though, to balance the grim. Bear River Smith had been found where Fate left him and brought in alive. He was at the field hospital at Shafter's headquarters near Sevilla, awaiting ambulance room to Siboney.

Pete Van Schuyler, Fate thought, little old Pete; all that education and money shot to hell. For what? What sense did it make? What sense did any of it make? First Houck, then Captain Capron, Bucky O'Neill, Blue Calhoun, O'Toole, Boone, Cuba Libre—where was the logic and the reason in all that? It had to add up. Somehow it simply had to have a total. But did it? Could it ever? Fate nodded his dark head, and was sure that it did, that it must. The fear had begun to come up in him again, but now it fled back and he was calm again. There was an answer. It lay somewhere between a little Cuban girl, a tall *yanqui* captain, a rich man's spoiled son, a Jewish street urchin and a humble, small, fearless Negro horse soldier. Yes, and maybe between them and a gaunt and lonesome, very frightened Arizona cowboy, too. A man knew that. He felt it so deep inside him that it had to be the truth. It didn't leave any room for question, any space for uncertainty. A man could lie down with that answer inside of him and be easy in his heart, set in his mind, peaceful in his soul.

"Baylen?" said Lieutenant Tiffany sharply. "Are you all right?"

The brevet-lieutenant heard Fate sigh gratefully in response, and heard his slow Southwesterner's drawl murmuring, "Yes, thank you, Tiffany; I want to say that I am surely pleased you got promoted, and that you was kind enough to come see me, and to tell me about Pete and Bear River—it was a right decent, friendly thing of you to do . . . sir." There was a pause and then what sounded to Tiffany like a relieved chuckle, and the quiet-voiced cowboy smiled up at him and said, "You know, Tiffany, I always thought you was a snob. . . ."

The new lieutenant returned the laugh. But when he

reached down to shake hands with the Arizonan and wish him luck, the gaunt figure did not move nor the gentle drawl reply. Tiffany knelt quickly. He peered closely into the pale face, felt for the shallow, reedy pulse.

"Soldier," he said to the nearest blanketed Rough Rider, "wake up. Go get the litter bearers up here on the double."

The man, not knowing Tiffany nor suspecting he was an officer, pulled his blanket more tightly about him.

"Go to hell," he growled. "Who was your nigger last year?"

Tiffany loomed above him in the darkness.

"Soldier," he repeated softly, "get up, God damn you, and go find help for this poor devil; I believe that he is dying."

Chapter Forty

But Tiffany was wrong. Fate went by field ambulance to the base hospital at Siboney, the flicker of life so low within him that three times during the transfer different doctors called him dead. Yet each time the indomitable heartbeat began again, the dogged respiration resumed. At Siboney he lay for a week drifting in and out of the last shadow. Then came the turn. By the second week he was consuming four meals a day and commenting at some critical length upon the quality of the cooking. Five days later he was visiting the other wards discussing with the convalescents of Regular Cavalry the comparative insignificance of their part in the final victory at Santiago. Since Fate's position featured a stirring peroration on the unquestioned superiority, both as man and cavalry commander, of Colonel Teddy Roosevelt, there was some natural slight disagreement from the regulars. This feeling reached its height the morning of Fate's release from the hospital and return to the regiment.

He was packing his things—the Red Cross had given him the only spare set of clean underclothing he had seen since leaving the Verde Valley—when one of the First Cavalrymen dashed excitedly into the ward. Roosevelt, he said, had just leaked "accidentally on purpose" to the Associated Press a personal letter pleading dramatically for removal of the malaria-stricken U.S. troops from Cuba. What made the act so mean was that only the day before, General Shafter and the staff, *including* Roosevelt, had got up an identical letter to send the War Department through proper channels, and not for press release. To this Fate wondered aloud what great difference it made who released the letter, so long as they all got safely home. His answer came indignantly from the trooper.

"Listen, cowboy," he cried, "be fair! Rough Rider or Regular Cavalry, can't you see what that letter of his will do? All the folks will hand 'Teddy' personal credit for getting the boys brought back. Now that's shameful!"

Fate shook his head, listening but not hearing.

"Soldier," he said, Arizona drawl as easy as the other's tones were strident, "you and me ain't got no fight. We ducked the same Mausers and run for the same holes up yonder to San Juan. But there ain't nothing you can say again Teddy Roosevelt that will cost him my vote. And, pardner, I know I ain't alone. When we get off that boat up there to New York City you ask the first person you see who won the war with Spain. Now I ain't about to tell you that it's entirely true, nor 200 percent fair, but what you're going to hear is, *'Teddy Roosevelt and the Rough Riders,'* and you can tighten your cinch on that until you cut your horse in two."

Three days later, on August 7, 1898, Fate marched with the regiment through Santiago, along the Alameda, to the dock where the transport *Miami* waited. There were no throngs at the wharf, no shipside ceremonies. They embarked quietly, sailed with the Caribbean tide and but a single cowboy conviction: Teddy Roosevelt's letter had done the trick and they were going home; it was as simple as that.

Their return was also a reunion. The troops that had been left in Florida came north by rail from Tampa, arriving August 10th at Camp Wikoff, the Rough Rider rest and quarantine center at Montauk Point, Long Island. A few days later the troops from Cuba disembarked. A welcoming crowd of 10,000 persons wildly cheered the *Miami* as she nosed in. The Florida companies stood stiffly at honor-guard dress and the band played "When Johnny Comes Marching Home Again." But the cheers grew thin, then died away, and the music stopped altogether when the malarial, dysenteried and filthy soldiers began to come down the plank. First the Florida troops, then the civilians, bared their heads and stood in silence.

At Camp Wikoff the disease and death rates climbed rather than diminished. The despondent men took to elaborating a reputation they had earned in good health, that of being a regiment of hard drinkers. One disgusted troopmate of Fate's fired off to the city papers a letter-to-the-editor naming his fellow heroes "a bunch of sodden, whiskey-soaked bums." When his staunch comrades learned his identity they nearly killed him; it was against the code of "the Terrors" to cast any doubts upon Teddy or themselves. The local inhabitants, along with the better because sober half of the regiment, were unquestionably relieved when, on September 13, the Rough Riders were at last "paid off" at Montauk.

The saviors of Cuba had been in service nearly five months. Each man got $15.50 per month, a total of $77. Even so, they now cheered more and were happier than when informed of the Santiago surrender. It was all over before 1:00 P.M.

A committee of awkward troopers waited upon T.R., asking him to step to the rough pine table placed in the center of the hollow square the regiment had formed outside his quarters. On the table beneath a horse blanket reposed a lumpy object. Colonel Roosevelt was escorted to the scene by Lieutenant-Colonel Brodie. William S. Murphy, a private of M Troop, the Indian Territory, made the speech. Known as an orator, Murphy was overcome and could not talk. The entire regiment began to weep. Some cynics standing near Fate Baylen suspected a bit of over-training at the canteen prior to the ceremony. But there were always poormouths of this breed, the Arizonan realized, and he told them to shut up. Murphy, meanwhile, managed to rally and get through his somewhat thickened presentation of the lump beneath the blanket—Frederick Remington's "The Bronco Buster" in bronze. Teddy then replied at campaign length, concluding emotionally, *"Now, boys, I wish to take each of you by the hand, as a special privilege, and say good-bye to you individually. . . ."*

When the last tight-lipped trooper had filed by and silently wrung his hand, Roosevelt left camp swiftly. His regiment, however, trailed him en masse to the depot and cheered him to the echo. When T.R., complete with glinting eyeglasses and faded campaign uniform, climbed aboard the railway coach which would bear him forever away from his college men and cowboys, there was not a dry Western eye in Montauk.

The Rough Riders themselves invaded New York City upon their release later the same day. Teddy's wide-eyed and wild-eyed frontiersmen, Fate Baylen bringing up the rear, did the metropolis as it had never been done before, not even excepting the "museum, art gallery and stock exchange." But the Big Town was too rich for the boys from Broken Bow and Buffalo Run. By the second day of the spree most of them had only their train tickets home to trade for drinking liquor, or the touch of something softer and still more expensive. With sundown and painful sobering, the last of them were on the cars heading west and the war for the Rough Riders was over. Or very nearly so. A final question still turned in the mind of Fate Baylen. Watching the Eastern night slide by the troop-car window, the Bell Rock cowboy frowned and shook his head. He had found some of the answers in Cuba but not this one. It was beyond such simple words as his own to phrase, he knew, yet it must lie somewhere. Glancing at the sleeping soldier next to him, he saw the familiar name stand forth in boldface type from the front-page editorial of a newspaper lying in the other trooper's lap. Reaching over, Fate took the paper, smoothed it across his own knees, and started his thoughtful lip-reading of the text:

". . . for Colonel Roosevelt, as for the new directions in his country's history which he has set in motion, the combat has only begun. Time will be the arbiter of the change but time will not alter the fact that T.R. has taken his nation out of the past, into the present. Nor will time deny that for all his weaknesses of vanity, guile, deviousness, bluntness and petulance, Teddy Roosevelt understands the greatest truths of his native land—that the fight for freedom is never won, and never can be. Teddy knows this heavy burden of democracy for what it is: to its safekeeping and advancement he has given the total measure of his strength, and to the flag which he loves beyond ordinary comprehension, he has paid the entire passion of his loyalty. A braver man has never lived, nor one more humanely frail and full of fault. Do not forget his name. Teddy Roosevelt. The Rough Rider. An American to cherish and remember . . ."

Fate looked at the paper a long moment after his lips had ceased to move over the words that he saw upon it. Then he nodded in his slow, careful way, replaced the paper in the trooper's lap, lay back with a weary smile and closed his eyes.

"That's right," he said, and went to sleep.

Bibliography

Alger, Russell A., *The Spanish-American War,* New York, 1901

Atkins, John Black, *The War in Cuba,* London, 1899

Bonsal, Stephen, *The Fight for Santiago,* New York, 1899

Chadwick, French E., *The Relations Between the United States and Spain,* 3 vols., New York, 1911

Coblentz, Edmond D., *William Randolph Hearst, a Portrait in His Own Words,* New York, 1952

Davis, Richard H., *The Cuban and Puerto Rican Campaigns,* New York, 1898

Dennet, Tyler, *Americans in Eastern Asia,* New York, 1922

Dyer, John P., *"Fightin' Joe" Wheeler,* Baton Rouge, 1941

Emerson, Edwin, *Rough Rider Stories,* New York, 1900

Freidel, Frank, *The Splendid Little War,* Boston and Toronto, 1958

Hagedorn, Hermann, *The Rough Riders,* New York, 1912

Latane, J. H., *America as a World Power,* New York and London, 1907

Mahan, Alfred T., *Lessons of the War with Spain,* Boston, 1899

Marshall, Edward, *The Story of the Rough Riders,* New York, 1899

Mason, Gregory, *Remember the Maine,* New York, 1939

McCurdy, F. Allen, and Kirk, J., *Two Rough Riders,* New York, 1902

Millis, Walter, *The Martial Spirit,* Cambridge, 1931

Pratt, Julius W., *Expansionists of 1898,* Baltimore, 1936

Roosevelt, Theodore, *The Rough Riders,* New York, 1899

Sargent, Herbert H., *The Campaign of Santiago de Cuba,* 3 vols., Chicago, 1907

Society of Santiago de Cuba, *The Santiago Campaign,* Richmond, 1927

Vincent, George E., and Miller, Theo. W., *Roughrider,* Akron, 1899

Wells, J. O., *Diary of a Rough Rider,* St. Joseph, Mich., 1898

Wheeler, Joseph, *The Santiago Campaign,* Boston, 1899

Wilkerson, Marcus M., *Public Opinion and the Spanish-American War,* Baton Rouge, 1932

Wisan, Joseph E., *The Cuban Crisis as Reflected in the New York Press (1895–1898),* New York, 1934

Young, James Rankin, and Moore, J. Hampton, *Thrilling Stories of the War by Returned Heroes,* privately printed in 1899

Documents

Annual Report of the Major General Commanding the Army, Washington, 1898

Correspondence Relating to the War with Spain, 2 vols., Washington, 1902

American Military History 1806–1953, Dept. of Army, July, 1956

Reading List from ROTCM 145-20

JESSE JAMES
DEATH OF A LEGEND

Beneath the bandanna, underneath the legend, Jesse James was a wild and wicked man: a sinister and brutal outlaw who blazed a trail of crime and violence through the lawless West. Ripping the mask off the mysterious Jesse James, Will Henry's *Death Of A Legend* is a novel as tough and savage as the man himself. Only a great Western writer like Henry could tell the real story of the infamous bandit Jesse James.

_3990-7 $4.99 US/$6.99 CAN

THERE WAS A SEASON

T.V. OLSEN

Winner Of The Golden Spur Award

A sprawling and magnificent novel, full of the sweeping grandeur and unforgettable beauty of the unconquered American continent—a remarkable story of glorious victories and tragic defeats, of perilous adventures and bloody battles to win the land.

Lt. Jefferson Davis has visions of greatness, but between him and a brilliant future lies the brutal Black Hawk War. In an incredible journey across the frontier, the young officer faces off against enemies known and unknown...tracking a cunning war chief who is making a merciless grab for power...fighting vicious diseases that decimate his troops before Indian arrows can cut them down...and struggling against incredible odds to return to the valiant woman he left behind. Guts, sweat, and grit are all Davis and his soldiers have in their favor. If that isn't enough, they'll wind up little more than dead legends.

_3652-5 $4.99 US/$5.99 CAN